The Bloodlines

B. S.

The Bloodlines

Olympia Publishers
London

www.olympiapublishers.com
OLYMPIA PAPERBACK EDITION

Copyright © B. S. 2023

The right of B. S. to be identified as author of
this work has been asserted in accordance with sections 77 and 78 of the
Copyright, Designs and Patents Act 1988.

All Rights Reserved

No reproduction, copy or transmission of this publication
may be made without written permission.
No paragraph of this publication may be reproduced,
copied or transmitted save with the written permission of the publisher, or in
accordance with the provisions
of the Copyright Act 1956 (as amended).

Any person who commits any unauthorised act in relation to
this publication may be liable to criminal
prosecution and civil claims for damage.

A CIP catalogue record for this title is
available from the British Library.

ISBN: 978-1-80074-979-5

This is a work of fiction.
Names, characters, places and incidents originate from the writer's
imagination. Any resemblance to actual persons, living or dead, is purely
coincidental.

First Published in 2023

Olympia Publishers
Tallis House
2 Tallis Street
London
EC4Y 0AB

Printed in Great Britain

1

There was a second-hand bookshop behind the church called Our Lady in Trondheim. Bergtora went in and looked around. A man came from the back of the store and asked if she needed help. He looked like a librarian with his brown shabby clothes and his long tousled hair. Bergtora asked him if he had a book written by OJ Høyem from 1862. "It's called *Nes* or *Bynes*."

"I sold the last copy yesterday," the librarian said with a sour voice.

"How many copies have you sold?"

"I sold three last week."

"How's that possible?" asked Bergtora. "Who is interested in a book from 1862. Who did you sell them to?"

"I sold the last book to a guy from Buvika. Let's see if I can find a copy for you elsewhere."

He put on his glasses and checked online. After a while, he said there was a book in Oslo, they could send it and she could have it within the week. Bergtora asked how much.

"$270," he said.

"It is a book mostly about farms and farmers during the nineteenth century," said Bergtora, resigned.

She didn't understand why the book was so popular, she decided to go and see if they had a copy at the library instead. On the way out, she saw a stuffed owl standing on the desk with a name tag around its neck. Bergtora had a dream the night before about the Hubro owl, this owl had a similar name. As far as

Bergtora knew, the owl represented death. Bergtora crossed the street and went through a small park, then she crossed the street again and went inside the library. It was an old building and the ground had recently been excavated by archaeologists, some skeletons still lay in the ground by the entrance.

Bergtora went upstairs to the Trondheim room where they kept the rare books. She wasn't allowed in the room, so one of the librarians went to get the book. Bergtora sat in a black leather armchair and waited, she almost fell asleep. The librarian couldn't find it, so another went to have a look. She found the book immediately, Bergtora understood why when she saw the book; it was so tiny, only 15 cm high and 7 cm broad.

Bergtora opened the first page and realised she had to read fast if she wanted to understand anything, the book was written in Gothic. Nothing caught her eyes until she read about a guy called Ravn Orm Lyrgja. It was a very frustrated OJ Høyem who attacked the historian PA Munch who claimed that Orm Lyrgja came from Bunes and not Bynes.

"In the oldest saga of the Viking kings of Norway, it said that Stein was one of the most considerable farms on Bynes."

Bergtora read further: *"Stein inhabited formerly by Orm Lyrgja whose wife Gudrun, Bergthor's daughter from Lundum, for her beauty's sake was called Lunda Solen, desired by Haakon to become his mistress.*

This indication is considered by PA Munch as an unreliable legend. On the other hand, he is of the opinion that Orm Lyrgja lived on Bunes up in Gauldal. Bynes is written in most of the old sagas about the kings incorrectly."

Bergtora could feel the wrath of OJ Høyem when he wrote: *"Bynes was not incorrectly written in most of the sagas about the kings. They had terrific sources to stick to, and it is strange that they all made the same mistake.*

One thinks of Orm Lyrgja sitting in the narrow valley on Bunes, then it seems a bit strange to hear Snorre say that Orm sent couriers to all four edges and asked his allies to attack Haakon. Gauldalen has only two edges."

Bergtora thought it wasn't the first-time names of places got mixed up. Lagertha was supposed to come from Gaula in Sogn and Fjordane. Bergtora flipped a bit in the book until she found out what Høyem had written about Lagertha.

"In 812 lived a shieldmaiden and ruled over the lower part of Gauldal on the farm Leiraa in Buvik which she owned, but she also owned the Langørgen farms both in Buvik and Bynes. Lagertha was her name.

On one of his conquests, the Danish king Ragnar Lodbrok visited her and landed with his fleet by the Gauldal river. His tents or Buerne he set up in Buvik, and that's how the village got its name. Three years he stayed with her and had a son with her by the name Fredleif which meant the last remnant of the peace. After a while, Ragnar spotted a greater beauty and left Lagertha. She on the other hand remained faithful to him, even though he had shamelessly left her. Her devotion and faithfulness was so big that she helped him with one hundred and twenty ships when he later once came in distress. Thus was a true trønderinne in those days."

What surprised Bergtora was that Ravn Valgardsson, who later was known as Floki, lived close to Lagertha at the same time.

Orm Lyrgja lived just down the road from Floki's farm, but that was about a hundred years later. According to Høyem, Floki's family farm was called Haarheim. It was the same farm that was called heim or Sudrheim in the sagas. Ravn Valgardsson left for Island and became one of the first settlers there, he also named the island 'Island'.

Suddenly, Bergtora came to think about what had happened the day before. She had been on Byneset, and walked past the farm Ravn Valgardsson came from just when a huge flock of crows lifted and flew over her head.

Bergtora returned the book and went outside, the weather was still grey. She walked along the river called Nidelva and crossed the bridge over to Bakklandet. The street she lived in had small wooden houses with different colours. Bergtora went into the kitchen and sat down at the table. The wooden kitchen table was round and brown, it looked old. The chairs were upholstered with grey green tweed with dark purple small stripes. The walls in the kitchen were painted in a dark eggplant colour. The lower cabinets were light blue, and the shelves above were wooden white.

The view was priceless, with the river and the gothic cathedral Nidarosdomen, usually called Domen amongst the locals. The huge green spire was always surrounded by a large flock of crows.

Bergtora decided she wanted to find out more about the last pagan Viking king named Håkon Jarl, he knew both Orm and Lundesol.

It wasn't as hard as she thought it would be, she found a book written by a Danish guy. He wrote that Lundesol was called Lundesol because she was so beautiful and came from a secret grove. Lunden was a halidom of worship, Odin's stone stood in the middle, with eleven other stones around, each represented by a god. It was not allowed for uninitiated to go into the grove. Her father was a blacksmith called Bergtor. His grandfather had forged the crown to king Halvdan Svarte, and Bergtor was forging the crown for Håkon Jarl, but Håkon died before it was finished.

Olav Tryggvason came sailing into the fjord just as the peasants gathered to attack Håkon Jarl on Orm's request. Håkon Jarl had cast his eyes on Lundesol, he expected her to be his mistress. Olav Tryggvason had stood on a large rock with his sword and shield overlooking the fjord when he decided he wanted to be Norway's next king.

Bergtora wondered if it could have been Høgsteinen Olav stood on. At that time, it had been a troll cauldron on top of the mound. Rocks and stones had made it a long time ago, when the ice retreated. It was believed to have healing powers, because of the green stone it was made from, there had also been a fort up there at some point.

Ravn came into the kitchen, he was Bergtora's boyfriend. He had tangled black hair to his shoulders and blue eyes. Bergtora's hair was tangled too, they had the same colour on their eyes, but Bergtora's hair was lighter than Ravn's, it was dark brown, but it had the same length.

"How you been?" asked Ravn and smiled at her.

"So and so," said Bergtora and poured him a cup of coffee.

"What," said Ravn, upset, "do I only get a white cup today?"

Bergtora looked at him and smiled, she took the white cup herself, and gave him a cup with the image of Uncle Blue from a children's book by Elsa Beskow. Bergtora preferred Aunt Purple herself.

"That's better," Ravn said, satisfied.

They sat in the living room, and Bergtora told him what she had found out. Ravn agreed that it was likely that it was Høgsteinen Olav Tryggvason stood on top of when he decided to be the next king of Norway.

"The story is there," he said.

Bergtora agreed, the story lay somewhere. She had found out that Lagertha, Ravn and Orm had lived close to each other. Maybe there was some truth to it, when some old folks said there had to be something in the water.

Bergtora wanted to open up her brain, so she fetched two glasses of whisky. Ravn took a sip, and looked at Bergtora. She looked scared.

"What is it?" he asked.

"The fear of failure," said Bergtora and took a deep breath.

"You see the patterns, what more do you need?"

Ravn didn't understand why Bergtora was so scared.

"How do I know if the patterns are enough?" Bergtora drank a large sip of the whisky glass.

"Everyone who writes gets the information eventually; the stories are there, you just have to find them."

Bergtora imagined Lunden lying towards the fjord. The light was silvery in grey weather and yellowish in sunshine. The best part was when the rays of the sun broke through the clouds and hit the water at full speed.

Ravn began to make beetroot soup, he was starving, and he didn't want to disturb Bergtora; he saw that the story had begun in Bergtora's imagination.

When he had finished, Ravn set the table with the pot of soup in the middle. He took a spoonful of sour cream in each soup plate. The soup turned deep pink. Afterwards, he poured blackcurrant juice into the glasses.

"Is it not missing roasted pumpkin seeds?" asked Bergtora.

"Clearly!" said Ravn and jumped up.

Bergtora wondered if Ravn was able to get up slowly from the chair, she doubted it. Her thoughts fell back to Lunden again.

She saw Lundesol going towards the stone circle, she put a flower wreath around Frøya's neck.

"Do you believe that all the Norwegian kings stemmed from Odin?"

Ravn looked at her and smiled. "No, but I think some did."

Bergtora ate the rest of the soup. The ingredients were cheap, but it became a luxurious dish if done right.

"You never use thickening?"

"Stick mixer," said Ravn and grinned, "that's the answer to a good soup, and a huge talent, of course."

"I like the sea salt from the Orkney Islands, there is a marine biologist who extracts the salt there."

"I have tasted it. Consistency is important, flakes are best, and of course if the salt comes from the high north."

"There is something special about the Nordic light, isn't it?" Bergtora said suddenly. "Frosta is known for the good vegetables. At the Farmer's Market, you can see the intense colours from afar."

"It's a combination of the length of light in summer, the fresh air and the minerals contained in the soil, it has the right amount of magnesium and chloride. The soil is calcareous, and therefore it hasn't inhibited the magnesium content."

"It's almost like the right side of the fence when it comes to vine culture," said Bergtora.

"You thought of something else?" Ravn looked at her excitedly.

Bergtora put on a record by the Cocteau Twins called 'Treasure', before she answered Ravn.

"The light over Trondheim. When I land at the airport, it's always the light that strikes me as enormously beautiful."

Ravn had seen the same thing. It was related to the

magnetism of the Earth, the magnetism in Trøndelag was extra strong, it bound the particles in the sunlight a few seconds longer than usual. Ravn got up and stretched.

"Time to go to Byneset and look at the light there. I just drank a sip of whisky. The alcohol is out of the blood right now," Ravn said, and looked at the watch.

"I just want to listen to the song "Beatrix" first. They come from a place where the Clyde and the Firth of Forth meets."

"Who?"

"Cocteau Twins. It's not far from Linlithgow."

"Linlithgow," Ravn said in astonishment. "What kind of place is Linlithgow?"

"I don't know, I just feel an intense horror when I hear the name. The church which is located in Linlithgow Palace has a steel construction on top, there is something strange about the whole place."

They went out on the cobbled street which meandered between the wooden houses. Ravn had parked the car in a small parking lot across the street.

"My cart awaits you," said Ravn gallantly and opened the door to an old dark brown Volvo. It had turquoise skai seats with a herringbone pattern. Bergtora put on sunglasses and a scarf which lay in the glove compartment. Ravn had made a sports car out of the car. He was wearing a black shirt with beige, brown and orange geometrical patterns. The black sling pants and the shiny shoes matched perfectly.

What Bergtora loved about Ravn was that he was so light-hearted. It wasn't just the wild hair and clothes, it was his whole personality. He was like a crow, incredibly smart but at the same time funny.

Bergtora suddenly thought of something.

"If light is important to get the best vegetables, how does it affect people?"

"They become more talented if they get the right amount of magnesium and chloride."

"How's that possible?" asked Bergtora, surprised.

"Some substances block the brain, and some don't. Beetroot increases oxygen uptake. There are eight hundred and forty-six billion glial cells in the brain, and they use calcium ions to communicate with each other. In the glial cells, there are water channels, and they transport vast amounts out of the brain. Beetroot makes that job much easier; it provides oxygen to the glia cells, which means glue in Greek. They were called glia cells because they were believed to be glued to the neural cells, that's something they have found out isn't true, but the name remains.

"The importance of the colours on the vegetables are something the brain researchers haven't fully recovered yet. We have the whole rainbow spectrum of colours in the brain. The carrot is the orange colour in the rainbow, the beetroot is as you have probably guessed, the red colour. And each colour is needed to make the brain reach its full potential."

Bergtora wondered which vegetable had the turquoise colour.

"That vegetable doesn't exist," said Ravn and smiled at her. "It's an interplay between what exists in the brain and the air we breathe. There are some small turquoise particles in the green stone found in Høgsteinen."

"The Earth has been almost destroyed five times before, and that was due to high CO_2 levels. The oceans get sour because of the high levels. Calcium brings that level down and maintains the balance. Clean water has a ph of seven, ph above seven are alkaline, and ph under are sour. I wonder if the water channels in the glial cells are alkaline or sour?"

"I have absolutely no idea," said Ravn. "All I know is that p comes from the Latin word ponds and means weight and h stands for hydrogen. A hydrogen atom consists of one proton, one electron and no neutrons."

They drove through the city and continued along the fjord towards Trolla. The fjord was medium blue, and the mountains were dark blue, the sky had a light ice blue colour. Bergtora leaned back in her seat and took a deep breath.

At this moment, she had absolutely everything she wanted. Bergtora wrinkled on the eyebrows, it was something that made its way to the surface, but she didn't get what it was.

The small white church from the twelfth century appeared. Ravn parked the car and took out the green and brown routed woollen blanket. He spread it out on the hill in between the farm called Olavstu and the church.

"It's not just on the vegetables the colours are important," said Bergtora and looked at him.

"No, they are important on much more than just vegetables. Just look at me," said Ravn while scurrying around. "The clothes reflect my personality; I think about what colours and shapes will suit the day every day."

"It's a talent," Bergtora said enviously.

"I know, you also had the talent once, but now you wear clothes that go straight down like torrential rain. You need sunbeams that spreads out. Shapes with geometric patterns, sunglasses and red lipstick."

Ravn took a deep breath and lay down on the woollen blanket. Bergtora sat and watched the fjord. She knew Ravn was right. It was easier to meet who you were supposed to meet if you showed who you were on the outside. Ravn had managed it perfectly.

"Stop worrying," said Ravn.

"I want a Jan Mayen sleeping bag, the one without a zipper that can withstand minus forty degrees," said Bergtora.

"If you buy one for me, I can buy one for you. We can lie and look at the stars."

She lay down on his arm and closed her eyes. It was so easy with Ravn; it was everything else that was difficult. Other people, expectations, what you should do or not do. Who to see and whom to do without. Not to forget those to avoid, the list was long.

"The dumbest thing you can do is complicate things," said Ravn and stroked her hair.

Bergtora felt everything let go, it was no big deal. It was enough with good food, a lovely bed and Ravn.

"And good coffee," said Ravn.

Bergtora nodded. Eventually, they fell asleep. The ravens began to gather in the trees towards the fjord. They sat completely still, there was not a gust of wind. The sky slowly changed colour, it was the beginning of the blue hour, the hour that turned into a deep blue before the darkness came. Something was going on, this much was certain. Ravn jerked occasionally, Bergtora did the same. Ravn suddenly sat up and stroked one hand through his tousled hair. The ravens started screaming and Bergtora woke up too. She reached for the thermos and poured coffee into two cups and gave Ravn one of them. She watched the ravens take off at the same time, they flew across the fjord.

"Always fascinating with large flocks," said Ravn.

Bergtora just nodded, she was numb after sleeping on the ground. It suddenly began to rain from clear skies.

"It is only temporary," said Ravn.

Bergtora shook her hair, it was already soaking wet. "Let's go home and light a fire and drink a whisky while we stare at the flames."

The rain had subsided. They stopped and looked at the fjord which flashed in gold and silver. The sun had just managed to break through a large dark cloud, it wouldn't last long.

"There you have the battle the sun must fight," said Ravn and smiled.

"The moonbeams are so different," said Bergtora. "Do you know why?"

"I do, the moonbeams go straight down and straight up, while the sunbeams goes around the sun."

"Sure?" Bergtora asked.

"Absolutely." Ravn had seen it many times, what amazed him most was the number of moonbeams, it was mostly seven or five.

Ravn started walking towards the car. Bergtora stayed a little longer. It felt like she had zero control, but still she had full control.

Ravn came back and took the basket out of her hands and said, "This is how it feels when you have faith. You know you will land on your feet; you always do."

"Do you feel the same?"

"More than you can imagine," he said resignedly.

"Whisky and a fireplace," said Bergtora and started running up the hill towards the car. Now it was Ravn who stood and looked at Gulosen. There were mountains surrounding the fjord and Høgsteinen, which lay to the right of the church by the fjord, and a farm.

"Ravn!" Bergtora shouted. "Come before it starts to rain

again."

Ravn set off, he just managed to get into the car before the rain poured down again. Bergtora had fortunately been foresighted enough to pitch the sunroof.

"Let's drive through Klett," Ravn said.

"They have added a gas station in the centre and managed to build roundabouts on all the surrounding fields. It's now officially the land of the roundabouts," said Bergtora resignedly.

"Not to forget the cafe which is so ugly that it is almost stylish, and it has the worst coffee ever."

"Wish I had seen Klett at the time there was a crown estate here, belonging to the Elgeseter monastery."

"There isn't much to brag about today, but imagine in ancient times when you came from Heimdalsmyra and got to see the light above Gulosen."

The next morning, they woke up to the sun coming into the bedroom. Ravn stretched his hand sleepily towards Bergtora and stroked her hair. She went down to the kitchen and made coffee. It was the best time of the day, dawn with coffee in bed.

The dawn with its dew, Bergtora thought. *The people who had survived the Fimbul winter, had survived on dew.*

They had decided to take an early holiday this year. It was mid-May, and the birds chirped in the trees surrounding the garden. Ravn had no problem leaving his job selling old cars, since he was the boss. Bergtora used to work in a coffee shop, but she had been laid off; it suited her perfectly. The coffee was ready, and Bergtora brought a cup to Ravn. He squinted at her and took a sip.

"What if we spend the holiday to dig into the past and at the same time create a future?"

"Good plan," said Bergtora. "A new job is what I want the most. I found out why Munch didn't believe that Orm came from Byneset, he believed that it was called Bynes much later than when the sagas were written. The name By on Byneset can be traced all the way back to the older Iron Age, it means farm. Bygrenda was the name of the hamlet that lay where By-viken lay. Just after By-viken comes Neset, which Byneset was named after."

"You believe that Byneset was not written down, and that is why Munch thinks it came much later?" Ravn asked.

"It says Bynes several places in the sagas, and Byneset was not written down incorrectly. Orm Lyrgja came from Stein on Bynes, and owned the land where the church stands."

"Then we have solved everything," said Ravn and laughed.

"I thought of something else last night."

Ravn looked at her questioningly.

"It's a saying I've heard several times. There is a farm a stone's throw from the church. The farm is called Lykken, but the ancients always said Lyrgja when they talked about the farm. They said the same thing about the farm below which is called Haugen, but they always said Haugja."

"Another proof," said Ravn.

"Like you said, the story is there, I just have to write it down."

It was midsummer in the year 810.

Ravn went down the hill from his farm, a large flock of crows flew over his head. He was on his way to Sjur's farm, which was right on the shore. Sjur had promised him a huge bonfire. Ravn hadn't noticed that Lagertha suddenly appeared behind him; where she came from, he had no idea. That was just the way it was, Lagertha appeared just as suddenly as she disappeared again.

"It's tingling in my stomach," Lagertha said.

"Mine too," said Ravn. "It's just like I have a strong feeling that we are going to accomplish great things."

Lagertha looked at him in astonishment.

"Do you feel that too?"

"We are at the beginning of something, it will stay in people's minds for hundreds of years to come."

"How do you know?" Lagertha was still amazed that he felt the same way.

"The same way you know," Ravn said dryly.

They arrived at the large bonfire that had been lit down by the shore. Sjur received them, he just nodded to Ravn before he hugged Lagertha. Ravn didn't blame him; everyone was in love with Lagertha. Ravn had long ago realised that Lagertha's heart belonged to a man who no one could compete with. Ragnar was expected later that evening, about the same time as the cairns on Hemnkjølen, Vassfjellet and Høgsteinen would be lit. The cairns were lit every midsummer, it was a tradition that was unbroken since the Stone Age. It was a sight that took Ravn's breath away, when the Viking ships came sailing into Gulosen with the cairns lit, and the full moon that stood just above Høgsteinen.

Lagertha looked at Sjur, his black hair down to his shoulders, and his grey eyes that slid quickly over her occasionally. She looked at his sinewy body and didn't understand why she couldn't settle with him.

Lagertha asked Ravn and Sjur if they wanted to join her on top of Høgsteinen. They could look at Ragnar when he came sailing with his ships. Ravn grabbed a jug full of beer; he had to drink a little so it didn't splash over the edge. Sjur and Lagertha were quick in their steps, and Ravn lagged more and more behind. Sjur grabbed Lagertha's arm.

"I think Ravn needs help," he said.

They sat down and waited until Ravn caught up. Lagertha took the jar from Ravn and drank some before sending it to Sjur.

"Now there's just enough left so it doesn't splash over the edge when I walk," Ravn said happily.

Lagertha was almost at the top of the mound, both Ravn and Sjur knew it wasn't possible to be invisible, but they could swear that Lagertha was from time to time.

Ragnar stood in the middle of the ship and looked at the cairns that were lit. Due to the cairn on Høgsteinen, Ragnar could see three people. They began to descend from Høgsteinen in the moonlight. The back figure was a bit wobbly, Ragnar guessed it was Ravn.

Ragnar and his men had to go the last stretch with water to their knees, it was impossible to row all the way, it was too shallow. They walked along the beach until they reached the bonfire. Lagertha came towards him, and Ragnar put his arms around her and hugged her.

There was no one else he respected so much, neither rulers or other kings. Ragnar wanted a wife who wasn't equal, he wanted to be the most powerful. It wasn't possible with Lagertha, she took the shine away from him.

Ravn came and shook his hand. Ragnar dragged him to the back of the fire.

"I know you can look into the future, what do you see?"

"I see a rift between you and Lagertha. You find yourself someone you think is an even greater beauty, but she is not. You are being brainwashed; why, I do not know. I only know it must be a greater plan behind all of this. Something that tells me it's not about you, but it has all to do with Lagertha."

Ragnar said nothing, he just walked over to Lagertha. Sjur came and stood next to Ravn. They looked at Ragnar and Lagertha who were obviously in a very difficult discussion. They went closer to hear what they were talking about.

Lagertha said she would never see Ragnar again. Ragnar asked if he still got the ships. It looked like Lagertha woke up for a moment.

"I don't know why I am giving you the ships, but the gods hopefully do."

Ravn looked at Sjur and asked, "Do you think the gods know?"

"None of us understands anything, so I do."

"The ships are ready; I wonder if Ragnar will take them with him?"

"Ragnar does not dare otherwise; he is afraid Lagertha will change her mind."

They saw that Lagertha was standing and looking straight ahead, it looked like she was in a trance. Ravn tried to make contact with her, but Lagertha didn't respond. Sjur went to Ragnar and asked what had happened.

"Lagertha gave me the ships, but she will never see me again. It's like she's paid off a debt, but I don't understand what debt."

"She wants to be free," said Sjur. "Lagertha believes that she can buy herself free from what her heart wants."

"You mean she still wants me?" Ragnar asked, astonished.

"It's not Lagertha who decides what she wants, it's her heart."

"I know you're a herse, but I didn't know you were wise as well." It wasn't enough for Ragnar to just have lived, he had other plans for his legacy, the ships played a part in achieving what he wanted.

Ragnar went to collect the one hundred and twenty ships, they lay close together in the innermost part of Gulosen. He had agreed to meet hundreds of his men; they had travelled from Denmark. The sails on all one hundred and twenty ships were hoisted as he approached. His ship took a half-moon turn, to greet the rowers. Ragnar raised his hand high in the air to signal departure. Soon after, the lurs sounded all over Gulosen. The hundreds of ducks that had been floating nearby flew in wing towards Høgsteinen.

Sjur, Ravn and Lagertha climbed back on Høgsteinen for the second time that day. It was time to see Ragnar off. Lagertha wiped a tear when she saw the ships pass by. The stars shone so brightly that it looked as if they were moving.

"Have you ever seen anything so beautiful as the ships moving under a black sky, with moonbeams in their sails," said Sjur in a low voice to Ravn.

"They are clearly an amazing sight, it's just a shame they have the wrong owner."

Sjur went over to Lagertha and took her hand.

"I'm ready for a fight," she said. "What about you?"

"I will join," said Ravn, "but I think it's best if Sjur stays here and holds the fort." Ravn knew Sjur wasn't a warrior, he was a farmer.

"Where do you want to go?" Ravn asked Lagertha.

"The island of the many stags, does that sound good?"

"Excellent," said Ravn, nonchalant.

"That's a strange word," said Lagertha and looked at him. "Where did you get it from?"

"I don't know," said Ravn and looked down.

"Probably a word from the future," Sjur said and smiled at him.

The next day it rained, but it was a warm rain. Ravn sat on a rock, there were three ravens surrounding him. Ravn looked like he was about to leave his own skin. Lagertha sat down next to him.

"I'm leaving after we've been to the island of the many stags," said Ravn.

"I know, I wish I could join you."

"You can."

"You know I can't."

"There's one thing I don't understand," said Ravn resignedly. "You can be with Sjur, and be happy with him, why don't you choose him?"

"Maybe because I can't. I do not choose to have love grief," Lagertha said just as resigned.

Ravn took her hand and squeezed it hard. If Lagertha had love grief, then she had love grief, she never did anything halfway.

They sat on the stone for a long time without a word. An era was over, and a new era was about to begin.

"What is your dream?" Ravn asked at last.

"Become someone that people remember for not doing anything halfway; if I have love grief, then I have love grief."

"That's the dumbest legacy I have ever heard," said Ravn and cracked out in laughter. Lagertha had to laugh too.

"What about you?" asked Lagertha after they finished laughing.

"One who can talk to ravens, maybe that's a good legacy."

Lagertha smiled at him. "Better than mine anyway," she said.

"Herse over the lower part of Gauldalen, and the largest shieldmaiden who has ever lived," proclaimed Ravn proudly.

"Your legacy is that there are ravens travelling with you, and one of them shows you land," Lagertha said slowly.

"I'm the one who's going to name the land."

"You forgot to tell me."

"Sometimes, I mix up the past with the present."

"What will you call it?"

"Since I have not been there yet, but as you know, nothing will do until I find the perfect island."

"So, what will you call it?" asked Lagertha for the second

time.

"Island, of course," said Ravn dryly. "What else could it be? Right now, I see one of my descendants sleeping and dreaming of us sitting here right now, chatting."

"Maybe he can be together with someone from my bloodline, then they can communicate the way we do."

"A lot is going to be lost, but Ravn, as my descendant is called, will have the ability to look back and forth in time. What can your descendant do?"

"She can do the same as him, that is what keeps them together." Ravn looked at the grey linen dress Lagertha was wearing. It was embroidered with rowan leaves and rowan berries at the bottom of the dress, around her waist was a brown leather belt. The brown leather boots were made of calfskin. Her long and almost white hair hung in a long braid on the side.

"I will always remember us as we are right now," said Ravn and kissed Lagertha on the cheek. "By the way, did I tell you that I think Ragnar is the dumbest man in the world?"

Lagertha smiled at him and squeezed his arm. The light over Gulosen had changed from gold to silver and the rain had stopped. That's why they sat on the same stone for so long, they wanted to see the change in the light.

2

Lundesol went and sat down with Orm. He sat on the same stone that Ravn and Lagertha had been sitting on more than one hundred years before.

"Håkon Jarl has cast his eyes upon you," said Orm.

"I have sent a message to all my allies in the immediate vicinity. Tonight, the cairns will be lit. I have also heard that Olav Tryggvason is on his way, he has been spotted in Trondheimsfjorden."

"Good timing," Lundesol said ironically.

"Bergtor will soon finish Håkon's crown, but he probably won't wear it."

"I think you are right. I had a dream last night, I dreamed that the heads of Håkon Jarl and his thrall were put on stakes on Nidarholm."

"That's probably true, your dreams usually tell the truth."

Orm didn't know if he was happy that Håkon would die. He just felt uneasy.

"I also saw that Olav Tryggvason stood on Høgsteinen. He had a shield, a sword and a crown on his head. I have no doubt, he will be the next king of Norway."

"These are turbulent times ahead of us, and then I don't mean that Håkon dies and Olav Tryggvason takes over the crown. I'm thinking of the old gods and the new ones."

"I like Frøya," said Lundesol. "She is funny, down to earth and has divine abilities. The Virgin Mary just seems boring and pious."

"I agree, it seems like they want us to pray all the time. We go to Lunden if we need to or feel like it. The blots are just as much for our sake as for the gods. It seems that the new god just wants us to submit."

"Subordinate perhaps. I don't think we need to submit. It's like potato or potato."

"Where did you hear that?" asked Orm, surprised.

"The men from Alba who came to visit last year, they discussed which was the nicest one of our ships."

"Which one won?"

"They couldn't make up their mind, they only said potato potato."

"I understand what they meant," said Orm and laughed.

Orm knew that Lundesol could look into the future. He asked her what she saw.

"It's a peculiar time ahead of us. People say all the time: If there truly is a god, he would not have allowed all the terrible things to happen."

"What?"

"We achieve things if we sacrifice the right gifts and ask for the right things, but we know that the gods are not omnipotent. In the future, an idiot says that God is omnipotent. God gets the blame for all the cruelty that happens, they expect him to fix everything."

Orm began to laugh. Finally, he lay on the ground and bounced while holding his hands on his stomach. It was the dumbest thing he had ever heard, how was it possible to be so stupid that one thought that someone could be omnipotent; no one could, neither God nor men.

"There's nothing we can do about it," said Lundesol.

"I will go and get rid of Håkon Jarl, then we can celebrate when I return."

Lundesol kissed him in response. She knew that the old was about to fall. The new era was different and much stricter, they cowed each other because of a god. Lundesol knew that it was the king who created peace, and not the gods. If there was peace and enough to eat, people were happy and could go on with their lives.

She hadn't told Orm that she had seen his death, he would die at the battle at Svolder. Olav Tryggvason sailed with one hundred and twenty ships to the battle, but it didn't go the way he planned. The ships disappeared one by one, and he ended up with just eleven ships. She didn't know for sure that Olav Tryggvason would die as well, but the chances were slim for survival with only eleven ships left to meet the enemy.

Lundesol knew that Lagertha had given one hundred and twenty ships to Ragnar, and she had seen a foresight about a battle in Largs, it was clearly the last battle a king called Håkon Håkonsson fought, he also had one hundred and twenty ships.

Lundesol looked at the big longhouse which they had just finished building. There were oak poles in the ground all the way around with curved walls at each end. The house was 88 feet long and 22 feet broad. The walls were made of hazel twigs which were smeared with clay and mixed with horse manure and dry straw, the floor consisted of hard-pressed soil. In the middle lay a fireplace, the roof had an opening where the smoke could seep out. People and animals lived together in the same house, only with the fireplace to disconnect them.

The longhouse lay a little up from the beach, behind lay a steep road. Orm used to say it looked like an old woman's throat. Since then, the road was only called the Old Woman's Throat. It went up to the road which went alongside the fjord all the way to Nidarnes. Lundesol went inside and lay down on one of the beds and fell asleep at once.

Orm came back the day after. It was completely quiet, he didn't see Lundesol anywhere, no one else either for that matter. Orm went into the house and saw that Lundesol was asleep. He kissed her lightly on the mouth. Lundesol opened her eyes and looked straight into his.

"Is it over?" she asked.

Orm nodded.

"And Tora?"

"She will manage."

Tora was Håkon's mistress, but also Lundesol's friend.

"Tora was the one who hid Håkon Jarl. It wasn't one of the warriors who killed him, it was his most faithful thrall, but you probably knew that already, since it was his head you saw on a stake alongside Håkon's."

Lundesol held her arms tight around Orm, she could see how tired he was. Soon he was asleep and Lundesol made herself carefully free. She poured herself some ale and drank it slowly as she watched the sun rays hit Gulosen. The birds chirped; it was mostly crows.

Lundesol thought maybe the crows didn't chirp, they had a completely different sound. They were the smartest birds, along with the eagles and ravens. There weren't so many eagles around Gulosen. She had seen a flock when she and Orm went to Frostatinget on Frosta.

They have the eagles and we have the ducks, magpies, crows and ravens, she thought. Lundesol was amazed at how many ducks there were who preferred to stick to the fjord of Gulosen. There were hundreds of them, and they constantly flew back and forth to Høgsteinen. Orm used to catch a couple of ducks every Sunday. It was something he had learned from the Danish, who loved duck breast. Lundesol always made a jam from the berries from the sea buckthorn which grew by the fjord. They grew as big as trees, even though they were a bush. She thought that's why people said berry tree about all the bushes that bore berries.

Lundesol closed her eyes. The sun rays were bright pink, shortly afterwards they changed to strong orange, and then turned into white. It was not often it happened, but when it happened, Lundesol always felt that the colours filled her body all the way down to her toes. She had never asked anyone about the colours she received from the sun. What she didn't understand was how one colour could be so strong and then suddenly switch into another. The shape was always the same, a large circle filled with a colour with a deeper tone in a geometric pattern.

3

"Ravn," cried Bergtora. "Would you like duck for dinner? I was thinking I could make jam from the sea buckthorn we picked at Gulosen."

"Don't use all of it," Ravn called back. "I'll use the rest to make a liqueur."

And I will mix the liqueur with vodka, Bergtora thought happily. Ravn began to peel some small round potatoes. The taste was impaired if you cut them in two. After he washed some carrots, the taste lay in the peel.

The carrots should preferably grow in light soil, so they were straight. Ravn used horse manure which had lain for two years and gotten really hot before the process to soil began. He mixed manure with clayey soil and straw – the secret lay in all the layers. The carrots were sown in a light sandy soil, and by the time they had grown three inches, they would meet the clayey soil mixed with manure and straw. The power the carrots had at that point was so strong that they went straight through the soil layer which was one inch. It did wonders to the taste.

Bergtora set the table by the river. It was one of those rare sunny days without a single breeze. She put on the green checkered cloth. Ravn had refused to buy a red checkered cloth; he didn't want to look like Lady and the Tramp. The table wasn't that big, but there was room for a couple of plates and glasses. Ravn was happy, this was the ultimate luxury for him.

"May we have a good summer," Ravn said and raised his

glass to the sun.

"What makes you so light-hearted?" asked Bergtora seriously. "Were you born that way?"

"I think my biggest secret is that I have insanely high demands on small things."

Bergtora looked at him wonderingly, but she understood what he was talking about. The food didn't have to be expensive, but it was deliciously prepared. The cloth wasn't made of polyester, it was a cotton cloth that he had ironed, that was Ravn in a nutshell.

"Holiday," said Bergtora, stroking her hand through her hair. "What do you think?"

"Lazy days with various chores and picnics. How are you doing with the surveys you are doing, have you found out something else about the epicentre?"

"I thought you could help me." Bergtora still couldn't grasp what it was that some places attracted people who accomplished greater things than others.

"There is an extra strong magnetic field around Høgsteinen that affects everything."

"I know you have explained it before, I just don't understand what's really going on."

"You are wondering who is really pulling the strings," Ravn said seriously. "Who has the power and knowledge to make things happen? By the way, Ardar is coming by, he has mostly been staying on his farm in Orkdal. I'm guessing he needs to see somebody at last, he's been living like a hermit for too long."

Bergtora had met Ardar many times during her formative years, they had mostly met at a concert, or parties with common friends. She was fascinated by the almost white colour of his hair.

"Ardar is a strange man," said Ravn. "I have known him

since we were fourteen. He is the same as before, only that he has become much stricter. There are certain rules on how things should be; people dance mostly after his tune."

Bergtora cleared away the plates and fetched an extra cup and a glass. Ravn could hear a car stop and a car door slammed shut. Ardar knew Bakklandet well, he and Ravn had rented a small house there, they lived together for a couple of years in their late teens. Ardar crossed the road and went down to the river. He gave Ravn and Bergtora a hug.

"You aren't afraid of the virus?" asked Ardar.

"We know you have been in a den in Orkdal," said Ravn.

He went to get another chair. Ardar sat down and Bergtora poured him some coffee.

"Milk?" asked Bergtora.

Ardar shook his head. He hoped Bergtora would say something, but she didn't. Ravn came back with a chair and sat down; he didn't say anything either.

What is wrong with them? Ardar thought. *Is it them or me?* After a while, he began to relax. If they managed to be quiet, then he would manage to be quiet.

"Nice view," he said after a long time. Ravn and Bergtora nodded and smiled.

Oh yeah, thought Ardar, *this is going to be fun.*

Bergtora saw that Ardar was stressed out because they didn't say anything. It was Ravn's plan, he said Ardar always controlled every situation no matter what happened. Ravn wanted to get to know him properly.

Ravn smiled at Ardar, and Ardar smiled back. Bergtora began to twist on the chair, she was bored. She got up without a word and went into the house, she had decided to do the dishes instead.

Ardar took a deep breath and said, "What is it, Ravn? Why are you being weird?"

"It's just as much about you," said Ravn and looked at him seriously.

Ardar smiled and said, "My famous shell, is that what you want to crack?"

"I want to get to know you," Ravn said.

Ardar wanted to leave and visit friends who didn't confront him, but he didn't want to be a coward, so he stayed. There was something refreshing about Ravn and Bergtora, they weren't like the rest of his friends, they were themselves. Ardar wished he could have what they had. He was just convinced that he gave people everything.

"Nobody gives people everything," said Ravn.

"How did you know what I thought?"

"Sometimes, I read people's minds."

"I had an aunt who could do that."

"There you go, there's more going on in Orkdal than you think," said Ravn and smiled at him.

"You think it's hereditary?" Ardar asked in astonishment.

"I know it is hereditary."

"Who did you inherit it from?"

"My ancestor's name was Ravn, and he goes back hundreds of years in time."

"Let me guess," Ardar said, laughing, "it was Ravn either on the plain, or Ravn up the hill or Ravn on the mound."

Ravn smiled broadly at him now. Bergtora came back with three bottles of beer.

"Finally, we can say something," she said.

"Who did you inherit it from?" asked Ardar.

"I have one ancestor, she goes hundreds of years back in

time," said Bergtora.

"Are you sure you two are not related at some point?" asked Ardar and laughed.

Ravn and Bergtora didn't say anything; they had always known that they were related, but they had never tried to find out how closely, or how far back it went.

Bergtor stood looking at Håkon Jarl's crown. It had been a little too big, he had used a large iron ring inside from one of Håkon's ancestors going back a thousand years in time. Bergtor had to remove a piece of the iron ring to make the crown smaller, he knew it was probably not a smart thing to do.

An owl flew into the smithy and disappeared again without a sound.

Bergtor knew it was a sign, he didn't have to finish the crown. It was possible he was to blame for Håkon's death, since he had cut the iron ring. Bergtor went down to Lunden and into the stone circle – he was one of the few who was initiated, it was his right to be there.

It was Frøya who became the chosen one. Bergtor lay down on the ground in front of Frøya and asked if it was so that he had caused Håkon's death. After a while, he felt the ground shake slightly, and a wind came into the grove.

Orm stood looking at Bergtor. "I just wanted to tell you that Lundesol is safe, Håkon's thrall killed him."

Bergtor sighed in relief and Orm helped him to his feet.

"Did you ask Frøya for help?" Orm asked in astonishment.

"I did," said Bergtor, and began to walk up the hill. Orm followed him.

"How about a huge celebration?" asked Orm. "We can make a blot to Odin on Høgsteinen."

"And Frøya," Bergtor mumbled.

Orm took his arm and stopped him. "Tell me what's going on?"

"It will come a time when Frøya becomes more powerful than Odin, that time lies far ahead, but it is important to be a step ahead."

Orm nodded, he was not surprised, he was just glad that Frøya would have her rightful place one day.

Lundesol came into the smithy and leaned against the bench.

"How would you feel if Frøya was more powerful than Odin?" asked Bergtor.

"About time," Lundesol said. "She is much smarter than Odin, she always has been."

"I know you sneak into the stone circle," said Bergtor. "It's time for you to be initiated before the moon begins to grow again."

Lundesol didn't say a word, she just ran down the hill and straight into the stone circle. Orm followed her. Lundesol was so happy that she didn't know which leg she should stand on.

"This is where I have my roots," she said.

"The only thing that stands between our roots is Høgsteinen," said Orm.

"What if we give Høgsteinen to Frøya instead of Odin?" asked Lundesol and squeezed his arm.

Orm didn't know if Odin would voluntarily give up the place of sacrifice, he knew Odin appreciated the beautiful view from the top of the mound.

"We will hear what the rest of the initiates say," Orm said, and began the long walk up to Høgsteinen.

Frøya looked at Orm, who was on his way up to Høgsteinen.

She hoped Lundesol was right, that it became her mound one day. Orm sat down and looked at the view when he reached the top.

Frøya couldn't resist the temptation, she went and sat down next to him. Orm knew for sure that he was alone at the top, but he felt that someone was sitting next to him. Orm turned his head gently to the side. He twitched when he saw it was Frøya.

"So, you know that Lundesol wants Høgsteinen to be your place?"

Frøya just snorted. "Do you think you can think a thought without me knowing what you are thinking?"

"Do you want this place?"

"What do you think?" Frøya asked dryly. "You know as the owner of Høgsteinen, you can decide who the mound belongs to."

Orm wondered how Odin would respond.

"Ask him," said Frøya.

Orm did so, and soon after it began to rumble, both in heaven and on Earth. Orm looked around, Frøya had disappeared. In front of him stood the towering figure of Odin. Odin looked at Orm but said nothing.

Orm posed the question one more time. Odin looked at him a long time before he answered, "Frøya is right, it is the owner of Høgsteinen who decides who it belongs to."

Orm breathed a sigh of relief. He couldn't wait to tell Lundesol the good news.

"Before you go you have to greet my ravens." Orm bowed first to Hugin, then to Munin.

"They want to say something," said Odin.

Hugin spoke first. "No one knows that we are also Frøya's ravens. Frøya wanted us to be invisible every time we were with her. She said it was much easier to achieve things if no one saw what was happening."

Munin continued, "What has happened, has happened, but what is to happen, has not happened."

Odin began to chuckle. He thought there was no limit to what Munin could say.

Munin just continued talking. "Many think they know what the future holds but they don't. There are incredible things about to happen. It's not until it has almost passed a thousand years that something will happen again; suddenly, someone starts to dig right up the hill, and the snowball will begin to roll."

"Like a stone rolling down from Høgsteinen," said Odin.

"Why is it so important that they start digging?" asked Orm.

"It's not that they start digging that's important, but what they find. In the century I'm talking about, very few people believe in me and Frøya. A punk from the other side of the Earth takes over. Piety and chastity will be paramount."

"That sounds terribly boring."

"The Viking ships will disappear, and at the same time the pride of creating something so beautiful. People's identities almost disappear as well. They can buy everything they want, but the craft and the endless hours of making things they need is no longer valued."

"We also exchange what we need."

"It's not the same, also the animals are not treated well in the future."

"We let animals we kill to honour you, bleed to death, I don't think that's so much better."

Odin scratched his chin. "It's the balance that is disturbed. I can agree with you that it's better to kill an animal fast, the blood taste just as good anyway."

Odin tried once more to explain to Orm what the future

would hold.

"Good food, money to buy everything you want no matter what. Good friends, family, relationships. Happiness everywhere, all the time. Do you understand?" Odin looked strictly at Orm.

"There is too much to fulfil. They don't appreciate life as it is."

"That's right," Odin said happily.

Ardar was completely put out. He had no idea he had shut down. He seriously believed that he was completely open and didn't hide more than most.

Ravn and Bergtora had gone inside to get more blankets and hopefully something hot to drink. Ardar hoped they came out with Irish coffee without cream. The crows fluttered around the green cathedral spire. What Ardar missed the most was somebody who made him feel like he had come home. Ardar could see that Ravn and Bergtora were each other's home.

Ravn came out with a tray with three cups, Bergtora had her arms full of blankets and sleeping bags. She kissed Ardar on both cheeks.

"What's that for?" Ardar asked in astonishment.

"You looked like you needed it," Bergtora replied.

She may be right, thought Ardar. He no longer felt that he wanted to flee. It was perfectly fine to be with two good friends who saw him for who he really was. Ardar felt he was content with his life.

"To be or not to be," Ardar said out loud and clinked his cup against Bergtora and Ravn's cups. The taste was much better than the original. "What have you used?" he asked Ravn.

"Single malt from the West coast of Scotland, then it needs no cream nor sugar."

"I know what you mean," said Ardar, "it's like moonshine; it's enough with coffee and ninety-six per cent spirit."

The clear full moon stood high in the sky. It was fourteen per cent bigger than usual.

"Did you say that the guest room was ready?" Ardar asked, smiling.

Bergtora nodded, and Ardar said good night and walked slowly towards the house.

"There's something I want to ask you," said Ravn. He took a deep breath before continuing, "I want to marry you, Bergtora, that's what I'm trying to say."

Bergtora smiled and said, "You know I want to as well."

Ardar came back again, he couldn't sleep. Bergtora asked if he wanted to sleep outside, and Ravn asked if he wanted a whisky. Ardar said yes to both.

Bergtora fell asleep first, Ardar and Ravn were wide awake. The full moon was huge, both Ravn and Ardar felt as if the moon drained all their energy out of them. They lay and chatted, the conversation was always different if it took place during the night, it was more open and heartfelt.

Ardar felt that the night was going to be long and good, it was almost like he and Ravn were teenagers again. The future had held different things then, everything was exciting. Ardar sat up and looked at Ravn.

"What?" asked Ravn.

Ardar told Ravn about his thoughts, that the future was exciting when they were teenagers, it was the next thought that had made him sit up.

"You're right," said Ravn. "We are not in charge anymore. In our youth we had a taste of life without any filters. Later the filter came into place, and it's impossible to see that we no longer decide anything, somebody is definitely pulling the strings. And you are wondering who it is?"

"That's more your department, isn't it?"

Ravn thought of all the obstacles that appeared all the time, it was possible to have a good time anyway, there would always be some trouble ahead. It was like a rock lying in the middle of the path. You could walk around, climb over, or sit down and wait for someone to come and remove it, or it just disappeared.

"Done thinking?" asked Ardar and laughed.

"There will always be a longing for the indescribable feeling you had in your youth. That feeling never comes back, no matter how hard you try."

"Why are they pulling the strings now and not before? It's like they wanted to see all the stupid things we were capable of."

"Or maybe they wanted to see young people full of hope. The whole of the world lay open, anything could happen. It was like an open door, and now it's closed because we are older, it makes absolutely no sense."

4

Lagertha came to Joen early in the morning, there was still dew in the grass. Joen asked Lagertha if she had a sword in mind. She explained the sword to him, the shape had come to her in a dream during the night.

Joen carved the sword on a rock. "Looks good," he said after a while. He had already planned to put some green stones on the hilt of the sword.

"Can you make it so strong that it will penetrate everything?" asked Lagertha.

"You have come to the right place. It's not just about the metal I melt, but what I add."

He showed her a grey powder.

"Do not tell me," said Lagertha and laughed. "It's actually greystone, isn't it?"

"It's the greystone that's the secret. If you're gonna be unbeatable you must have a sword that kills with one stab, but the sword must be light, since you're gonna use it for many hours."

Joen looked at Lagertha and stroked his hand over his chin. It was something he had been wondering for a long time, but he didn't know if he could ask. Curiosity prevailed.

"What do you think it is that makes you go on a tokt again and again?"

"Love grief," Lagertha replied. "It doesn't matter if I live or die."

"And Fredleif?" Joen asked cautiously.

"Sjur takes care of him, I'm not a good mother. All I can think about is that Ragnar chose another."

Joen looked at her for a long time.

"It may be that Ragnar was intimidated. You are equal and it can be scary. If I were you, I would take a closer look at Sjur. First of all, he is much more handsome than Ragnar, he is beautiful, smart and funny. What more do you want?"

Lagertha just shook her head and went down the hill to Lunden. She went into the stone circle and straight to Frøya's stone, Odin was unreal to her.

Lagertha had a shield with her which was made of birch bark, a couple of bricks were attached underneath so it came up a little from the ground, the freeze in the ground early in the spring was notorious. It was a shield in the sense that it protected her from the cold which came crawling up off from the ground.

Frøya was patient, she waited until Lagertha had sat down on the shield with Odin's stone as support before she started chattering. Lagertha could hardly believe what she heard. The sun was rising above the horizon. Gulosen would sparkle in the sunlight any moment now. Frøya saw that Lagertha had great difficulty digesting what she had said.

"It's true, that is what's going to happen."

"It was you who gave me the dream," Lagertha said finally.

Frøya nodded. "Without the sword, nothing would be possible. It was I who gave Joen the dream of mixing in greystone powder as well."

"What about Odin, why doesn't he know how to make the best sword?"

Lagertha could feel the stone in her back moving. She could feel how annoyed Odin was.

"Odin is not as smart as me. As soon as you get to the battlefield with your long and almost white hair, you have already won the second you need to kill those around you."

"So that's why I'm still alive?"

"Among other things, but the most important quality is that you are fearless, and you do not think about the consequences."

"How do men think?"

Odin's stone moved again.

"Let Odin answer," said Frøya.

"There is no difference in either hair length, hair colour or fearlessness. The only difference is that you are a woman. When men see you, they act instinctively, they don't want to kill you, they want to multiply. Once they have that thought it is already too late, you have managed to kill them."

Lagertha laughed for a long time. "Do you mean to say that men are so primitive?"

"Men don't kill because they want to, they kill because they have to, they'd rather lie in the arms of a lovely woman in peace."

"Give me a break," said Frøya angrily.

Lagertha suddenly realised that Frøya loved Odin, but he had chosen another. She wondered if it was safe to stay in the stone circle.

"Stay seated," said Frøya to her. "I'm so tired of men, and especially you," she said to Odin in a thunderous voice.

Lagertha could feel the stone move again, but this time it was Odin who trembled with fear. She felt like laughing, but she didn't dare.

Frøya continued with a thunderous voice, "You and your idiotic son Tor who rides across the sky with his hammer and makes thunder, you are both equally primitive, completely brain dead. I'll tell you one thing, Lagertha will not only be remembered as the greatest shieldmaiden that has ever lived, she will also be remembered as the one who ended the era of you and your idiotic son."

Frøya was so angry, but she had to stop and take a breath. Odin took the opportunity to say a few words.

"Do you think that Lagertha will lead to my downfall?"

"Not right away, it becomes the task of one of her descendants. Her name is Lundesol, and she is born here in Lunden. Bergtor, the most famous blacksmith who has ever lived is her father."

Lagertha was suddenly worried. "And Joen?" she asked.

"Joen is not the most famous, but the best blacksmith who has ever lived. Joen will be forgotten for posterity, no one will look for your sword, they don't know where to look."

"Where will you hide it?" Odin asked curiously.

"Underneath my farm," Lagertha replied. "So Joen is the best blacksmith, and I'm the best shieldmaiden?"

"Of course," Frøya replied. She turned to Odin again. "Since men are so primitive, and it is us who give life to you. What is it you think you can do better than us?"

Odin knew he was on thin ice. He didn't dare to tell her she was the one in his life. Frøya and Lagertha was equal, but there were no men tough enough to be with them. Frøya had followed his thoughts.

"There is one for you," she told Lagertha, "but it's not Ragnar." Odin didn't have enough courage to be with Frøya, he stopped breathing, she still scared the crap out of him.

Lagertha suddenly figured out who Frøya could be with. "Forget Odin," she said. "There is one who is tougher than Odin and Tor combined."

It started to drizzle, and they could see a huge, bright and double rainbow which stood like a bridge on the glossy calm Gulosen. Frøya laughed out loud and disappeared.

There were tough enough men, Lagertha thought, *you just had to look for them in the right place, and the right place for Frøya was obviously in the middle of Gulosen.*

Lagertha got up and went up the slopes to the smithy.

"How is it going?" she asked Joen.

"I need another week, but otherwise it's going well."

Lagertha sat down on a stump that stood on the outside. Joen asked Lagertha what was on her mind. Lagertha told him about the quarrel between Frøya and Odin.

"I saw the incredible rainbow," said Joen. "It's the first time I have seen a double rainbow. Did you know that the rainbow continues into the fjord, it makes a circle. Heimdal is a steady guy, it's about time Frøya forgot Odin. He is too full of himself, that's why he can't be with Frøya, he doesn't know how to give her enough room."

"That sounds strangely enough right. Do you think the same applies to me and Ragnar?"

"Definitely," Joen said and smiled. "There is no doubt that the greatest love that is rare and survives everything is equal. This is where the difficult point lies. Equal love from both, and both are equally strong, but they need to make room for each other, Odin didn't make room for Frøya, and Ragnar didn't make room for you."

"How come you're so smart?"

"Look at that view," Joen said and smiled.

Lagertha had to smile too, she understood what he meant.

5

Bergtora woke up and sat up in her sleeping bag, her eyes were still sleepy, it was clear that she wasn't in this world yet.

"I remember something I read," Ravn said.

"It's a conversation between the dwarf Alvis and Vingtor. Alvis wants to marry Vingtor's daughter, but Vingtor wants to kill him, so he asks him a lot of questions, because Alvis knows everything. If Vingtor asks him questions until the sun rises, then Alvis will turn into a stone when the sun rays hit him. Vingtor asks Alvis what they call the night, and Alvis replies."

Ravn drew a deep breath before he continued, "*Men call it Night. The gods say Darkness and the most holy gods say Hood. The giants name it Lightless, the elves Sleep's Soothing and the dwarfs the Weaver of Dreams.*"

"It is clear that Bergtora has been in the land of the Weaver of Dreams. Don't you think?" Ardar said and laughed.

Ravn nodded and smiled. Bergtora received a steaming hot coffee from Ravn. Both Ardar and Ravn had enough sense not to start talking to her until she had drunk the cup.

"Tell us about the dream," said Ravn when the cup was empty. Bergtora told them about Lagertha and her sword, and Frøya who left Odin in Heimdal's favour.

"I have to say," said Ardar, impressed, "to me it sounds like your dream has happened. Is it a talent or is it innate?"

Ravn looked at him sharply. "What do you think?"

Ardar became insecure, he was always insecure when Ravn

was sharp.

"I don't know," he finally said.

"What do you think?" Ravn asked, still sharply.

"Innate," mumbled Ardar.

Ravn was satisfied, he hated when Ardar made himself more stupid than he was. The sun broke through the cloud layer. It was always unbeatable when it happened, it was just as if hope came along every time the sun managed to break through the layers.

"I'm excited about what will happen next," said Ravn. "What do you think, Bergtora?"

"I have no clue, the information comes when it comes, it's impossible to force, but you know that."

"Are you sneak informing Ardar without him noticing?" said Ravn and laughed.

There was so much Ardar wondered, but at the same time he didn't want anyone to know that he believed in something that wasn't scientifically proven.

"Just ask," said Bergtora.

"I'm wondering if you two get the information in the same way."

"Between us, it's the same way," said Ravn, "but that's very rare, mostly it's different."

"How do you receive the information?"

"A place, or birds that are gathering, or that something repeats itself."

"It's a pattern?"

"The pattern leads you to something. A classic example is when Bergtora passes by the Høyem farm on Byneset, and a large flock of crows flies in a circle over Bergtora for so long that she finally leaves. The very next day she reads in an old book that Ravn Valgardsson came from that particular farm. You probably know that Ravn was associated with ravens, if you connect the crows and Ravn, then you will see the pattern."

"Somebody is showing you something from the past, but how did you know where to find the book?"

"The book was suddenly there, I wanted to find out more about how they built the church," replied Bergtora.

Lundesol looked at Orm while he slept. She tried to move her legs, but nothing happened.

"Help!" she shouted loudly.

Orm woke up and looked at her in astonishment. He jumped out of bed and held her tight.

"I can't move," Lundesol said worriedly.

"I know, you're stiff as a stick. I'll be back."

Orm ran to a small house by the sea, Marta who lived there knew the strangest things, she was as old as the mounds. "Come fast," said Orm to her. "Lundesol has frozen."

Marta staggered to her feet. Orm most wanted to carry her and run back to Lundesol, but he knew it was disrespectful. Finally, after a long while, Marta reached Lundesol.

"Look at that, look at that," she said over and over again.

"What?" Orm asked, annoyed.

Marta didn't reply, she said the two words endlessly while she splashed water on Lundesol and waved a green tassel around her. Orm saw that it was a bundle of nettles. He also noticed the large ball of fat that the woman had in the middle of her head. The long grey hair hung loosely down her shoulders. Orm wondered if she had a broomstick standing outside her door. Lundesol moved her head, shortly afterwards she moved her fingers and, finally, she was able to move her legs. Orm asked Marta what had happened to Lundesol.

"That, my son, was witchcraft, not from the past, and not from the future, but from just now. There are some who see Lundesol as the symbol of the new era. She got Håkon Jarl killed, the last pagan king is gone. Håkon insisted that he was a Jarl, but that's just humbug, he was a king who didn't have time to put on his own crown. Bergtor finished the crown in the same second as Håkon Jarl drew his last breath. Olav Tryggvason also came sailing into the fjord at the same second. Lundesol froze because there are some who wants to freeze time."

"Who are you talking about?"

"Odin. On the next full moon, you shall go up on Høgsteinen eight o'clock in the evening and ask Frøya to protect you."

Orm thanked her and promised to give her a goat. Marta went back to her house, and Lundesol and Orm decided to go up to the mound, they always did if something special happened.

"Exciting times," Lundesol said when they sat on the top and looked out over the fjord.

"It is possible it will be a little too exciting."

Orm told her what he had found out from Marta. He was going to die at the battle of Svolder. Lundesol asked if Marta had said anything about a current danger.

"We have long enough to finish the ale," said Orm.

They started laughing. That's how it was, one lived and one died. The sun was setting, and it was getting cold. A large flock of ducks lifted from the plain down by the fjord and flew back to the outlet of the river Gaula.

"Did you know that the gods say Beer instead of Ale?" asked Orm.

Lundesol nodded and said, *"The Vanir call it Foaming. The giants name it Cloudless Swill, and in Hel it is known as Mead. Suttung's sons call it Feast Draught."*

Lundesol and Orm went down to the bonfire on the beach; some of Orm's men sat around, they were in a glorious mood. Olav was there too, he was Orm's best man and friend, they could have been brothers; both had light, long hair and blue eyes. Lundesol wasn't so different from them, she had the same colours. They decided to while away the evening swilling horns of ale.

"When will there be a wedding?" Ardar asked excitedly.

"Soon, my friend, soon," Ravn said. "I just need to get some things sorted out first."

"Is there anything I can help you with?"

"Not really, I just have to arrange the flowers and fix the food, set the tables and get all the torches in the ground. Find a normal wicker, invite people, make Bergtora's wedding dress and wash my suit and the car."

"Let me help you with the music."

"The barn we are going to borrow is soundproof, it should work well. We are going to have a great bonfire on the beach as well as a barbecue and, of course, barrels of beer."

"Is that all?"

"No, of course not, there will be cake as well. How are your baking skills?"

Ardar just shook his head, and Ravn took the hint, he went to find someone who could bake a cake. Ardar stretched as long as he was, he felt that it was going to be a good day.

"Isn't it very unusual for the groom to arrange everything?" he asked Bergtora.

"Maybe, but then Ravn isn't very ordinary, is he?"

"He's very unusual," Ardar said, smiling. "His femininity makes him strangely enough more masculine."

"Isn't that funny," said Bergtora and laughed.

"What's so funny?" Ravn had returned without them noticing.

"Nothing," said Ardar, and they laughed even more.

"It's gonna be a marzipan cake with raspberries, strawberries and vanilla cream. I found a pastry chef next door; can you believe it? He works at the cafe where you used to work."

"Maybe that's why he said yes," said Bergtora and laughed.

Ardar still felt it was going to be a good day, he never used big words, but he had to say a beautiful day out loud. He heard Bergtora laughing behind him.

"Hard to say?" she asked.

"Big words," Ardar said, smiling at her. She gave him a cup of coffee.

"Do you have any wishes for the wedding dress?" Ravn asked.

"Not really, as long as it's not uncomfortable."

They could see that Ravn was lost; he was obviously thinking about the dress.

"Let's go for a walk," said Bergtora to Ardar.

Bergtora and Ravn's house was located in such a way that it was pleasant in all directions as soon as you left the house. The small wooden houses in different colours lay in a row on both sides of the road, while the grey cobblestones meandered between them. Bakklandet was laid out according to the terrain, while further towards the fjord, the ruler had decided how the roads should look.

They came to a square, there were four intersecting streets right there, it was the city's nicest hub. They crossed the river and walked underneath the red wooden portal at the end of the bridge, it was still there after one hundred and sixty years, it was called the portal of happiness.

Bergtora and Ardar were on their way to the West wall of the cathedral, that was always an unbeatable view. There were benches at a suitable distance from the wall with a square in between.

They sat down on one of the benches and looked at all the sculptures that stood on the wall.

"It's still a beautiful day," Ardar said.

"You sound more and more weird," Bergtora said and looked at him.

Ardar stroked his chin and said, "I'm starting to get poetic, and possibly old. I know I have asked you before, but what was it about Ravn that made you understand he was the one?"

"I never decided, you don't have to weigh the pros and cons if you know it's right."

"That is true."

"You are worried you won't experience it, but you don't have to be, there's only one thing that will prevent it from happening."

"What?"

"Some idiotic lady move in with you and make you terrified of being alone."

Ardar got up.

"We're going back," he said. "I know what to give Ravn as a wedding gift."

6

Lagertha looked beyond the plains, it was early spring. The birch had buds, but not mouse ears yet. She was soon going on her first journey that wasn't a tokt, with one ship and twenty-two rowers. Lagertha had found a place reminiscent of Neset, it lay on the west side of an island sheltered by a peninsula.

The sword was finally finished, she picked it up from Joen, and headed down the hill towards Lunden. Frøya was waiting for Lagertha when she entered the stone circle.

"There is a rowan by the burn Rowan in Lochranza," she said, "it's the most sacred tree in existence. Ranza is the masculine word for rowan, and the place is masculine, but the burn that runs through is feminine.

"The trip you are taking will have ripple effects, not only into the next millennium, but the millennium after as well. You will meet an old lady named Ailsa. She comes from an island which is located between two countries. The name of the island is Ailsa Craig. Ailsa means stone in Cymric, and Craig means stone in Gaelic. Ailsa Craig was once a peak in the same mountain range as Høgsteinen a long, long time ago. It was transported to Norway by the huge masses of ice that floated across the land and sea. Ailsa has a blue stone, and Høgsteinen a green stone. It's important that the connection between them is hidden for the next 1203 years."

"1203," Lagertha said slowly. She added 810 which was the year they were in, and got 2013. It was the same numbers.

Lagertha wanted to ask Frøya if it meant something, but she had already disappeared.

Ravn woke up and looked around, he was alone. His thoughts had been on a long journey, it was the photons and atoms that had captured his interest. Ardar and Bergtora came back.

"I know what to give you as a wedding gift," Ardar said.

Ravn was excited, this gift felt personal.

"A trip," said Ardar. "I have booked a trip for you, me and of course Bergtora. I've rented a house, we're going to Corriegills for three weeks."

"And where is Corriegills?" asked Ravn.

"It's located on the west coast of Scotland."

"It is a fantastic gift," said Ravn. "How did you find the place?"

"It was easy, I closed my eyes and spun the globe."

"I didn't think you were the type to spin the globe," said Ravn, smiling at Ardar, who looked at his hands.

"I was tired of being me, to put it mildly," Ardar said. He was still looking down at his hands.

"When do we leave?" asked Ravn.

"We can go right now. I met a captain at Kjeglekroa yesterday, he said he would leave for Glasgow today. He will take us across the Clyde to the quay in Brodick, it's not far from Corriegills. I have my luggage in the car."

"Then we have to pack," said Ravn.

"It's warm there," said Bergtora. "You don't need winter clothes."

"There are clothes there," Ardar said.

"What!" said Bergtora and Ravn at the same time.

"The house I rented is fully furnished, and Margaret who I

spoke to said her father who lived there just died, all his clothes are still there. We could use them if we wanted to."

"I can pack nice and colourful shirts, and nothing practical," said Ravn happily.

"I'm just packing some dresses," Bergtora said and went upstairs.

"The house is magnificent, it's a typical old Scottish house with the pipe on the short outside wall, two chimneys, a dark blue AGA in the kitchen and, of course, a deer antler in the hallway."

Bergtora came out shortly afterwards and said she had finished packing. Ravn went inside and Bergtora and Ardar watched Domen on the other side of Nidelva. The crows started to gather.

"Both you and I, and Ravn for sure, knows this is going to be a trip to remember," said Ardar.

"Not only that," said Bergtora, "it will also change us."

"I thought we could go to a pub at the hotel Ormidale, but unfortunately, it's closed. A huge greenhouse is part of the main building. They have had a disco there every week uninterrupted since the '70s."

Ravn came back and said, "We can have our own disco party; I have packed my sling pants. It is common that the bridesmaid gets clothes from the bride and groom. We have arranged an outfit for you, since you are the only guest and best man."

He gave Ardar a parcel. Ardar unwrapped the gift. It was a pair of purple sling pants, green suede shoes, and a bright yellow shirt with a white geometric pattern consisting of circles, some had dots and some had streaks. Ardar got tears in his eyes. He wasn't sure about the pants and shoes, but the shirt was a hit.

"Go and try them on!" said Ravn. "See if everything fits."

Ardar came back as a new man. His white long hair matched the white pattern on his yellow shirt. The sling pants looked fashionable.

"You need a brown leather jacket," said Ravn and ran inside. He came back with a short jacket from the '70s.

Ardar tried it on.

"The green shoes are too much," Ravn finally said.

He ran inside and picked up a pair of dark brown shoes. Ardar put them on and felt strangely well.

"Now you are ready to meet the only one on the CalMal ferry," Bergtora said.

"You did your homework," Ardar said impressed. "I've done mine too. You will not come on board the ferry unless you have an urgent errand on the island. That's why I talked to the captain. Margaret said the larder and the basement are full of food. Her father used to be a gourmet chef; we could use it all if we wanted to. Co-op is open if we need anything, and there's also an old Aston Martin in the garage we can borrow."

"It's starting to look like a real holiday," Ravn said, and asked what colour the car was.

"Green."

Ravn ran inside, and Ardar took off his brown shoes, he knew Ravn would come out again with the green shoes.

"I was right," said Ravn out of breath, "there was a bigger plan behind the shoes."

"Does the car have four round headlights?" Bergtora asked.

"Yep!" Ardar said lightly.

"I need sunglasses and a scarf to wear over the hair," said Bergtora.

Ravn and Ardar had already packed their sunglasses, Ardar went to the car and picked up his luggage and Bergtora locked the door. They strolled between the low wooden houses on their way to Nyhavna. The captain said they had to make a stop in Wick, which was in Caithness. He didn't say why and Ardar didn't ask, he knew it was useless.

Orm thought it would be nice with a change of scenery, he wanted to test his newest ship. It was made of oak, the carvings were exquisite, a raven was in the bow and one in the stern.
It had five thousand five hundred nails and iron rivets. It was 21.5 metres long and a little over 5 metres at its widest. There were seventeen frames, and on the outside, there were twelve oak strakes on both sides. The ship lay well in the water.

Orm had had many long and tough discussions with the shipbuilder whether the ship was too low or not. The most common was to have sixteen strakes, especially out on the high seas. Orm felt it was enough with twelve strakes, the ship would be much easier to manoeuvre that way.

The sail had a deep blue stripe in the middle, sky blue stripes on the sides, and some in gold occasionally. It was made of linen and was attached to a 13-metre high mast. When the weavers started weaving, everybody knew nobody could disturb them, they were free from all other work tasks until the sail was finished. Good shipbuilders you could find everywhere, but a good weaver was very hard to come by.

Marta had insisted that Orm was the one who should learn how to make a clear blue colour. The plants had to be sown every year, they couldn't survive the cold winter. Orm was only four the first time he collected the leaves from the woad. He and Marta got up before the sun three days before the full moon, the dew had to be on the leaves still, that was of utmost importance. Then they would put the leaves in a big cauldron and stir all the time.

Marta always yelled when it started to boil, she scared the little beasts away. The first colour that fell to the bottom of the cauldron was white, after a while it changed colour to blue. Marta used pee from drunken men to make the colour last. Orm had to promise Marta that he wouldn't tell anyone the big secret.

Orm had decided to bring Olav, Lundesol and twenty-two rowers. It wasn't a tokt he was going on. He wanted to take the same trip as Lagertha had been on. He went up to Høgsteinen. It was early in the morning; the sun had not risen yet. He reached the top just as the first sunbeams passed the horizon. Orm felt in his bones that he had made the right decision. He thought of Lagertha, and what she must have felt, going on the same trip over a hundred years earlier.

"If you want to know, I can tell you," said a voice.

Orm noticed that Lagertha was sitting next to him on the rock. It was the first time he heard her voice; it wasn't so different from Lundesol's.

"How are you?" Orm asked.

"Not bad. You know the feeling everyone has when they're alive, they feel there's a great wisdom waiting for them on the other side."

Orm understood what she meant. He wondered what Lagertha's point was; she was dead, after all.

"There isn't an answer on the other side, you have all the answers when you're alive. Most of the time the answer is right in front of you. It's like a ship passing by, sometimes you have to get on board. It's too late no matter what you do, if the ship has sailed, time can't change the decision you should have made. I wish the feeling of predictability didn't exist; life would look completely different if it didn't."

"If I only win that battle and finish that ship and get the one

I want, then everything's perfect," Orm said and laughed.

"It's a great and completely incomprehensible feeling," Lagertha said slowly.

"Do you really mean that, even though you're dead?" Orm asked in astonishment.

"I see how that feeling is the governing feeling, I cannot for the life of me see it's leading anywhere." Lagertha sounded disillusioned.

"Maybe for the death of you?"

Lagertha looked at him from the side and frowned.

"You said for the life of me, but you're dead."

Lagertha nodded and laughed a little. "There isn't much difference," she said. "It's the same thing that happens over and over again, no matter where you are."

"Do you mean it seriously, that there's no big difference?"

"That's exactly what I mean. I understood you intend to follow in my footsteps."

She looked at him inquisitively, Orm could feel her gaze.

"Nobody can follow in your footsteps," he said finally. "I'm just going to the same island you went to. Olav needs some fresh air."

"And a beloved one?"

"Yeah!"

"I can help you," said Lagertha. "There's a nice lady who lives in Lochranza, located on the North end of the island. You have to pass Catacol first. It's named after Frøya's coal black cat by the way. There's a nice poem her father wrote, Olav can learn it and say it to his daughter. Do you want to hear it?"

Orm nodded.

Lagertha began to say the words as the sun left the horizon and began to rise in the sky.

"*Arran of the many stags,*

the sea reaches to its shoulder; island where companies are fed, ridges whereon blue spears are reddened.

Wanton deer upon its peaks, mellow blaeberries on its heaths, cold water in its streams, nuts upon its brown oaks.

Hunting-dogs there, and hounds, blackberries and sloes of the blackthorn, dense thorn-bushes in its woods, stags astray among in oak-groves. Gleaning of purple lichen on its rocks, grass without blemish on its slopes, a sheltering cloak over its crags; gamboling of fawns, trout leaping.

Smooth in its lowland, fat its swine, pleasant its fields, a tale you may belive; its nuts on the tips of its hazelwood, sailing of longships past it.

It is delightful for them when the fine weather comes, trout under the banks of its rivers, seagulls answer each other round its white cliff; delightful at all times is Arran."

"Nice!" said Orm when Lagertha had finished. "The only thing I didn't understand was gambolling of fawns, I haven't heard that one before."

Lagertha pointed to some young deer that ran playfully around Lunden.

"There you have gambolling of fawns," she said.

"Do you think that you and Lundesol would have been friends if you had lived at the same time?"

"I know we had," Lagertha replied. "She will travel with you and Olav, I travelled with Ravn and Sjur."

Orm didn't quite understand the point.

Lagertha explained to him what she meant. "Both Lundesol and I thrive best in men's company, we find that women's presence is deceptive. The lady that Olav finds will also be Lundesol's good friend."

"How is it to live between death and life?"

"I will disappear soon, it's time to move on."

"How was it between you and Sjur of Stein?"

"It was actually very good." Lagertha did not sound happy when she talked about Sjur.

"He was not the one?"

Orm already knew the answer when he asked. He could see that Lagertha slowly faded away. Orm wondered if Lagertha still had a broken heart, but it was too late to ask, she was already gone.

7

Ragnar stood in his ship; he was on his way out of Korsfjorden. Why he had said no to go with Lagertha was a mystery, Ragnar knew it was going to be an adventure. After all, they were going to the island of the many stags.

Last time Ragnar had been there, he had dreamed of moving there with Ravn and Lagertha. He knew Ravn longed to live on an island. Bynes was only a peninsula, it wasn't enough for Ravn, he wanted water on all sides.

Ragnar was happy with the ships Lagertha had given him, he just couldn't understand why it wasn't enough. Was it he himself who messed up his life or was it Lagertha? That was the big question, Ragnar didn't know, but something had gnawed at him for a long time. Did it matter what he did or didn't do? He came to the conclusion that it didn't. Ragnar hoped time would tell. He didn't know that in the second he thought time would tell, Ravn and Lagertha had a conversation about exactly the same thing.

"Let's talk about it one more time," Ravn said. "Ragnar said no to you, but yes to a hundred and twenty ships made from the finest oak, and you both think it's perfectly normal?"

"None of us do."

"You are independent, you look after yourself, it makes absolutely no sense, but you are in love and that's a disease in itself, so you are not to blame. Ragnar does not have that disease, but he needs the ships."

Lagertha thought for a long time, she tried to figure out if she felt exploited. There was a hurt feeling that he would rather be with someone else. It didn't matter if he got the ships or not, something inside her was dead.

Ravn jumped up and said he had a solution. "We will find a new and better guy for you on the island with the many stags."

Lagertha almost believed it could be true.

"Anyway, we're leaving tomorrow," she said. "Sjur is coming as well."

"Sjur," said Ravn with a grimace.

8

Bergtora went up the long and narrow stairs that led up to the deck. Ravn and Ardar were already on deck, they wanted to see the first sign of land.

"Your dress is similar to the beetroot soup with pumpkin seeds I made the other day."

"How do I look?" Bergtora asked excitedly.

"Very nice," said Ravn. "This used to be the land of the Pictish tribe, the Cat people, maybe they worshiped Frøya."

They could barely distinguish land from the sea, they would soon arrive in Caithness.

The captain brought a package to a resident of Trøndelag who lived in Wick, that was the only reason they stopped here. The boat docked at the quay, and Ardar and Ravn couldn't wait to go ashore.

"Stay right where you are," said the captain. Ravn and Ardar looked at each other, Ravn saw that Ardar had the same thought as himself. Without a word they followed the captain down the gangway.

"We're just excited about who the emigrant is," Ardar said when the captain looked at him.

"He was supposed to be on the quay. I reckon he'll find me or us. It will be easy," the captain said dryly. "Since you two look like somebody straight out of Carnaby Street."

A guy came walking and smiling. The captain gave him the box. They didn't exchange a word, they just looked at each other excitedly.

"Coffee?" the emigrant asked at last.

"Love to," said the captain. "I have a couple of blind passengers with me, is that okay?"

The emigrant nodded.

"What's your name?" asked Ravn.

"Emil Skagen. Named after the Swedish rascal and the Danish shores, and here comes the trønderrose," he said soon after. Bergtora came down the gangway. After greeting her, Emil cross-turned and went with straight legs straight into the air.

"Don't ask if he has been to the Red Square in Moscow," said Ardar quietly to Ravn.

Fortunately, Emil walked only a few meters with straight legs. They approached a typical old Scottish house with hollyhocks facing the street, they weren't in bloom yet, but it was going to be a beautiful sight later on.

Emil showed the way through the gate and into the garden. A small stream meandered like Nidelva and the River Thames through the garden. Blue irises stood straight and beautiful on both sides of the stream. A wooden table in the garden was set for six people.

"I would have understood it if the table was set for three people," said the captain. "I'm assuming you have a wife."

"I do."

Alma came out of the house and walked towards them. *She's too good for Emil,* thought Bergtora, she exchanged glances with Ravn, he thought the same. None of them had seen that Ardar turned pale as soon as Alma came out. He was pale before, but now he was almost blue.

Alma stopped and stood as she was frozen to the ground with a tray in her hands. Emil was so preoccupied with himself that he didn't see what was happening. He took the tray out of Alma's hands and put scones, cream and raspberry jam on the table, as well as a large teapot.

"Be seated, and please supply yourselves," he said.

The table was round, none of them needed to send anything. Emil unpacked what was in the box. There were five pairs of Selbu mittens in different colours, as well as ten large brown cheeses from Gudbrandsdalen. Emil gave one pair of brown and white Selbu mittens to Alma, and tried on a black and white pair, they fitted perfectly. Three pairs in small sizes lay on the table, the Selbu roses were red, orange and pink on a white background.

"I was once in the village museum in Selbu," Emil said. "What I didn't know, was that there were many men who knitted as well. They composed patterns with moose, birds, routes and the Selbu rose of course, it was absolutely amazing.

The men's sweaters were shorter and wider than they are today, but much nicer. I want to start knitting one day, but for now, I'm importing Selbu mittens to my family, due to this wonderful captain, who is willing to stop here on such an important errand."

The captain didn't answer, he was too busy eating scones. Alma and Ardar were happy with the flood of words from Emil, they hoped he didn't see what was going on between them. They drank tea and ate scones and pretended like nothing had happened.

They glanced at each other from time to time. When they finished eating, Ardar offered to help Alma clear the table. Ardar walked slowly across the lawn and into the kitchen, Alma was everything he had ever wanted.

"I heard you were on your way to Arran," said Alma. "Maybe I can come and visit you while you're there?"

Ardar just kissed her lightly, they both knew that it wasn't reversible what they experienced.

"Already back," Emil said, when they returned.

Ravn wondered if it was more than okay that Ardar had fallen for Alma. He decided to ask Emil.

"Alma is of another calibre than me, we don't fit together. I have long waited for an opportunity to tell her that I have met someone else." He looked at Alma and said, "You can go to Arran if you want to, I will take care of the kids. You have endured enough from me over the years."

Alma kissed him lightly on the cheek and went to pack. Ardar sat and looked straight ahead, with his eyes wide open.

"Do I have a girlfriend and three daughters I have not met yet?" Ardar looked at Ravn.

"You have," Ravn replied seriously.

"I'm happy, but terrified," Ardar said.

"Alma has everything you need," said Ravn. "She knows the importance of a small amount of vanilla together with the sugar in the cream, she also knows that Suki tea from Ireland is of utmost importance, serving scones. The last taste to bring it all together was the wild raspberry jam."

"The tea was lemongrass and ginger."

"I could also taste a delicious butter underneath the jam."

"I'm not scared anymore," Ardar said as he drank the tea.

Alma was ready, she wore a yellow dress with a brown leather belt at the waist. In her hand, she held a brown leather bag. The colours matched well with her long copper-coloured hair and green eyes. Ardar just smiled his secretive smile. Bergtora and the captain got up and said goodbye to Emil. At the same time, three girls came running around the corner of the house. They stopped suddenly and looked at the guests.

Alma introduced them. Holly was the oldest, she was eight, then Emma in the middle who was six, and at last, four-year-old Fiona. Emil said that Alma was going away for a while. The daughters started to howl.

"I don't mind if they join us," said Ravn.

Bergtora and Ardar agreed. The captain was already on his way to the ship. Bergtora helped Alma to pack three bags in a hurry. They ran down the street and caught up with Ardar and Ravn who walked in a long, long line with Fiona, Emma and Holly between them.

"I knew he was coming today," said Alma to Bergtora.

"When I woke up today, it was like D day."

"You mean like the landing in Normandy?"

"It could have been a life of grief, if we hadn't taken a chance."

Bergtora nodded, she understood what Alma meant. It was now or never in some cases, and this was one of them. She looked at Ardar, there were bounces in his steps, he was happy. The captain stood on deck and shook his head and tried to hide a smile.

"I reckon we arrive at Arran during the late hours of the night, there are plenty of cabins," he said.

Ardar stretched out his hand and helped Alma on board.

"How would you like to sleep in mine and Bergtora's cabin tonight?" asked Ravn of the daughters. They just jumped up and down, that was answer enough.

Ardar woke up the next day to seagull cries. There was a lady on his arm with long copper-coloured hair. Ardar felt the anxiety rising in him, but it only came halfway. The joy took over, he didn't bother to be afraid anymore. He kissed Alma when there was a knock on the door. It was Ravn with two cups of coffee.

"One should think it was you who were to marry, and not me and Bergtora."

Ardar smiled and Alma just laughed.

"I'll make it up to you," she said. "Ardar told me that you have planned to get married in the middle of the Standing Stones. I could make the food if you want me to?"

"I will not say no thanks," said Ravn and smiled. "I had actually managed to find a guy in Trondheim who was willing to bake the cake, but then Ardar invited us on this trip, so I cancelled. It would be great if you could bake a cake, any one will do. The captain said we had to get a permission to get married in the middle of the Standing Stones. I have already sent one, that's the beauty of being on a ship in the middle of the North Sea, you can still send an application to the mainland. Anyway, I asked your daughters if they wanted to be bridesmaids, they just jumped high into the air."

"I hope we aren't in the middle of the North Sea anymore," said Ardar and sat up, "that means we are going backwards." He gave Alma a cup of coffee, Ravn took the hint and closed the door silently.

He hoped the application would be ready in time, usually it took up to two months to get one. Maybe they could get married first, and then get the permit.

9

Orm and Lundesol stood in the ship waiting for Olav. Orm had named the ship Volven. The rowers were ready, but time went on and Olav didn't come. Eventually Orm went ashore to find him. Olav sat on a rock engrossed in his own thoughts.

"We're all waiting for you," shouted Orm.

"I'm not coming, I want to end my days here," shouted Olav back.

"You're not dead yet," shouted Orm, he was furious.

Olav sat still.

Orm dragged him to his feet and kicked him in the ass.

"You don't have to say anything, but you will walk, I won't carry you."

Olav barely walked. Orm got more and more furious.

"Most of all I want to throw you in the rubbish heap," he said, "but I want to leave. You don't want to know what I'm capable of."

"I know that," said Olav, his voice sounded hollow.

"You can cry on the ship, but you will get on board."

Olav gave up, he didn't have enough strength to fight Orm, he felt completely empty.

Olav sat down in the ship as far away from Orm as possible. Lundesol gave the rowers a sign, and soon Olav and Orm lay in the cold water and huddled; at first, they were furious, but then they started to laugh. Olav and Orm laughed so much that they were about to drown. Two rowers had to help them back into the ship, and the journey could continue at last. Olav was actually looking forward to the journey.

They approached Korsfjorden. Olav looked at Lundesol who stood with her loose fluttering light hair like a sail in the wind. Olav sighed heavily. He knew there was only one Lundesol, he hadn't managed to hide his interest. Olav had to get his shit together, or there was a fat chance he would be thrown overboard again. He stared feverishly at the water, his mind racing.

There was a flock of seagulls following the ship, they were wonderfully quiet, it was almost as if they had a plan. There were two carved ravens on the ship. Olav was amazed that it was the seagulls that followed them, and not the ravens. The ship lay well in the water, not too deep and not too shallow, but just right. The exciting part would be how the ship would cope with its first storm on the high seas.

The blue hour was on its way, soon the stars would show the way. Olav was glad the rain didn't pour down. Orm came and stood next to him.

"I have always known about your love for Lundesol. All men are in love with her, they can't help it. I'm just glad it was me Lundesol chose. She is important to me, but so are you. I need your friendship. This trip has one purpose, and that is to get you back on your feet again. You mourn Lundesol, but it will soon end. Lagertha said there was a woman for you who lives on the North end of the island, she said you should learn a poem before we arrive."

Olav just nodded; he was glad Orm had taken control of his life.

Orm said the poem first:

"*Arran of the many stags, the sea reaches to its shoulder; island where companies are fed, ridges whereon blue spears are reddened.*

Wanton deer upon its peaks, mellow blaeberries on its heaths, cold water in its streams, nuts upon its brown oaks.

Hunting-dogs there, and hounds, blackberries and sloes of the blackthorn, dense thorn-bushes in its woods, stags astray among in oak-groves. Gleaning of purple lichen on its rocks, grass without blemish on its slopes, a sheltering cloak over its crags; gamboling of fawns, trout leaping.

Smooth in its lowland, fat its swine, pleasant its fields, a tale you may belive; its nuts on the tips of its hazelwood, sailing of longships past it.

It is delightful for them when the fine weather comes, trout under the banks of its rivers, seagulls answer each other round its white cliff; delightful at all times is Arran."

It wasn't the easiest poem to learn, but it helped that Olav felt completely empty, there were no disturbing thoughts that made it difficult. Finally, Olav could recite the poem.

"Gamboling of fawns," he said, "that's something I would love to see again."

"You didn't see the young deer in Lunden?"

Olav shook his head, he had been too busy looking down in the ship.

"Now when you can recite the poem, you are well equipped," said Orm. "You only need one more thing."

He pulled a necklace from his pocket. It was made of silver, with a green stone in the middle, surrounded by five rose petals made of gold. Olav didn't know what to say, he just looked at Orm. Lundesol came over to Orm and asked him what Lagertha had said about the woman Olav was to meet.

"You get a good friend named Arnhild," said Orm and pulled her down on his lap and put his arms around her.

Lagertha, Ravn and Sjur were on their way. They sailed from the same place as Orm sailed from a hundred years later.

Gulosen was yellow from the strong sunlight. Further out in the fjord, the colours were different. It was a silver veil in the light blue sky, with an almost beige fjord below.

Lagertha had never seen such a special beige colour on the fjord, she made Sjur and Ravn aware.

"It's Gulosen that crosses into Korsfjorden and becomes beige," Ravn said dryly.

Lagertha wondered whether the beige was going to change when they got closer, the answer came faster than she thought. It came closer and closer, both the ship and the colour were drawn towards each other. Sjur and Ravn stood and gaped.

"Is it an epicentre?" asked Lagertha.

"That's possible," Sjur said, "but for what?"

"We are getting the answer right now," said Ravn.

The ship didn't glide as easily on the water as before, the wind suddenly became calm and abruptly stopped. The wind had gone down into the fjord and disappeared.

"Do you think this is the beginning of a maelstrom?" asked Lagertha.

"Hard to say," said Sjur, "we have to wait and see what happens."

They filled the horns with ale and sat down. None of them knew how long it would take before the wind returned. Lagertha loved the unpredictability that always happened when they were dependent on the wind, but this was something more than exciting, it was just strange.

The horns were empty, and Lagertha got up to look at the water. A change had taken place, there were foam peaks, but there were no waves. It just got more and more strange.

"I want to find out if the water feels different," said Ravn and took his clothes off.

Sjur started to undress too, Lagertha stopped him.

"Wait and see what happens to Ravn first," she said.

Ravn jumped out into the fjord; the foam had adhered to his hair. Lagertha and Sjur couldn't help but laugh. Ravn swam further and further away from the ship. Finally, Lagertha shouted that he should return. Ravn turned right away, and Sjur helped him on board.

"So?" Lagertha asked, looking excitedly at him.

Ravn took some of the foam from his hair and tasted it. He gave a little to Sjur and Lagertha as well.

"Salt," said Lagertha.

"Not only salt," said Sjur, "there's something else, something I've never tasted before."

"Then you haven't tasted much soil," said Lagertha, "it tastes like salty soil."

"So true, so true," said Ravn. "It's salty soil."

"We drink some more ale," said Lagertha, "then we'll see what happens."

Ravn started to say a stanza from the "Lay of Alvis".

"*Men call them Wind. The gods say Waverer and the most holy gods call it Neigher. The giants name it Wailer, the elves Roaring Traveller, and in Hel it's known as Blustering Blast.*"

"I agree with the gods," said Lagertha.

It was evening, and then day again. That's how it went for three days.

"Why not let the rowers get us out of here?" asked Sjur from Lagertha.

"I have always managed to get out of Korsfjorden with the wind only, it means bad luck if you don't, didn't you know?"

Sjur just shook his head.

Lagertha remembered what her ancestors always said, that poison could expel poison. Perhaps the same applied to the soil that was in the fjord. Lagertha fetched the sack of soil she always brought with her. In case she had to stay in a barren place for a long time, she could sow something in order to survive.

Lagertha emptied the sack into the fjord and said aloud, "Come, wind, and lead us out on the open sea!"

The wind rose from the fjord, and the ship accelerated. A flock of ducks flew over their heads, they were also on their way to the open sea.

"It was the wrong time," said Lagertha, "but now we are where we're supposed to be."

"How do you know?" asked Sjur.

"There can't be another reason for the fjord to swallow the wind." Ravn wasn't sure that Lagertha was right, but he knew his dreams would give him the answers. He didn't remember his dream the next day, there was only one thing that had stuck, there were some who had difficulty walking, it was necessary to provide support.

Ravn told Lagertha the little he remembered.

"The wind disappears and returns, we need support to move forward, it's not very uplifting," she said.

"We are nowhere near finding out what it is about," Ravn said, "what did you dream?"

Lagertha thought for a long time. "I actually dreamed something," she finally said. "A flock of ducks flew in wing, they flew between the high mountains, the narrow valleys and the great oceans."

"Were you worried?" Ravn asked.

"No, it was just wonder that the birds showed the way. Time and distance disappeared."

Sjur came and sat down with them.

"Tell us about your dream," Ravn said.

"It was a living skeleton that wandered over the Earth, he left the image of himself behind."

"Explain," said Ravn.

"The skeleton went through a forest and came to the sea, then it went on to a meadow. The forest existed both by the sea and the meadow, but it was not real."

"It's the dimensions," Lagertha said suddenly. "The thin veil is getting thinner. What we experience is almost like a dream, but not quite. We don't know if we are dreaming or awake."

"Sounds reasonable," said Sjur.

The ducks flew in a wing far ahead, and the ship had finally gotten out of Korsfjorden.

10

It was not far from the ferry port and to the house they had rented. Ardar walked ahead with long steps, he needed to clear his head. Ardar liked Alma and her daughters, but would he willingly move to Caithness?

"You don't have to move," Bergtora said; she walked beside him, Ardar hadn't noticed her.

"You can keep your house in Orkdal. You can stay there every summer and Christmas. If you want to come to Trondheim, you can stay with us."

"It sounds much better when you say it than it did in my head."

"Think about the alternative. You alone in a large trønderlåne in Orkdal."

"Depressing."

Bergtora just smiled at him.

Alma came and took Ardar's hand, she didn't say anything. Soon the daughters walked hand in hand with them as well.

"They look like a duck family on a trip," Ravn said to Bergtora.

"I just hope Ardar doesn't get cold feet."

"If he does, he's so stupid that he doesn't deserve Alma."

They arrived at the house; the key was under the flowerpot. Ardar unlocked the dark blue front door. It was a spacious house with two floors. The view was stunning, there were slopes down to the fjord.

Fiona sat down on the stairs and watched the ducks walking around on the grass. Ardar sat down next to her. Fiona took his hand. He stroked her long red hair.

"You're Ardar," she said with Scottish rolling Rs.

"Sounds good," said Ardar, "I like it."

The ducks came close to them, Ardar went into the kitchen and found some old bread. Fiona threw the bread as far away as she could. Ardar put the bread crumbles right next to him, he wanted to study the ducks.

Holly and Emma began to run after the ducks, they quacked and fluttered around. Fiona just laughed.

"Come," she said to Ardar, "let's go for a walk."

Holly and Emma came running as well. They walked to the end of the road, then turned left. After a while they came to a path, it went steeply upwards. Two cats came walking after them, one red-speckled and one black and white. The path went up and up, finally they reached the top, there was an island in the bay low below.

Ardar couldn't free himself from the thought that he had been here before, he lay back in the grass and closed his eyes, after a while he fell asleep. Ardar saw himself on the island, he had long almost white hair and yellow clothes. "Come and eat, a lady shouted."

There was a small stone house among some solid deciduous trees, he could see the smoke rising from the chimney. Ardar and a slightly younger girl and boy ran into the house and obediently washed their hands, they had great respect for Flora who obviously was their mother.

Flora changed the washing bowl with a cauldron of venison. Soon their father, named Oak, came and joined them. Ardar woke up abruptly. There was a straw in his nose. "Let's go home," he said.

The girls ran along, Ardar let them, it was impossible to miss the way, he needed some time alone.

Bergtora was his younger sister in the dream, but the younger brother wasn't Ravn. Ardar wondered who he could be, his brother had not shown his face.

He saw the smoke from the chimney a long way ahead. It smelled like venison cauldron as soon as he opened the front door. Ardar stood in the hallway, it was a dream and a truth at the same time.

Ravn stuck his head into the hallway. "Are you coming?" Ardar told him the dream.

"I know it must be hard for you," said Ravn. "You hate everything that isn't one hundred per cent rational, you have a built-in anxiety that you are going crazy, which I find very strange, for you are one of the toughest guys I know. It is words and behaviours from idiotic people that destroys what you are experiencing, you don't want to be like them."

Ardar knew that Ravn was right, he had met too many idiots. He also knew that Ravn and Bergtora were the only ones he could tell what he had experienced.

Ardar had forgotten all about Alma. He gasped when he saw her sitting at the table. The cauldron was the same as the one he had seen in his dream, and it smelled the same.

Ardar couldn't look at Alma, he was too shocked. Ravn gave Alma a sign that she should leave him alone. After they had eaten, Ravn and Ardar went out on the porch, Bergtora and Alma stayed in the kitchen, Alma made coffee.

"How did you manage everything?" asked Bergtora.

"It's easy when the ingredients are of top quality. It's obvious that a master chef used to live here. There was enough Italian cheese to make a cheesecake, and I found some wild raspberries in the freezer. What's wrong with Ardar?"

Bergtora told her about Ardar's anxiety about everything that wasn't rational. If there was anything inexplicable, he freaked out.

"How will he manage to be with me, what will happen when the infatuation passes?" Alma looked worried.

"He has to change, or it will end," said Bergtora, she saw no other solution.

Neither Bergtora nor Alma had thought it would be a problem, but the problem was out in the open, it wouldn't go away by itself. They went out with the cake and the coffee.

"We will have a good week," Ravn said, satisfied.

Alma poured the coffee and Bergtora gave them a piece of the cheesecake, they helped themselves with the raspberry sauce.

"Hear! Hear!" Ardar said, raising his cup to Alma.

"Bergtora told me why you are so afraid of experiencing something out of the ordinary. Why do you give a damn about all those you don't want to be compared to?"

Ardar said nothing, and they ate the cake in silence. Bergtora brought all the dirty dishes to the kitchen and fetched a whisky bottle and four glasses.

"Perfect timing!" said Ardar.

"Bergtora is the queen of timing," Ravn said and smiled.

"Okay!" Ardar said. "I will tell you about the dream, I don't feel weird anymore."

"I wonder who our brother was," said Bergtora after Ardar had finished. "Were there no characteristics?"

"He had red clothes. You had pink and I yellow."

"It sounds like you and your brother belong together," said Alma to Bergtora. "The colours are almost the same."

"It's not me who was in the dream," said Ravn. "Who have you been hiding?"

Bergtora said nothing, but she knew who her brother was. Bergtora could see that Ardar also had guessed who he was. Ardar knew that Casper and Bergtora knew each other, but he had no idea that Bergtora and Casper had a history together, Casper had never said anything. A tense atmosphere spread along the porch.

"We are going for a walk," Alma told Ardar, she pulled him up from his chair.

They went to the lower part of the garden and sat down on a tree trunk. Ardar let his mind wander, he played different scenes in his head again and again. Every time he had seen Bergtora and Casper together, Ardar saw that they were struggling not to look at each other. Every time Ardar had talked to Bergtora about Casper, she had never followed up with a question or a sentence, she had just pretended not to be interested, it was striking how uninterested she had been.

Ravn came, and Alma got up and went back to the porch to Bergtora.

"I think I have lost Ravn," said Bergtora. "Casper was the one, but we met too early. We already knew each other from way back, hundreds of years ago. I know Casper had the same feeling, even though we never talked about it. We were too young; it was simply the wrong timing."

"Or the right timing. Timing doesn't always make sense."

"We are here because me and Ravn got the trip as a wedding gift from Ardar. How ironic is that?"

"What's going on, Ardar?" Ravn asked. "Who was the brother in your dream?"

Ardar knew there was no point in lying to Ravn, he told him about Casper.

"I always knew that Bergtora had a secret. We all know how dangerous the first love is, it's the love that beats everything."

"Now you are more pessimistic than me," said Ardar.

"Am I?" Ravn asked, looking hard at Ardar.

Ardar had never seen Ravn like that before. He got up and went up to the room he and Alma shared. He had decided to call Casper.

"Hello! Ardar, that was a long time ago!" Casper answered right away.

Ardar told him where he was and why. Casper's voice was no longer cheerful.

"Why are you calling me?"

"Why do you think?" Ardar said harshly.

"You know as well as I do, love is not something you can control."

"I know," Ardar said resignedly. "I just don't know what to do, the wedding between Ravn and Bergtora is tomorrow."

"Do you want me to come and find out what's between me and Bergtora?"

"Yeah! It's about time you figure it out, I'll send you the address." Ardar hung up and stood thinking for a long time, then he went down to Ravn. Bergtora and Alma came also.

"He'll be here," said Ardar.

"Why?" Bergtora asked, but she already knew the answer.

"When does he come?" Ravn asked.

Ardar said he didn't know, but Casper would probably not waste much time.

Bergtora looked over to the mainland, she cursed Ardar, but at the same time she knew he had done the right thing.

Ravn got up and left, he planned to go up to the island's highest peak. Ardar ran after Ravn, he owed Ravn that much.

"You'll be fine," Alma said.

"Do you think?" Bergtora was not so sure.

"I know it's gonna be fine," Alma said. "It's just unexpected, all the guys come at once."

Bergtora knew it was true, but she had never believed in it.

Arnhild stood and looked at the fjord. A flock of crows sat on the ground; it was amazing how many hours they spent in the same place. The crows only lifted once in a while, but now they did. They flew across the fjord for a while before they turned left. They just disappeared out of sight when a large ship came sailing, it was a beautiful black ship with sails in different blue colours with golden stripes in between.

Arnhild held her hand up so the sun wouldn't dazzle her. Three pairs of hands flew up in the air at the same time, they thought she was greeting them. Arnhild laughed and waved back.

"There you have the lady of your dreams," Lundesol said to Olav.

"Are you sure?"

"Can't you see the deer herd?"

"The island of the many stags, let's see if she knows the poem."

Olav jumped ashore before the rowers had gotten the ship completely to the shore and walked calmly towards Arnhild. Her long brown hair fluttered in the wind, the sun rays lit up some lines of copper in her hair.

Arnhild looked at him with a curious expression, it was just as if the man with long blond hair and blue eyes knew who she was. Maybe he knew her family, her father had told her that her ancestors came from a place called Orkdal. Olav went straight to her and took her hand, then he said the poem he had learned during the crossing.

"Arran of the many stags, the sea reaches to its shoulder; island where companies are fed, ridges whereon blue spears are reddened.

Wanton deer upon its peaks, mellow blaeberries on its heaths, cold water in its streams, nuts upon its brown oaks.

Hunting-dogs there, and hounds, blackberries and sloes of the blackthorn, dense thorn-bushes in its woods, stags astray among in oak-groves. Gleaning of purple lichen on its rocks, grass without blemish on its slopes, a sheltering cloak over its crags; gamboling of fawns, trout leaping.

Smooth in its lowland, fat its swine, pleasant its fields, a tale you may believe; its nuts on the tips of its hazelwood, sailing of longships past it.

It is delightful for them when the fine weather comes, trout under the banks of its rivers, seagulls answer each other round its white cliff; delightful at all times is Arran."

Lundesol and Orm had come ashore and were standing next to Olav. They looked at Arnhild while Olav finished the poem. When he had finished, Arnhild didn't know what to say. The herd of crows returned and settled on the plain again.

"*Fint skip*," she said at last.

"You speak Norwegian," said Lundesol.

"I have ancestors from Orkdal."

"It's close to where we come from," said Olav. "Do you want to join us and meet your family?"

Orm kicked Olav hard on the calf. "You're going too fast," he hissed.

Arnhild smiled for the first time. "Come!" she said. "I want you to meet my mother."

Olav saw if he could see a ring on her finger, but he saw none. They went to a stone house behind the herd of deer. A lady in her fifties came out of the house.

"This is my mother," Arnhild said proudly.

Ailsa greeted them in turn. When she came to Lundesol, she said, "You look like the shieldmaiden who threw our ancestor into the sea. She has been described so often that she lives on in our memories."

"She is in our family," said Orm. "Lundesol and I also come from the same tree."

"I come from the outer branch, while Orm comes from the trunk," said Lundesol and laughed.

"The ring is closing. And now you have come to rob my only daughter?"

"How did you know?" Olav asked in astonishment.

"You drool, and secondly, I had a dream last night."

"You can also join," said Lundesol and took Ailsa's hand.

Ailsa laughed and said, "That was what the dream was about. Lagertha came and said there would come a beautiful ship to get me, with blue and golden stripes in its sail. And here you are. I'm ready; what about you, Arnhild?"

"Why didn't you tell me about the dream, was it because you didn't think it would come true?"

"I just wanted to see with my own eyes if your suitor was right for you."

"Olav knows the poem, "Arran of the many stags"."

Ailsa looked at the three who had come with the ship. Their hair was so fine fluttering in the wind with the sun rays in the golden white. Orm's hair was a little darker than Lundesol's.

Olav had the colour of a ripe wheat field.

"Can I touch your hair," asked Ailsa of Lundesol. Lundesol nodded, and Ailsa touched her silky soft hair.

"Come inside," said Ailsa. "I have a soup that was just ready, and the bread is freshly baked. The ale is also ready, I have used a secret ingredient, it's white heather."

"It's probably no longer a secret," said Orm dryly.

Ailsa just laughed. They sat down around the long oak table. Orm never ceased to wonder why he could find people he already knew. He wondered if his uncle who was a very difficult bachelor was a match to Ailsa. He discussed it with Lundesol.

"I'm sitting right here," said Ailsa, "why don't you ask me?"

"Maybe because you haven't met my uncle, but Lundesol has," Orm said calmly.

"What do you think?" Ailsa asked Lundesol.

"I don't know you very well, but it seems to me that you have been out on a winter's night before, you make good food, and you are beautiful to be so old."

"Thank you," said Ailsa dryly. "When do we leave?"

"Can we sleep first?" asked Orm.

"I would like to see the island," said Olav. "What if we stayed for a week? If the island is anything like the poem, we won't have any problem finding food."

"You can't kill the sacred white deer," said Arnhild. "I will come with you and show you where we can hunt."

Olav finished the meal and thanked Ailsa for the food, he couldn't wait to see the island and get to know Arnhild better. Arnhild got up and went to find what they needed. She gave Olav a bow and arrow. They went outside and looked up at the mountain behind the house. The deer roared at each other, and the eagles flew high in the sky.

"The crows live down here with one herd of deer, the other herd lives up on the mountains with the eagles."

"Where is the habitat of the white deer?"

"It lives in a valley called Glen Rosa. The glen is pink, yellow, blue, brown and purple, and sometimes turquoise, you will see what I mean when we get there."

"Down there is the valley called Glen Rosa," said Ravn and pointed. Ardar looked down on the valley with the river in the middle between the mountains.

"Nice," Ardar said and walked on, they were almost at the top.

"Gaelic is a beautiful language," said Ravn. "We can soon see the peaks of Caisteal Abhail and Cir Mhor."

"It's written Eilean Arain on the ferry, do you know what it means?"

"Isle of Arran. We never say the island before the name, if we say the island, it's because it's the name of the place. Øya av Frøya," Ravn said it out loud. "It sounds strange, but it's probably because we aren't used to it."

He stood on top of Goat Fell and looked at the Clyde and the mountain range around him. Soon Casper would arrive, there was trouble ahead.

Bergtora looked at Alma for a long time.

"How is it that I should have married Ravn yesterday, and you have known Ardar for a day or two, now you are more together than me and Ravn are?"

"Things are moving fast. Maybe it's you and Casper who should be together. Ravn and Bergtora, Casper and Bergtora. Ravn and Bergtora sounds better. Casper and Bergtora sounds settled."

Bergtora began to laugh. "I'm glad you've solved the problem; I actually feel you're right."

"I know I'm right," Alma said seriously.

"Let's make supper," said Bergtora.

"If you put the kids to bed, then I'll make supper."

Alma didn't say it to be kind, she just knew that cooking

wasn't Bergtora's strength, there were too many strange flavours according to Ravn and Ardar.

Bergtora found Emma, Holly and Fiona, and promised them a long fairytale. Alma went into the pantry; it was like an old-fashioned grocery store with wooden shelves on all the walls. On the bottom shelf the whisky bottles stood in a row like soldiers. On the shelf above was a box of Blonde from the local brewery.

There were many cheeses on one of the shelfs that she hadn't seen before, she found a cheese with hazelnuts which had been stored for five years, a well stored ham was hanging from the ceiling, and the homemade flatbread lay in a cloth on the small wooden table in the middle of the room.

Alma set the table with wooden plates, the whisky glasses stood in the middle together with the whisky bottle, then she lit the large silver candlesticks with white candles, she wondered when Ravn and Ardar would show up. Bergtora came and sat down in one of the bright yellow armchairs. The fabric was most likely from the island Harris, Barra, Lewis or Uist. The tweed was allowed to be called Harris Tweed if it was made on one of those islands. Alma poured a whisky to both of them.

Bergtora thought of Casper. A life with him was going to be predictable. Casper pretended to be a rebel, but in reality, he was set in his daily chores. Bergtora missed Ravn, she hoped it wasn't too late.

"Have you finished thinking?" asked Alma.

Bergtora nodded and filled up their glasses. At the same time, Ardar and Ravn began to descend from the mountain, it went surprisingly fast. Soon, they were by the brewery and the other artificially companies that were housed in the surrounding buildings.

"I like pink stone houses," said Ravn out of the blue.

Ardar hadn't noticed the two pink stone buildings they passed. He looked more closely at them, Ravn was right, they looked amazing.

They decided to walk along the fjord back to Brodick. There was wet sand and waves on the fjord, it wouldn't be long before the rain shrouded. There was no one out walking, not even to walk the dog. They passed a closed pub, on a sign in the window it said you were allowed to bring the dog. They walked along the boardwalk with stone houses in different colours. It was almost a feeling of being on a desert island. Ardar asked Ravn if he felt the same.

"I am a deserted island. If you had asked me yesterday, I would have had a different answer. Who do you think Bergtora will choose?"

"No one rules over love."

"You are wrong, you can definitely decide who to love, as long as you understand that it's possible to love two at the same time, then you choose a lifestyle."

Ardar thought about whose lifestyle he had chosen. Ravn won superiorly. Casper was surrounded by mystery, people thought he was so exciting, but he wasn't. Casper was himself so seldom, that Ardar wondered if he had seen wrong the few times it had happened.

They approached the house; they could see the lit candlesticks a long way away.

"It looks like a home," Ardar said.

"It is a home," Ravn said. "Right now, it's yours, and maybe mine." Ardar turned and looked at Ravn.

"We will find out," he said. "It looks like the sky is about to explode soon."

"*Men call them Clouds. The gods say Change of Showers and the Vanir say Wind Kites. The giants call them Hope of Rain, the elves Weather Might, and in Hel they're known as Helmets of secrets.*"

"Right!" said Ardar and looked up at the sky.

The rain began to pour. Ardar and Ravn started running, but it took a few seconds before they reached the front door. They went in and shook off the rain on the Persian rug in the hallway.

"How is it possible to get wet so fast?" said Ardar, shaking his hair once more.

Alma got up when they entered the living room, she dragged Ardar into the kitchen without saying a word.

Ravn took a deep breath and walked over to the whisky bottle and poured himself a full glass, then he sank deep into the purple armchair and stroked his hand over the fantastic fabric.

Bergtora looked at Ravn, but he didn't look at her, his courage had fallen with the rain. If she chose Casper, he would fall so deep and heavy that he didn't know if it was possible to recover. Bergtora clinked her glass against his. Ravn met her gaze; he saw what he longed to see. Bergtora had not left him, she had chosen him.

"What do we do with Casper when he arrives?" he asked lightly.

"We throw him in the sea," said Bergtora. "And don't give me that Alvis Lay again."

Ravn just laughed.

"Can we come now?" Ardar cried. "I'm starving to death."

11

Lundesol was excited about whether Arran lived up to her expectations. Orm gave her a sword when she said she wanted to go alone.

"Remember right into the heart, and do not hesitate."

"It won't be a problem, people seem peaceful here."

"Be back before the sun goes down," Orm said seriously.

Lundesol looked at him angrily. Orm just laughed, Lundesol hated admonitions.

They went separate ways. Orm to provide food and Lundesol to wherever the path led her. She walked to a bay called Bred-Vik, the wide bay, then she turned her back to the fjord and began walking inland towards a valley called Glen Rosa. When she reached the high mountains on both sides of the glen the sun had almost disappeared. The strong shadows went by the mountain sides at full speed.

Lundesol noticed an almost square stone in the river. She took off her shoes and sat on the stone while she stuck her feet into the river. The water was clear but icy cold and sent shock waves through her. It suddenly became windless and there was no sound to be heard.

Lundesol noticed that she was holding her breath. After a while she started breathing again, and she took her feet up from the river and let them dry in the sun. Then she put her shoes on and started walking towards Lochranza.

There was an ominous feeling throughout the glen, not a

single bird chirped, at this time of year they used to go crazy. Lundesol turned around over and over again, she had a feeling somebody was behind her, but she couldn't see anything, she just felt a presence, and the presence wasn't good.

"Do you know where Lundesol was heading," asked Arnhild of Ailsa.

"She went to Glen Rosa."

Ailsa made a drink for Lundesol when she returned. It contained white heather that bloomed at the wrong time of year. It was important for the flowers to get the qualities they had. It was planted in secret in a sheltered place known only to the initiates, it bloomed three months too early.

"Do you think she must bathe in blood?" Arnhild asked.

"I don't think so, the sticky spirits only appear when a person is weakened."

It became darker and darker, and no Lundesol appeared. Orm was concerned, but Ailsa consoled him and said that Lundesol knew what she was doing.

12

Lagertha still didn't understand why the beige colour had occupied parts of Korsfjorden, and why it had taken the wind and then suddenly given it back again. The morning was still dawning, Lagertha was the only one who was awake, she decided to ask Frøya.

"I know what you want to ask," Frøya said. "Beige is a colour that is little appreciated, but it's special. You find beige on rocks, sand and tree trunks, but very rarely in the sky or the sea. What you saw was the sand in the depths of Korsfjorden. You got an insight into what the sea can do. There are countless stories about the wind that suddenly disappeared, and then returned again."

"The sea is the guardian of the wind?" asked Lagertha.

"Who else would dominate the wind. You're coming to Arran soon. Ravn and Sjur will sleep as long as they have never slept before, it gives you the chance to explore the island alone."

Lagertha could see they approached a plain where there was a flock of crows, yonder there was a herd of deer. Above them rose the high mountains. The sun had not reached the horizon yet, but it was just about to happen.

The ship came close enough to land, so Lagertha could jump ashore. There was a house on the outskirt of the plain. Lagertha brought a jug of ale and two horns, in case she met a morning bird. She could see a man sitting outside the house when she got closer, he was smoking a pipe. Lagertha stopped right in front of him.

"Ale?"

The man just laughed and pointed to the bench next to him. Lagertha sat down and poured in the two horns. Just as she handed him the horn, the first rays of the sun hit the flock of crows.

The man handed her the pipe. Lagertha wondered what it was that made her know this man, she had been right here many times before.

"You have been here, and not just in your dreams, you have truly been here."

"Lagertha," said Lagertha.

"Michael," he said, shaking her hand.

Then we have clarified that, Lagertha thought, *I wonder what the next thing will be.*

"It will probably be that we get married," Michael said and laughed.

Lagertha looked at him in astonishment. She certainly didn't feel like laughing, instead she felt her feet getting cold. Lagertha asked if she could put the blanket that lay beside him over her feet.

Michael nodded and went inside the house and picked up some wool socks and big leather boots as well. Lagertha gratefully accepted.

"There's a saying," said Michael. "If you meet the elected one of your heart, you will get cold feet."

Lagertha looked closely at his grey eyes and the black shiny hair that went straight to his shoulders.

"Maybe you're right," she said.

"I sat and watched the wonderful ship that came sailing, and you jumping down from the side of the ship."

"I like heights," said Lagertha and laughed.

"You're beautiful with your almost white hair and your blue eyes that are as unfathomable as the sea itself. Is it weird that I would like to marry you?"

"Actually, it's strange," said Lagertha. "I only have eighty ships left, I was stupid enough to give away one hundred and twenty ships, but I have three farms."

"I think we can manage," said Michael and laughed.

They saw that there was hectic activity on board the ship. Soon, Ravn yelled all over Lochranza, "Lagertha! Where are you?"

Lagertha got up and shouted back, "I'm here."

Ravn saw her and jumped down from the ship. He came running towards them. "I was so worried," he said breathlessly.

"Why?"

"You were gone. No, that was not it, I dreamed I lived on an island and you on another. I was afraid I would never see you again."

They saw that Sjur was coming towards them. Lagertha went to meet him, she wanted to explain everything to him before he met Michael.

"You do not have to explain," said Sjur and stroked her hair. "I understand, we are just good friends, no one decides over their heart." Sjur brought ale and two horns.

"Good thinking," said Lagertha.

Michael and Sjur measured each other with their eyes, when they were done, they shook hands. Michael asked if it was okay if he and Lagertha got married.

Both Ravn and Sjur swallowed the ale before they had to cough. Ravn was usually never short of words, but now he was. Lagertha and Michael knew it was necessary to give Ravn and

Sjur some time to digest what they had just heard. The sunbeams had reached them with full force.

"It seems like the sun agrees," said Sjur.

"With the sun no one can argue," said Ravn, and raised his horn.

"Thanks for letting me be your best man," said Ravn to Lagertha. Lagertha just laughed, Ravn was himself again.

"I'll take care of your ships and farms if you want to stay here," said Sjur.

"I hope you understand that I can take care of you," said Michael to Lagertha.

Ravn looked at him angrily and said, "Lagertha needs no man to take care of her, she is the best and most infamous shieldmaiden who has ever lived."

Ravn sat back heavily and leaned his back against the wall.

"Nice house you have, by the way," he said lightly.

13

Arnhild wanted to hear what Lundesol had to say when she finally arrived.

"It went well until I was about to leave the glen, then I turned around and looked yonder into the valley, a huge brown bear came at me at full speed, it panted and snorted with its mouth open. I was sure it was the end, but suddenly the bear stopped and turned back just before it reached me."

"Strange," said Ailsa. "In all the other stories throughout the years, those who have met the brown bear have been attacked, but in your case it turned around. Do you know why?"

"I had a feeling the bear became aware of someone who was behind me. I know it sounds silly, but it felt like it was a male presence."

"It does not sound stupid. That is what I've been suspecting all along, there are some who look after the glen."

Arnhild sat and stared at the door, Ailsa saw that she was not with them anymore, she was far away. Ailsa asked Lundesol for help.

"I always have a barrel of blood standing in the shed, in case we get a visit from sticky spirits."

"The bear did not invade me, but its sticky spirit came here and invaded Arnhild?"

"That's right," said Ailsa. "Help me get enough blood drained over Arnhild."

Ailsa took her outside so she could sit on a rock, then they poured almost the whole bucket of blood over her, but Arnhild didn't react.

"Look for a place where the blood hasn't gained access."

"Let's put her on the ground," said Lundesol.

They could see where the blood hadn't gained access, it was on the shoulders underneath the hair, in the armpits and under her feet. It helped when they covered the missing parts, Arnhild became herself again.

Olav and Orm came from the plains holding torches in their hands. Olav slammed the rabbits he had caught on the ground and ran over to Arnhild.

"Sticky spirits are a shitty bunch," said Ailsa.

"Looks like you need to go for a swim," Olav said, looking at all the blood.

"I'll come too," said Orm.

"And I," said Lundesol.

Ailsa understood that the cold sea didn't bother them much, she sat down on the stairs. She could see them walking down the path in the moonlight. The moonbeams reflected in the sea, it was beautiful.

14

Casper sat at a table by the window, looking at the narrow road with cobblestones meandering past. Krambua was one of the few places that was still open, it was an old pub with brown wooden interiors and floors. Casper never understood how English pubs could stay clean with all the dirty old carpets on the floor. He knew one pub in Trondheim with carpets, and it was owned by an English guy. He was waiting for a friend who came all the way from Orkdal, it could take a while. Casper thought of all the times he and Bergtora had met. Time was like a worm going back in time. Most of the meetings he had with people were hidden inside the worm, he didn't remember them, with Bergtora it was different.

Casper played a sequence from Bakklandet over and over again. He had played basse with some comrades when she appeared. Bergtora had short, bleached hair, bright red lipstick and it looked like she had soot around her eyes. She wore a white shirt tucked in the skirt. Two narrow leather belts hung obliquely over the black skirt. She looked classic and rebellious at the same time.

Basse was the strangest and most natural game. The circles were already there on the black asphalt, or you could use chalk to draw a new circle depending on how many circles you needed, it was one circle per person, and it was approximately 3.3 feet in diameter. Everybody played, it didn't matter how good you were, it was just great fun.

You used the inside of your foot to kick bassen over to another circle, if you managed, then everybody moved to the next circle, and the game would continue until you had a winner.

You were not allowed to use your hands, and bassen had to fall into somebody's circle over the height of the knees, that was the rules.

There were specially two places it was played, and that was in the old working class areas Lademoen and Bakklandet. An old huge bright red rendered school from the 1800s, lay on top of the hill in the city overlooking the fjord, that was one of the great arenas as well. It was a perfect game during the summer, the midnight sun made it light day and night. Bassen could land in your circle three times, and then you had lost. The circle was then called the dead circle. If bassen landed in the dead circle, then you were dead as well. Bassen was made from a bicycle host which was cut into small rings and made into a ball with a string tightening them together.

Casper remembered that Bergtora didn't talk to him, but to a mutual friend. She glanced at him from time to time, and he met her gaze. As she walked away, he kicked bassen in front of her. She kicked it backwards with her foot. Casper was sure that Bergtora felt that everyone was looking at her when she nonchalantly moved on without turning.

Arnljot came and sat down on the other side of the table, Casper was far away.

"What's on your mind?" Arnljot asked.

Casper told him about a meeting with Bergtora, when he and some friends had played basse.

"I was there," said Arnljot, "and I won. Bassen ended up just within your circle, don't you remember?"

Casper laughed and said, "We had a long discussion about

whether it was on the line or not."

"I noticed that Bergtora was looking at you," said Arnljot. Casper looked at Arnljot's long almost white hair. Some got white hair when they turned grey, maybe that was what had happened to Arnljot.

"Are you all right?"

"It's going brilliantly," Casper replied monotonously.

"I can see that," said Arnljot dryly.

Casper began to twist. He told Arnljot about the conversation with Ardar.

"I know I should go to Arran, but I'm scared."

Arnljot just nodded. If Casper refused to listen to his heart, then there was nothing he could do about it. He drank the rest of the beer; Casper did the same.

"I have planned a trip," said Arnljot.

"You have, where?"

Casper looked at him with astonishment. Arnljot was the most home-loving friend he had, he never went anywhere voluntarily. "To the island where you ought to go."

Arnljot meant what he said, he had decided to go. Casper writhed on the chair. It was he and not Arnljot Ardar had invited, it was going to look like he was a coward.

"I will join," he said firmly.

Casper was satisfied, he needed a shell to hide under, and that was exactly what Arnljot had given him. Arnljot ordered another beer, Casper did the same. This time, they chattered to each other. Casper had heard of a pirate bar in Edinburgh that they had to go to. The owner had a parrot on his shoulder, and they had live music.

"And we will drink Captain Morgan, right?" asked Arnljot.

"Of course, what else?"

"They have a beautiful tearoom with Mackintosh furniture in Glasgow."

"You must be joking?"

"No, it's very nice, I went there a long time ago, but I'm sure they have the same splendid tea and cakes still."

"Cheers for pirate bars and tearooms," said Casper and raised his glass towards Arnljot.

Arnljot just laughed.

"I suddenly remembered something," Casper said. "Ardar said the ferry only brought people who had urgent errands to the island, but he thought the same skipper they had used, was back at Nyhavna."

"Do you think everything is closed?" Arnljot asked.

"I don't know, maybe the skipper knows."

Casper ordered more beer. They had to go to Nyhavna and see if they could find the famous skipper. Either way, it could certainly wait a bit.

15

Bergtora stood leaning against the kitchen counter. Ravn stroked his hair. He didn't know what to do or say, so he kept his mouth shut.

Bergtora stroked the hair away from his face and kissed him. Ravn hoped and lost hope, it could be a welcome kiss or a farewell kiss. He opened his eyes and saw in Bergtora's eyes that it was a welcome kiss.

"Are you sure?"

Bergtora nodded.

"What made the difference? Casper hasn't arrived yet."

Bergtora told him about the names that didn't match.

"You are right," Ravn said excitedly. "It's completely wrong with Casper and Bergtora, but is it enough?"

Bergtora looked at him feverishly, she didn't know what to say.

"Don't think," said Ravn. "It's good that Casper is coming so you get to meet him. It's not your choice, we both know that. Let's go for a walk, so you can clear your head."

They went where Ardar had been earlier in the day along with Fiona, Emma and Holly. It was a growing crescent moon, but it was still just a narrow crescent. Ravn took Bergtora's hand, they were together tonight, and now was now. Bergtora had a strange feeling again. She knew the island and the island knew her.

"I have the same feeling," said Ravn, "it's a very reassuring feeling, it's like the island takes care of us." They approached the top of the hill.

"It is a very turbulent starry sky," said Bergtora. "Sometimes, the starry sky is majestic, but it's certainly not tonight."

"You're right, it's a troubled starry sky."

"Let me hear," said Bergtora.

"What?"

"What did Alvis say about the stars," said Bergtora and laughed.

"He doesn't talk about the stars, but you can hear about the Earth, sun, moon and Heaven instead."

Bergtora just smiled at him.

"Men call it Earth. The Aesir say Field and the Vanir say the Ways. The giants name it Evergreen and the elves Grower. The most holy gods call it Clay.

Men call it Sun. The gods say Sunna and the dwarfs Dvalin's Delight. The giant's name it Ever Bright, the elves Fair Wheel and the sons of god All Glowing.

Men call it Moon, but the gods say Mild Smile. It's known in Hel as Whirling Wheel. The giants name it Rapid Traveller, the dwarfs Gleamer and the elves Time Teller.

Men call it Heaven. The gods say the Hight and the Vanir say Wind Weaver. The giants name it High Home, the elves Fair Roof and the dwarfs Dripping Hall."

"Some of the words are funny and some say something. The dwarfs obviously didn't like to leave their great hall underneath the mountains since they called heaven the Dripping Hall."

"Maybe they only stayed in places where it rained all the time."

"Or they scared the kids, and only took them outside when

it rained."

"Don't forget they never saw the sun; they died if the sunbeams hit them."

Ardar was all alone in the kitchen the next morning, the others were still asleep, he put on some coffee and looked out the window. He jumped high into the air when he saw two guys staring at him, it was Casper and Arnljot. Ardar tried to breathe normally again.

"You scared the shit out of me," he said when Arnljot and Casper entered the kitchen.

Casper and Arnljot just laughed.

"The coffee is ready," said Ardar, and put three cups and the press jug on a tray. "We will drink it in the garden."

"It's so beautiful here," said Arnljot, captivated.

"There is no nicer place," said Ardar.

They looked at the old deciduous trees that stood proudly in a row to the right of the garden.

"How did you get here; did you find the famous skipper?"

"We drank a couple of beers in Krambua," Casper said, "then we strolled down to Nyhavna and a boat came and docked. We asked the captain if he happened to be going to Arran. He looked at us in astonishment before answering that he had just taken a group there. One of them looked like you, he said, pointing at Arnljot."

"I asked if his name was Ardar," said Arnljot, "and the skipper could confirm that, so we had found our man."

"How long did you have to wait before he was ready to sail again?" Ardar asked.

"He sailed right away. Luckily, we had enough money, and the captain made a stop on the mainland, so we could buy a toothbrush."

"He made another stop as well," said Arnljot, "he had to deliver a package to a guy in Caithness."

"You're kidding, the same thing happened to us. Did you meet the guy?"

"No," said Casper. "We were walking down the gangway when the captain turned around and said he would throw us overboard if we followed him. We dared not to follow, so we got back on board again."

Ardar just smiled his secretive smile.

"Have you seen any dolphins?" Casper asked curiously.

"I saw a pod that left for the next village just before you arrived."

"It must have been the same dolphins we saw," said Arnljot. "They came as soon as we started walking towards Corriegills."

"It's a strange sight," said Ardar, "that's for sure."

"Fill us in," said Casper. "What has happened in your life?"

Ardar told them about Alma and her daughters, and that they would probably stay in two places, Caithness and Orkdal.

"Caithness," said Arnljot. "Do you mean it has something to do with the captain refusing to let us ashore?"

"There were three of us who got off the boat, and seven who returned."

"You found them in Caithness?" Arnljot asked in disbelief.

"I did. The man the captain delivered the package to, was with Alma, it's his daughters too. Come and visit us in Orkdal when we have moved there."

"You have kept the farmhouse."

"I have, it's not too far from where you have your roots."

"Your farm is nicely located, with rolling fields down to the fjord and the mountains at the back. It's exactly the kind of location a farm should have."

"Have you been there lately?" Casper asked Ardar.

"Lately it has become a lot, it's nice to feel your roots from time to time."

Arnljot became almost nostalgic, he thought of the long white houses called a trønderlån and the red barns. A trønderlån was 16.4 feet on the short end, depending on how long the timber was, and it could be up to 131.6 feet.

It was likely that they had continued to build with the same measurements as the long and narrow Viking houses had. First, they built the rooms they needed, and then, as the family grew, they just added some more rooms, and made the house longer and longer.

A trønderlån had two floors, and usually it had the best view towards the landscape or seascape. The red barn lay on the other side of the yard, with the third house located between the trønderlån and the barn. It was a store house called a stabbur, which was small, but it still had two floors. At the top of the stabbur you found all the hams hanging after they had been salted. It needed the right cold temperature and windy lofts to contain their delicious flavours. Most stabbur had a mellow yellow colour.

The yard had a tree in the middle, and it was common knowledge that in the old days, you should give ale to the little people who lived in and around the tree. Around mid-winter, you had to place a huge plate of porridge in the barn if you wanted to keep the little people happy.

As soon as you approached Trøndelag you could see poplars popping up. It looked like someone had just thrown them up in the air, and then decided to plant them wherever they landed. They looked natural around and in between the white trønderlån, the red barn and the yellow stabbur.

Casper asked Arnljot what was on his mind. Arnljot told him about the poplars. Casper nodded; he had observed the same thing. "You mean the poplars that look like pillars, right?"

Arnljot nodded. "As far as I can remember, they are called Populus tremula 'Erecta'. The stalk that attaches the leaves to the stem which makes the leaves trembling and quaking are due to the flexible flattened petioles."

"It only applies in the country," said Casper. "In the cities, the poplars have been given a natural place. It may be wrong to say natural since they are planted in a row."

It was a conversation that only trønderne could have, Ardar thought, but he had to smile. He already missed trønderne's inherently chatty way of looking at the world, they could chatter about absolutely everything.

"Exciting life you have all of a sudden," Casper said to Ardar, he sounded almost envious.

"Two days ago, I had nada," said Ardar.

They saw that there was life and movement in the house. Three little girls came running into the garden. They stopped abruptly when they saw the strangers.

"Come and say hello to my two friends from Norway!" Ardar said to them.

They came closer and stood staring at them. Casper started laughing. The girls were obviously fascinated by Arnljot's long hair. They asked if they could braid it.

Arnljot nodded.

Holly went to get a brush, hair pins and hair ties, while Emma and Fiona discussed what would suit Arnljot best.

Bergtora stood in the window and watched Casper. She went down to the kitchen where Alma was making breakfast.

"I'm going outside," said Bergtora.

Alma smiled and nodded.

Bergtora wore a dressing gown on top of her nightgown. The hair was tousled, but Bergtora didn't care, she would get dressed after she had drunk coffee, and met Casper.

Ravn woke up, he hurried to the window and saw that Bergtora was approaching Casper. Bergtora thought Casper looked good, but she felt nothing. She thought it was because she was so tired and needed coffee. Ardar gave her a cup.

"Never try to talk to Bergtora until she has had a cup of coffee," he said.

Casper and Arnljot just laughed.

"You look nice," Bergtora said to Arnljot.

Casper pulled his hand through his short brown hair. Bergtora wanted to do the same. She became aware of Ravn standing in the window. She waved to him, but he didn't wave back. Bergtora drank the last sip, and said she had to go and get dressed.

Alma was done making breakfast, she shouted that they had to come and eat. Casper and Arnljot strolled slowly up towards the house. Alma came and met them, they greeted and Casper and Arnljot gave a look of approval towards Ardar, they liked Alma. Arnljot had ended up with a braid around his head, he looked like a milk maiden.

"No worries," said Alma, "it doesn't last long. After breakfast, you will probably get a new hairdo." Arnljot was amazed at the feeling a braid around his head gave him, it made him feel powerful.

"There are a lot of emotions in hair," Alma said. "It is much more important than people think."

"I get what you mean," said Casper. "I just cut my hair short, and I feel weird most of the time."

Ravn entered the room, and everyone stopped eating except Alma's daughters. Alma got up and gave him a cup of coffee. Ravn looked at the vacant chair next to Bergtora, he sat down. Ravn knew it was rude not to greet Casper and Arnljot, but he didn't manage to meet the gaze of Casper. It was Arnljot who broke the silence.

"I have a car I think you will like, it's a turquoise Ford from the '70s. It has seats in artificial leather in a strange salmon colour. I thought that was up your alley. You can get a test drive when we return to Trondheim. I don't really want to sell it, but I need money."

"I have a car," said Ravn.

This is going well, thought Bergtora. Alma sent around the dish with scrambled eggs and ham.

"We just stopped by," Casper said, "we're leaving again tonight. There wasn't much that was open in Glasgow, but we found a room located in a Victorian row of houses, behind Glasgow School of Art, it's owned by a guy from India. That's probably why it's still open, they are used to being open no matter what happens."

Alma said she had stayed at the hotel once. "It was truly horrible. The mattress had plastic under the sheet and was rock hard. If that wasn't enough, there was a fan on the ceiling that made a terrible noise. The room didn't have a window, and it was dirty."

"Anything else?" Casper asked, laughing.

"It has posters on the doors where it says: If you feel unsafe, run to the reception, and if that still wasn't enough, the hallway stinks of perfume. On the other hand, the people who run the hotel are very nice, and the location is the best."

"The location is important," said Arnljot.

"We'll survive," said Casper. "We have slept in worse places."

"I don't doubt it," said Alma, "but there's plenty of space here." Ardar kicked her on the calf, but it was too late.

Ravn got up and left, Casper went after him. He had expected to find a furious Ravn, but not one who was crying. They sat down on some logs behind the house.

"I know why you're crying," said Casper, "but it's not up to us, it's up to Bergtora."

"You'll survive if she chooses me, I won't."

Casper knew Ravn was right. He would survive, but Ravn would be a living dead.

"I don't know what to say. The only thing I know that can cheer you up is a car. If Bergtora chooses me, then I will give you Arnljot's car."

"You think a car cheers me up?"

Ravn was stunned. He understood that Casper had no idea how much Bergtora meant to him. Ardar came out with two cups of coffee, Ravn could smell the well-known aroma of whisky. He hoped it was half and half in the cup.

Casper and Ravn drank in silence, there was nothing more to say. Bergtora came and walked silently towards them. The silence lasted and lasted; Casper began to get impatient.

Finally, he said, "You have to choose, Bergtora."

Bergtora looked at both of them. Casper had been in her dreams and in her thoughts, but Ravn had been in her life. She knew what the right choice was. She asked Ravn if it was okay if she and Casper went for a walk. Ravn nodded and looked down. Bergtora wanted to go up to the same mound she and Ravn had been to the night before.

They walked down the road, and Casper took her hand.

"I know you're wondering why I didn't fight for you, there's neither an explanation nor an excuse. We met and it was too good to be true, I got scared and chose another."

"Where is she now?"

"She's at home waiting for me. I came to find out if there was still something between us."

Casper looked at the dressing gown Bergtora was still wearing. She had replaced the slippers in favour of sneakers. The hair was still tousled. He had never stopped loving Bergtora, finally he asked straight out.

"I have tried hard to forget you," said Bergtora, "but you have always reappeared. I've cursed you many times, but never hated you."

"Because you love me," said Casper quietly.

"Because I love you," said Bergtora.

This was the day when she and Ravn should have been married on Machrie Moor. Bergtora stopped abruptly.

"There's only one place I can find out how I feel, and that's on Machrie Moor. I want Ravn to be there too."

"And the rest?"

"We take everyone with us, we can bring a picnic basket and beer."

They turned around, and Bergtora took a quick shower while Casper gathered the troops; she hoped no one had managed to escape yet.

There was a family that was gone, they had gone to the beach in Brodick. Alma had packed a large picnic basket too; it was clear that they had planned to be there a while. Ravn and Arnljot were the only ones left. Ravn helped Arnljot to get all the hair pins out of his hair.

"Back already?" Ravn asked, astonished.

Casper told Ravn about Bergtora's plan before he started to prepare the sandwiches. Ravn thought it was a cruel plan, but he understood at the same time why. If they went there, it was impossible to hide anything. He started brushing Arnljot's hair with a firm hand.

"It feels like I'm getting married today," said Arnljot.

"You know what they say about the dolphins?" asked Ravn.

"No."

"If you see a pod of dolphins, you can make a wish, but only if there are seven dolphins."

Arnljot said he and Casper had seen a pod of dolphins.

"I wished for Bergtora when I saw the seventh dolphin, Casper doesn't know that one can make a wish," Ravn said quietly so Casper couldn't hear him.

Arnljot wasn't so sure, Casper had folded his hands and closed his eyes just when the last of the dolphins disappeared. Bergtora came down the stairs wearing a dark purple dress, yellow shoes and black sunglasses. Ravn put on a leather jacket and light brown shoes. Casper was already waiting in the green car.

"Aston Martin," said Arnljot, captivated.

"With four round headlights," said Ravn.

"It will be a nice day," said Arnljot, before he remembered what the trip was all about.

He put on the CD player, and soon they heard: *"Two black clothed men stood guard by a coffin, in grief and sorrow over the friend they lost."*

16

Lagertha looked up at the high mountains in Lochranza, the eagles flew high. It had been a long time since she had seen any eagles, they were seldom in Gulosen, they thrived best in the fjord arm which lay further north.

Michael had decided it was a good idea to take a trip to Machrie Moor. Since he only had two horses, they decided to take the ship instead.

Ravn had already left them, this wasn't his adventure anymore, another island was waiting for him.

"I know she has chosen you," said Sjur to Michael. "I was just so sure it was my turn when Ragnar left."

"It is no one's turn when it concerns the heart," said Michael, "I thought you knew that."

"I do, I just want to feel whole."

"Everyone misses a home and someone they feel whole with."

"I was so sure Lagertha was the right one."

They didn't reach Machrie Moor until it was almost dark. The wind had disappeared, and it hadn't appeared again before the blue hour arrived.

They pulled the ship up on the beach and went ashore. It was already pitch black, there was no help in neither the moon nor the stars. It started to drizzle, the puddles were slowly filled with rainwater, they could see half a meter of the path in front of them, but that was enough.

"It's almost completely quiet," said Lagertha, "but I can hear some water trickling."

"There is a steep slope down to the river on your left, and the moor is to your right, in case you wonder," said Michael.

Eventually, they reached the highest point, and the path began to descend slightly.

They saw three stones in front of them. Michael had brought some dried meat, and Sjur had brought sealskin bags. Lagertha carried three horns and ale. It quickly got cold, the drizzle had stopped and the stars had made their entrance. Lagertha stroked away some drops that were trickling down her nose and laid down in her sealskin bag. Michael and Sjur did the same, and soon they were asleep.

It was Sjur who woke up first. It was just before the sun rose. It was completely silent. He thought of a stanza he had heard and said it in a low voice. *"Men call it Calm. The gods call it Quiet and the Vanir says Winds Hush. The giants name it Sultry, the elves Day's Lull and the dwarfs Day's Refuge."*

Sjur wanted to start a fire before he woke up Lagertha and Michael. While he collected dry wood from some dead trees nearby, he mumbled another stanza.

"Men call it Wood. The gods say Mane of the Field and in Hel it's known as Seaweed of the Hills. The giants name it Fuel and the elves Fair Limbed. The Vanir call it Wand."

He placed the smallest branches together with some bark and hit two stones together hard. Michael and Lagertha were still asleep.

Sjur said quietly to himself while he watched the flames, *"Men call it Fire. The gods say Flame and the Vanir say..."*

Michael looked at him and said he should continue. He had never heard anything like it before.

"*Vanir say Wave. The giants name it Hungry Biter, and the dwarfs Burner. In Hel it's known as the Hasty.*"

The first rays of the sun managed to get over the horizon just as he said Hasty. Lagertha opened her eyes and looked around; she saw for the first time the majestic stones with plains all around. The colours were exceptional with the purple, yellow, blue and brown variations. The mountain range lay far away in a horseshoe behind the stones.

"It is truly beautiful here," she said.

"Isn't it time to go back home soon?" asked Sjur.

"It is," Lagertha replied, "we just have to pick up the rowers in Lochranza first."

"I don't think we'll forget," said Sjur dryly.

"What if we make a stop in the middle?" said Michael. "It's a piece of land I want to show you, it's not far from Bred-Vik."

Lagertha and Sjur agreed, they wanted to see as much of the island as possible before they returned. The sun was alone in the sky, all the potential clouds had decided to move on. When they reached the ship, the wind had turned and was blowing in the right direction, it didn't take long before they reached Bred-Vik. They dragged the ship as far as they could up on the beach, and Lagertha made a knot on the rope after she had laid it around a huge stone. Everywhere on the island was beautiful, it didn't matter where they went.

The land Michael wanted to show them was a gift from his great-grandmother. She had said just before she died that a maiden from the high north would arrive one day. Michael had to show her the land. The hallmark was the colour of her hair. When Michael asked her which colour he was to look out for, it was too late, she was already dead.

The road meandered towards Glen Rosa, as did the burn that

lay on the edge of the plains. Michael strolled around the plains, he looked for the peacock that lived there, but all he could see were some squirrels.

Lagertha and Sjur went down to the burn. Lagertha took off her shoes and dipped her feet in the burn, it was completely silent, only a few birds chirped. *I could stay here*, she thought.

"I thought so too, the first time I was here," Michael said and sat down next to her.

Now we will never get out of here, thought Sjur.

"I have a suggestion. You give me your ship. Since Ragnar got one hundred and twenty ships, I can get one. I'm going home and you're staying here."

"Tempting," said Lagertha, "but I have plans to pick up at least five ships while I'm home, you can keep the rest, you can also keep my farms. Fredleif can join me if he wants to, if he returns one day, I would appreciate if you gave him the Lerånd farm."

Michael took a deep breath. "You have a son, when were you going to tell me?"

Lagertha saw the change that happened to Michael; if she had been a man, Michael would never have reacted.

Michael roared at her now, "You don't understand anything! It's not because you're a woman. The fact that you are leaving your son, that's appalling."

"You have misunderstood," Sjur said angrily. "Who do you think has been like a mother and father to Fredleif when Lagertha has been out fighting? Who do you think Fredleif will miss, do you think it's Lagertha? Are you prepared to be both a father and a mother to Fredleif?"

Michael just looked at him in shock, he had never heard of a father who was both father and a mother to a child as long as the mother was alive. He took a deep breath and took off his shoes and stuck his bare feet into the burn. He gasped at how cold the water was, it came straight from the mountains which still had a thin layer of snow on top. His thoughts cleared from the cold water, and he realised Sjur was right.

Suddenly, Michael understood everything. Lagertha was a good mother, she realised her limitations and made sure Fredleif was looked after by a man she trusted.

17

Arnhild, Olav, Lundesol and Orm went to Bred-Vik via Sand-Vik. They were on their way to the place where Lagertha had lived on the island. They continued inland on the island from Bred-Vik. Large black clouds gathered over their heads.

"Isn't it strange," said Orm. "Usually, the clouds gather in one direction or another."

"It is very unusual," said Arnhild, "I've never seen it before." Despite the clouds continuing to gather, it was unusually quiet. The first thing that struck Olav when they arrived, was how peaceful it was. It was an atmosphere there that made you just want to sit down and listen to the silence.

"Let's go to the burn," said Arnhild to Olav.

They sat down on a large rock and took off their shoes. The water was freezing cold, but it felt good. The blood in the body gained momentum. Lundesol sat down next to Arnhild. She also dipped her feet in the water.

"Maybe I should give this place my name," said Orm.

They sat in silence and looked at Orm who was concentrating so hard that he had a hard time standing still. At last, he said, "*Orm i dal*. I want people to remember that once upon a time there was an Orm in the glen."

"That's good," said Arnhild, "dal means glen, and this is a glen. Ormidal sounds good."

"I don't want to write Orm was here. It is a better description for posterity that Orm was in the glen."

"Maybe it will last," said Olav, "who knows."

Orm was satisfied. He knew it was going to last, he had found the perfect name.

Bergtora went for a walk on the beach in Brodick. The others had returned to the house, Bergtora wanted to be alone. She decided to go inland on the island. Ormidale it said on a wooden sign by the road. *Strange name*, Bergtora thought to herself. What amazed her the most was how at home she felt. Suddenly, she missed Ravn by her side.

Ravn had let Bergtora go alone, but he had followed her. To Arnljot and Casper, he had said that he needed to be alone. It was not completely true, he wanted to be with Bergtora. Ravn found Bergtora by the burn.

"There you are, I wanted to ask you something. Do you think it's possible that genes can have a photographic memory?"

"If your ancestors have been here, it's in the cells' memory. Here, it is very likely that Orm, who obviously has been in the glen, has been sitting."

"Or not," said Bergtora and laughed. "Maybe it was Lagertha and Lundesol."

Ravn took a deep breath. "Have you decided?"

"I choose you."

"Dare I ask what the deciding factor was?"

"We can talk about absolutely everything."

Ravn looked down, then he smiled widely.

"Does it hurt," asked Bergtora.

"A little!" Ravn said, and both began to laugh.

18

Lagertha stood and looked at Gulosen. She didn't know if she would ever come back, she went to Lunden. Ravn was there.

"I'm leaving," he said. "I want to stay in a place with water all around, but you know that. I have almost found the perfect place before, but this time I'm not coming back."

"What's so special about the islands?" asked Lagertha.

Ravn looked at her in astonishment. "It's the feeling of being in a ship instead of being landlocked. You don't need a large fortune if you live on an island."

Lagertha understood what he meant.

"If we never meet again, know that you have been in my life for the crucial years," she said meekly.

"Those between young and early adult," said Ravn and laughed. "What are we going to ask the gods for?"

Lagertha looked at the stones and the surrounding landscape.

"What about good soil for the generations to come?"

"I would like to ask for good health as well."

"God, we are terribly responsible and boring."

"One day, there will be two people sitting here, just as we do now, and they're going to be just as close as we are."

"Always close," Lagertha said, squeezing him hard.

Ravn had to swallow hard. He loved Lagertha, but he was no longer in love with her, it was a brotherly love.

"We can do it," Lagertha said quietly. "We just have to send each other a thought from time to time."

Ravn felt that he was about to cry. It was an era that was over, he both dreaded and rejoiced in the future, but most of all he rejoiced. Ravn suddenly jumped straight up.

"What are we doing? We have the best ships that have ever been made, we can visit each other."

Lagertha had a feeling she wasn't going to see Ravn again, but she didn't have the heart to tell him. It did not always turn out as expected.

Lagertha got up, she had one last prayer. "I have never asked you for anything before, Odin, but I want you to let your ravens follow Ravn on his journey to the unknown."

Both Lagertha and Ravn had to smile when they saw the ravens that came flying and disappeared behind the trees. Lagertha knew the ravens belonged to Frøya too, but she felt it was most proper to ask Odin this time.

"It's going to be just fine," Ravn said. He didn't understand how Lagertha could be so calm no matter what happened. It wasn't her he needed to reassure, it was himself.

19

Casper asked Arnljot if he wanted to go for a walk. Arnljot went to get his jacket. When he returned, he saw Casper was leaning against the wall of the house, his guard was down. Arnljot went inside the hall again and made sure to make extra noise with the front door. Casper was his old self again, and they walked towards Brodick.

"Bred-Vik," Casper said, "it's what it's really called."

"And Sand-Vik instead of Sannox," Arnljot said, "via the Gaelic name Sannaig."

"Then that's solved," said Casper and laughed.

Arnljot pointed at the fjord, and Casper could barely see a man swimming back and forth. There was a policewoman waiting for him as he came up out of the water. She gave him a sermon, the index finger pointed constantly at him. The man cracked with laughter; he held his hands on his stomach bending forward. Arnljot and Casper could hear his laughter echoing all over Brodick Bay.

They went over to him and asked what had happened. The man still couldn't speak, he laughed too much. Finally, he said the policewoman had said that he wasn't allowed to exercise. Arnljot and Casper started laughing too, it was completely beyond, but that was probably why the island was still virus-free; they took it seriously.

They turned and walked back, it had started to drizzle. Ardar sat and waited for them when they came back. There were three glasses on the table, as well as a Cherry Cask from the Arran distillery.

"I found it in the basement," said Ardar.

They clinked the glasses together for a man who had newly died, but obviously had a very good taste when he was alive.

"Do you want to hear a fairy tale from the Grey Antiquity?" asked Casper.

Arnljot and Ardar nodded.

"One day, one of the trolls said: I thought I heard a cow moo. Then a hundred years passed. Then the other troll said: It may well have been a bull. Then a hundred years passed. Then the third troll said: Should you continue to chatter like that, then I can't stand it any longer."

Casper finished the glass and poured himself a new one.

"Here's another one," he said. "If your relatives are not after your taste, then rather use up your fortune, enjoy it yourself and let your friends enjoy it. Often one saves for the hated what one has intended for the loved one."

"That can't be from the Grey Antiquity," said Arnljot.

"No, it's from Håvamål, Odin's own kvad."

Arnljot and Ardar understood that Casper's girlfriend was the hated one, and Bergtora was the beloved one.

Casper fell asleep with his head on the tabletop, while Ardar and Arnljot went upstairs, they were both tired.

Alma was the one who found Casper the next morning. She made him a cup of strong coffee. Casper was glad it was Alma who got up first; sometimes, it was easier to talk to a stranger when life was difficult.

Alma stroked his fringe away from his forehead, she wanted to see what colour his eyes were. She was amazed to see that they were green, she had been so sure they were blue. One who had green eyes couldn't look as unsuspecting as one with blue eyes, but that was exactly what Casper did, he was completely open, Alma could see right into his soul.

It was a nice morning, the sky was light blue and clear. Alma appreciated the sunny day, but she knew it was the opposite for Casper. She wondered if he was going home.

"I'm not," said Casper.

Alma knew she hadn't said it out loud.

"I dreamed last night that the id gateway must change," Casper said, "it doesn't work."

"It's how people see you, and how you are. You have created a life for yourself, and then I mean created, it's something you've made."

"I envy Ardar, Arnljot and Ravn."

"Why Arnljot?"

"He has potential."

"And you don't?"

"Not without Bergtora," said Casper firmly.

"You can be my friend; I can give you potential."

Casper smiled broadly; he knew Alma was on to something. It was the people around you who helped you define you. Casper needed Alma more as a friend than he needed Bergtora as a girlfriend.

"I accept," he said, smiling even wider.

"Does it hurt?" asked Alma.

"A little," Casper replied, rubbing his jaws, it had been a long time since he had smiled so widely. "It was you who said that Arnljot and I could stay here, and now you're suddenly my friend."

"Let's go for a walk before the others wake up, I want to show you a path."

They went to the brewery and continued uphill, then they turned into a path that went to the left. Casper quickly understood why, little red squirrels were bouncing and running at full speed over the branches. The path meandered along a field, the large deciduous trees were impressive.

Alma stopped, and Casper looked up. In front of him stood the most amazing tree he had ever seen. On the bare branches were huge white flowers with a pink tinge, they were at least 1.6 feet, some of the flowers had fallen from the tree and lay on the ground. Behind the tree stood a rhododendron, Casper had always thought it was a bush, but this tree had to be at least 46 feet. The flowers had a faint yellow-pink colour. It was like a picture from a fairytale, where the illustrator had imagined the most incredible trees that didn't exist.

Casper saw a tree he had in his living room; it was a birch fig which stood alongside a huge eucalyptus tree. The climate was completely different here than at home; there couldn't be much frost in the ground during the winter.

They walked over a bridge, the river had split in two a little yonder. Alma was exceptionally quiet; Casper didn't ask why. The path went slightly uphill, there were trees on both sides. They passed a wooden sign that said Glen Rosa.

Alma stopped suddenly and looked down at the river on the right side of the steep path. It had become more and more wild and inexhaustible the higher up they went. Casper felt the same turmoil that was in the river, he breathed heavily and sat down on the path, Alma sat down next to him.

"What's going on?" Casper asked anxiously.

Alma told Casper what had happened here 988 years ago. Casper felt the blood rushing around his body, he was alive, but on the small sandbank on the other side of the river, it had once been a violent death, a mass slaughter. The bodies had followed the river's wild trek down to the fjord.

"Arran was once the secret and hidden island of the druids," Alma said. "In the year 1032, all the druids suddenly disappeared. The clan who extinguished them stood on this side of the river with their bows fully drawn, and they killed all the druids who stood on the other side, all at the same time."

A white deer came walking down the slope sides on the other side of the river. It paused for a moment and lifted its head and looked at Alma and Casper, then it turned and disappeared at full speed.

Casper began to see pictures in his head. He was wearing red clothes, Ardar yellow and Bergtora pink. They were on their way down to the river where the other druids were standing. Ardar died first, then he and Bergtora were thrown into the river. The river accelerated, it got heavier and heavier loads.

"We're leaving," Alma said firmly, taking Casper's hand and pulling him up.

Casper looked at her in shock. "What was that?"

"It was you on Arran in the year 1032. You can ask Ravn if you are wondering about the scientific aspect of it. How the photons take care of events that have happened, and how the images may reappear if the same person comes back to the same place. The event is saved in the cells, it's like putting a memory stick in a computer, it's no stranger than that."

"I think you explained it quite well."

Alma thought hard about something, there was something about the events that had taken place, and the numbers 1032 and 2020, there was something missing.

"Put them together," said Casper.

"3052," said Alma.

Casper started to see numbers in his head. It was the day, the month and the year, 2705+2020. He added them together and got 4725. Then he divided it with 2 and put the numbers 23625 consecutively and got 22356. Casper lifted his eyebrows when he saw the number.

He showed Alma the numbers.

"It's the same number I saw on a number plate earlier," he said. "How is that possible?"

"Somebody wants you to open your mind and change who you think you are."

"It has to do with my dream," said Casper.

"Not only that, you are back on the island where you used to live with Bergtora and Ardar."

"Is it possible that it's related to the number of druids who died here in the year 1032?"

"It is possible," Alma replied thoughtfully. "If you remember what I said before about the cells which preserve information, and that some particular information is stored in your cells. Your brain recognises numbers, that means something."

Casper thought it might not be their job to understand any of it, maybe the numbers were meant for someone else, someone who picked up the information through them.

"Come on!" Alma said suddenly. "I need coffee."

She's not so different from Bergtora, Casper thought with a sigh. They walked in silence until they approached the end of the trail. The red squirrels jumped from the deciduous trees that stood by the field, and over to the solid deciduous trees on the other side of the path, it looked like they had a fixed route.

"That's all you need," said Casper, and gave the red squirrels a long gaze. The squirrels knew him and he knew them, Casper was sure of it, this was a path he had walked many times before, it had been here a long, long time.

Ravn was awake, he went down to the kitchen and looked around, there were two coffee cups on the table. He looked at the press jug that still contained coffee. Ravn pored himself a cup and grimaced at how strong it was, he put on some more water. Ardar and the kids played in the garden. Bergtora and Arnljot were still sleeping. This indicated that Casper was still on the island.

The water boiled and Ravn made himself a normal cup of coffee. He knew that Bergtora and probably Arnljot had greatly appreciated a cup of coffee in bed, but he wanted to be alone with his thoughts.

Arnljot suddenly stood in the doorway with very tousled hair. He sat down, folded his hands and said, "Please let the hair fairies play outside until I have had a cup of coffee with Ravn."

Alma and Casper came into the kitchen. Alma told Ravn about what had happened on the trip.

"As simple as a carrot is called yellow and is orange, but no one thinks any more of it," said Ravn.

"That only applies in Norwegian since it's called a yellow root," said Arnljot, "not in English."

Alma understood that Ravn's brain needed significant amounts of coffee before it started working. "Your first coffee?"

Ravn just nodded.

The hair fairies came rushing in and the peaceful morning was broken for Arnljot's part.

"Go out and play," Alma said firmly. She saw that Arnljot had had enough. Arnljot looked gratefully at Alma, but he quickly looked down. Alma looked at Ravn, he could see that her feelings were raging inside.

"We're going for a walk, boys," he said. "Let Alma have

some peace and quiet."

Alma wrote down the numbers she and Casper had discussed. Bergtora came down from the attic with more tousled hair than Arnljot. Alma was glad the daughters were outside playing. Bergtora cast a glance at the numbers.

"Add 3052 and 4725," she said.

Alma did and looked at numbers with astonishment. "I've got 7777," she said shocked.

"What do the numbers stand for?" asked Bergtora.

"All the druids on the island disappeared in the year 1032. We live in the year 2020. If you add them together, you'll get 3052."

"And the second number?"

"It's the 27th of May today, and the year 2020. If you add them together, you'll get 4725."

"It means we go back in time, but we don't know which day the druids died, is it possible it was the 27th of May?"

"Makes sense. Emerald is the stone that is connected to the month of May."

"The stone has a connection to Frøya. Vanadium, which makes the stone green, has the atomic number twenty-three and is in group number five. Then we have the number 235. Vanadis was Frøya's name, and Vanadium is named after her. It is used as an iron alloy, and it gives greater strength and resistance to iron."

"Casper saw a number he remembered, it was 22356. If you take the last and the first number, you get eight. Maybe it has to do with something eternal," said Alma.

"Let me try something," said Bergtora, she had a strong feeling that it was related to the first and the last number. 22356, didn't make any sense because of them. "Maybe we are looking for the eternal number eight. If you divide 4725 with 2, you get

2362.5 And if you divide 3052 with 2, you get 1526."

She added the two numbers together: 1526+2362.5. She was right, the number became 3888.5. The last and first number was eight.

"I always wondered what the two and the six stood for?" said Alma. "It didn't make any sense, but now it does."

"I always make my mind up before I find the numbers," said Bergtora, "that way I know if it's true or not. In this case, I wanted to find the number eight in the first and last number. Then I saw that the middle part contained the number eight three times. We have found the missing number, and it is the eternal number four times. Another strange thing is, I checked the number of how many that had died from COVID so far in Norway."

"And today the 27th of May the number was 235?"

"It was."

"Well, it makes sense," said Alma. "Death and eternity. What else do we need?"

"4725, is the 27th of May and the year 2020. What happens if you take the years 1032 away. What is left?"

"3693," said Alma.

"If you add the last and first number, then you get 666."

"How do you turn the nine into a six?" Alma started to laugh just after she asked, it was obvious.

"It has always been the same number," said Bergtora. "It's a secret not many people know about."

"How do you know?" asked Alma.

"It wasn't only the druids who didn't write down their biggest secrets, the Vikings didn't either."

"So, the Devil is present," said Alma.

"It was originally somebody else's number," said Bergtora, "but somebody misused it. Think about it, why would the Devil use it if he didn't take it from God? What would be the fun in that?"

Lagertha stood in her ship watching the incredible light above Gulosen. She had only taken with her rowers who wanted an adventure. None of them had a farm they were to inherit; they were warriors who wanted a new life. There were twenty-two rowers on each of the five ships.

Lagertha sailed first with the other four in wing behind. She tried to hide a tear, but it was trickling down her nose. Fredleif wiped it away and looked wide-eyed at his mother. It was the first time he had seen Lagertha cry.

"Don't be sad," he said. "We'll be back, I know we will."

Lagertha squeezed him close to her. It was okay if they did, and it was okay if they didn't. She took a deep breath and looked at the long line of blue mountains that lay further and further behind them, they were on their way out to the open sea. Lagertha couldn't wait to feel the big waves beneath her, they gave her a peace of mind.

She started to say a stanza from the "Lay of Alvis":

"*Men call it Sea. The gods say Smooth-lying and the Vanir say Waves. The giants name it Eel Home, the elves Drink Stuff and the dwarfs call it the Deep.*"

"What do you call it?" asked Fredleif.

"I call it strangely enough the Deep. I thought I would call it the same as the Vanir, since Frøya is one of them, but Waves isn't right for me. What about you?"

"I think it's just Drink Stuff," Fredleif said and laughed.

20

"I dreamed of you last night," Bergtora told Casper. "Every time I have made a decision and determined that it's not us, then life plays a trick on me."

"Tell me about the dream."

"You had a car from the '70s with green round taillights, there were four of them."

"Four warning lights, but they were green instead of red, that means go instead of stop. It's like you said, we make up all the excuses in the world not to be together."

"Do we have a choice?" Bergtora asked, taking a deep breath. She feared the answer.

"You know the answer," Casper replied.

He fetched two beers from the pantry and carried them out into the garden. They sat down on the lawn and looked at the medium blue fjord and the ice blue sky. Alma came and sat down with them. The trees rustled gently with the leaves in the cool breeze.

"It was so strange that you remembered a number plate," Alma said to Casper. "Now the same thing happened to me."

"You saw a number plate with only sevens," said Bergtora.

"How did you know?" asked Alma.

"You wouldn't have bothered to tell us if you saw another number plate."

"And now when you have seen it, it makes all the sense in the world," said Casper and laughed.

Alma and Bergtora had to laugh too.

Lundesol walked on a path with old deciduous trees. Most of the trees stood in clusters, they revealed an atmosphere that she had never experienced before. The red squirrels ran at full speed across the branches. Lundesol wasn't surprised when she saw Ailsa sitting under a tree. Lundesol went and sat down next to her. They saw some druids galloping past.

"They're in a hurry," said Ailsa. "They know something is going on, but no one has told them that it's in the year 1032 it's going to happen." Ailsa wouldn't tell Lundesol that there were several things that had to become part of her consciousness before she could leave the island.

"Do you want to meet Flora and Oak? They are two very good friends of mine." Lundesol nodded and got up. They started walking back on the trail, then up towards Goat Fell. Lundesol saw several cows with insanely long horns and fringes. Flora and Oak's farm lay at the end of the enclosure. It had started to drizzle, but it was still warm.

Flora stood in the doorway waiting for them. They could smell the freshly baked bread a long way away. Flora gave Ailsa a hug, and greeted Lundesol, Oak did the same.

Flora had already set the table with bread and newly picked raspberries. Oak came with a small barrel of ale from the storage room. "It contains white heather," he said.

Lundesol liked the taste, it was subtle, mild and rich at the same time. It was completely different from the ale Ailsa made. She could taste a sandy soil and a hint of salt wind. Maybe it was the white heather that opened up her palate, she truly believed so, otherwise the ale was out of this world.

"So, you like it," Oak, said and smiled.

"It's divine," said Lundesol, "I can probably taste if the moon was full or not when you made it."

"Have a guess," said Oak.

"A crescent moon," said Lundesol.

"That's absolutely right," said Oak.

"Tell us about the place you're from," said Flora.

"The climate is much better here, we have meters of snow every winter, and the summer is not much to brag about. Sometimes we don't even have the feeling that it has been a summer, because it's so short, especially if it rains all the time.

The water is icy cold all year-round. The mountains are higher and the fjords much deeper, the land has a wildness to it. The colours are much clearer and sharper, the mountains have all the blue colours in them, the fields are golden and the fjord has the same colour as the sky, mostly silver-grey and sometimes golden, if we are lucky enough to see the sun. I can see people sitting outside in the cold drinking ale in the future, and they have a word for it as well, they call it outside ale. Anyway! In the summer it's bright all day and night, no one goes to bed before they have to. It's like living in a dimension of thin, transparent air."

"Sounds like a different very cold world with more depths and highs," said Oak. "How do you survive the winter?"

"Because of Orm. Our lives are intertwined, he has long hair just like me, and it's almost as white."

"Sounds amazing," said Flora. "Maybe I will meet a man with long blond hair one day."

"That is possible," said Lundesol, "there are many where I come from."

"Either I have to go, or he must come here," said Flora.

"You stay," Oak said abruptly.

"Time to go," said Ailsa and got up.

"Nice to greet you," said Flora to Lundesol.

"Come back whenever you feel like it," said Oak. They stood in the doorway and waved at Ailsa and Lundesol.

"What amazes me is that the Norwegian king hasn't cast his eyes on Lundesol," Oak said.

"Maybe he has," Flora said thoughtfully.

21

Casper let out his breath slowly. There were so many rounds he and Bergtora had gone, and there were so many rounds they still had to go.

"One step ahead and two backwards," said Bergtora.

"And just as far," said Casper.

"What are you talking about?" asked Arnljot. He and Ravn came into the kitchen to get more beer. Casper recognised Ravn's feelings, Ravn didn't want to enter the kitchen alone, but he didn't want to miss anything either.

"We're talking about life," Bergtora replied.

Ravn knew her well enough to know that it was a rewriting of the situation, they had talked about their relationship. Ravn knew that Bergtora struggled with the fact that what she said didn't necessarily turn out that way. She was just a piece, and right now he was not standing on the board with Casper.

Ravn picked up a beer and went outside again, Arnljot did the same.

"Don't think of Ravn," Casper said. "What would have happened if he hadn't been here?"

"Then I would have done this," said Bergtora and gave him a long and passionate kiss.

Casper reciprocated the kiss both once and twice. "Do you want to go for a long walk, just the two of us?"

Bergtora felt that was exactly what she needed. Casper took Bergtora to the path where he and Alma had been earlier in the day. Casper sat down under a large maple tree and leaned his back to the trunk; it had seven trunks that wound around each other. Right next to it stood a solid willow tree. Bergtora sat down next to him.

"We have no choice," Casper said.

"I know, we have to be together whether we want to or not."

"Who should tell Ravn?"

"Ravn knows," Bergtora replied, "he's packing his things and leaving right now. He's taking the midday ferry."

Bergtora was right, that was exactly what Ravn did. He had capitulated. There was no choice, Bergtora could choose him over and over again, but Casper would always be there, with Bergtora, or in her mind.

Ravn was on the ferry, Arran got smaller and smaller as the ferry approached Ardrossan on the mainland. His wedding had been interrupted by Bergtora's first love which apparently had never disappeared.

Ravn was in shock, the blood flowed inside his body, but that was all. Emotions and brain capacity ran on a minimum. He would never feel that life was worth living again, he was a living dead.

He saw a beautiful lady with long red and black hair, it looked completely natural, she turned and sent him a big smile. Ravn knew it was an invitation, he sent her a blank stare back, she probably thought he was brain dead.

His thoughts flowed, and eventually he felt his legs float too. Ravn leaned on the railing and sat down on a chair. An old man was sitting on the chair next to him.

"It hits hard," he said.

"What hits hard?" Ravn asked.

"Love grief," the man replied.

"No kidding!"

"It's hard to begin with. Then it gets heavier and heavier until it becomes unbearable, before it flattens out and becomes heavy again."

Ravn couldn't believe what he heard, was it meant as a comfort, or a help overboard?

"Nothing helps," the man said heavily.

"Thanks," Ravn said sarcastically.

"You could try to dedicate your life to the poor; it is a poor consolation, but some say it helps."

"What's your name?" Ravn asked.

"I'm just here to help you," the man replied monotonously.

Ravn got up and left. He saw the beauty with the long red and black hair, she looked at him once more, that made him even more depressed.

Ravn had no plan whatsoever to move on. He wasn't going to commit suicide, but the years ahead of him were endless years of pretending everything was fine. From now on, he would look forward to the day it was all over.

Frøya saw Ravn that sat on the ferry and felt completely alone. She knew that he had shut down. As long as nothing mattered anymore, no one would get through to him. Frøya could have told him the secret of moving on, but it was too late. A thousand years had gone by before she understood how everything was connected.

The only thing Frøya could do was to convey it to someone that Ravn listened to and who was open. Ravn was going to come home to a great empty space. Frøya knew it was urgent; if he fell into the great empty space, he would never get up again.

She saw that Arnljot sat down next to him. Arnljot had intended to stay on Arran, but he was worried about Ravn. He had left the car on the pier, and put the key under the left front wheel, then he had sent a message to Casper. Ravn hardly noticed that Arnljot was sitting next to him, but Arnljot noticed another presence he had never known before.

"Frøya," he heard a voice say, "that's my name."

Arnljot looked around to see if anyone else heard the voice. Everyone was sitting quietly, doing their thing.

"Ask me anything," Frøya said.

"How can I get through to Ravn?"

"You have to make him understand that there are bigger things behind it all, he's just a piece in the game. Take him on a car trip to Orkdal in your turquoise car, he will greatly appreciate it. Be a good friend, Casper no longer needs you, but Ravn does. You and Ravn are free to enjoy and see life in a slightly different way.

I can't tell Ravn that he is lucky, for his life has been cut to the bone. From now on Ravn will find out where true happiness is to be found."

"With all due respect, Ravn knew that before too."

"Now it has been cut to a minimum. Imagine high and low tide, Ravn had the high and low tide, now he only has the low tide left. Everything is still there, but it's much smaller, it takes more time to discover what's hidden in the sand."

"I understand," said Arnljot. "You want me to show Ravn the world as it is when it's low tide."

"That's exactly what I want," Frøya said proudly.

Arnljot squeezed Ravn's hand hard. Ravn looked at him for a moment, before he smiled and said, "You have no idea how happy I am that you don't say anything foolish to make me feel better."

Arnljot thought that Frøya was right. It didn't help what you said, but what you did, he was looking forward to getting to know Ravn better.

Bergtora looked at Casper, she felt that Ravn went further and further away from her for every second that passed. She tried to feel whether there was something different in the grief she felt for Ravn compared to the grief she had felt for Casper. There was no difference.

Then she felt the love she had for Casper compared to the one she had felt for Ravn. There was no difference either. The difference would be in how they were to live with. Ravn she had tried to live with, but not Casper, she understood that it was the crucial point.

It was too early to conclude since she hadn't been with Casper a whole day yet. Time would tell what would happen next. She wondered if she had a retreat, if it turned out that she and Casper couldn't live together.

Bergtora decided to stop thinking. Luckily the kitchen was a mess. Casper wanted to lie in the hammock and finish reading the book he had started on. Bergtora went into the kitchen and saw that Alma was doing the dishes.

"Let me do it," said Bergtora, "you don't have to both cook and do the dishes."

"I thought you wanted time off today."

Bergtora took a deep breath, she needed time to get her head around that Ravn had left, and Casper remained.

"I need to do something practical."

Alma took off the apron and gave it to Bergtora, then she went outside to get some fresh air. It wasn't just Bergtora who needed to think things through. What shocked Alma the most was the fact that she could imagine being with Arnljot. She had felt it the same second Casper said the car was on the pier and Arnljot had gone home with Ravn. Ardar was on his way to the pier to pick up the car with the kids.

Alma thought of the wicker of hair Arnljot had had around his head, then she went back and felt the feeling she had had when she saw Ardar for the first time. It wasn't comparable.

When she saw Ardar for the first time, she had longed for something else. The relationship with Emil was over a long time ago, they both knew it. Alma tried to put Arnljot in Caithness instead of Ardar, she was shocked. Had she met Arnljot first, then Ardar wouldn't have stood a chance.

She had to talk to Bergtora, and quickly before Ardar returned.

Bergtora listened silently to the flood of words.

"You're in the same situation I was in, a couple of days ago," she said.

"I have to choose, but how do I know if Arnljot is interested?"

"Just like you knew Ardar was, you just know."

"I don't know what I am doing," Alma said, rubbing her hands tightly against each other.

Bergtora took off the dishwashing gloves and took out her mobile from her pocket. She wanted to hear if Arnljot was interested or not.

Alma thought Bergtora would give her the mobile, but she didn't. She breathed fast and nervously while Bergtora waited for an answer. Finally, Arnljot answered.

"I made up an excuse when I saw it was you," he said. "You don't have to worry; I will take care of Ravn."

"That was not why I called," said Bergtora.

Arnljot asked if anything had happened.

"You can safely say that. Would you have tried to date Alma, if it hadn't been for Ardar?"

"Do you need to ask?" Arnljot replied.

That was answer enough. Bergtora said to Alma that Arnljot was interested.

"That was what I was afraid of," Alma said.

They heard the unmistakable sound of an Aston Martin not far from the house.

"What should I do?" Alma asked, perplexed.

"You pretend Ardar is Arnljot," said Bergtora. They both burst out laughing.

Soon after, Ardar entered the kitchen. Alma didn't know what to say, and for once Bergtora was out of words too. It was Emma who saved them. She came and asked if it was okay if she tipped Casper out of the hammock.

"As your future stepfather, I clearly say yes," said Ardar.

He had expected a smile from Alma, but she didn't smile, she just looked scared. Ardar wanted to ask her what was wrong, but something stopped him. He strolled nonchalant out into the garden after Emma.

"Tell Ardar I'm going for a ride," said Alma to Bergtora.

She quickly got out of the kitchen and started the car. She drove first to Brodick, then she followed the road for a while before she turned left and drove the road that went like a worm across the island. There was a small horseshoe bench on top of the mountain.

Alma got out of the car and looked at the mountains which lay like a horseshoe behind the bench, with the Firth of Clyde in front fare below. She could see the ferry which was halfway across the fjord.

Alma imagined Arnljot sitting on deck with Ravn. The

display on the mobile shone, Ravn, it said. *Maybe Arnljot has confided in him*, Alma thought. She answered, it wasn't Ravn's voice she heard, it was Arnljot's.

"Can you talk?" asked Arnljot. Alma said she was alone.

"I didn't want to make any trouble for you, so I borrowed Ravn's mobile. I understood that you're wondering if you're with the wrong guy, is that correct?"

Alma said yes.

"What do you suggest we do?"

"What can we do?"

"How sure are you?"

"Absolutely sure, what about you?"

"Absolutely sure," said Arnljot.

"The ferry goes back again almost immediately, but if you get off the ferry, you won't get on again. You are allowed to leave the island, but not vice versa."

"Hang on a minute," said Arnljot.

He went to ask one of the staff on the ferry if it was okay for him to go back again.

"That's fine," he said shortly afterwards, "I'll be back."

Alma didn't say anything, she just ended the conversation. She looked out over the fjord with an empty gaze and held her breath while she wondered if it was too good to be true. Eventually she had to breathe, but it took a long time before she breathed normally again.

"Where's Alma?" Ardar asked Bergtora.

"She wanted some air," said Bergtora, "she didn't say where." Ardar felt the unrest spread throughout his body.

"The two of us go much further back in time than you and Alma. Tell me what's going on."

Bergtora didn't have to think twice. Ardar deserved to know what had happened. He was right, they went way back in time. Bergtora took off the dishwashing gloves once more.

"I think you know."

"Is it as bad as I think it is?"

Bergtora nodded.

"How did it happen, what did I miss?" Ardar shouted.

Bergtora told him what Alma had said. If she had met Arnljot first, she had no doubt she would have been with him still.

"It's your fault, if you had been sure of your relationship with Ravn this would never have happened."

"They would have met sooner or later."

"Do you know if they have talked?"

Ardar looked strictly at Bergtora.

"You know there's a chance Arnljot is coming back with the same ferry," said Bergtora.

They looked out of the window at the same time and saw that the ferry was on its way back. Ardar screamed that he would pack up and leave if Arnljot came back.

Casper came into the kitchen and asked what all the fuss was about. Bergtora explained as best she could, she hoped Ardar would calm down, but he had already gone to the attic to pack. Casper and Bergtora heard the car coming back again, they went outside to meet Alma.

"Arnljot is coming back again with the ferry," said Alma.

"Give me the keys," said Casper, "I'll replace Ardar with Arnljot." Alma wanted to walk away, but she owed Ardar enough to say a proper farewell. She stood waiting by the car until Ardar finally showed up. He walked fast against the car, but Casper stopped him.

"You owe it to yourself to say goodbye," he said. "You'll

regret it, if you don't."

"It was good as long as it lasted," Ardar said angrily.

"Sorry," Alma said, "but it had only gotten worse and worse to end it."

Ardar came to his senses again. "I know," he said. "It was honest of you to do it this way, give me some time, then we can talk." Bergtora and Alma stood watching the car drive down the road.

"Then another one is off," said Alma.

Bergtora took her arm, and together they went back to the house.

"Ardar intended to go to this house alone," said Alma, "and now we are seven people that shouldn't have been here."

"We still have two weeks left. Ardar told me he has paid the rent. It was a wedding gift foremost to Ravn, and now Ravn and Ardar are gone, how unbelievable is that?"

"Unbelievable," said Alma. "Maybe we should find out more about the dead man."

Bergtora suspected that Alma wanted something else to think about for a while.

They went up to the attic, it was large and airy with chests and boxes that stood along the walls. The cobwebs hung limply in the corners of the room; they pulled out a box each.

Bergtora opened a small cigar box with old letters and cards. The first letter she read was almost incomprehensible, the explanation came midway through the letter. The woman was obviously drunk at the time she had written the letter. It was a declaration of love with a childishly drawn heart at the end. Bergtora gave the letter to Alma.

She read it and looked at the return address, it said Blairmore.

"It's actually just on the other side of the hill, maybe Fiona is still living there, we can go to Blairmore as soon as they are back with the car."

"Are you not jumping ahead a little too fast?" Bergtora asked. "Don't you wanna spend some time with Arnljot first?"

"He can come too, we can all go."

Bergtora nodded.

"That's the first letter you read," Alma said. "Isn't it a little creepy? In a way we found what we were looking for."

"Intuition," said Bergtora and laughed. "Sometimes, it's good to have."

"There we have the gentlemen back already," said Alma.

They heard the car park, and the car doors slammed shut. They heard wild cheers from the garden. Bergtora and Alma went to the window and saw that Arnljot was forcibly placed on a chair.

The brushes went at full speed in his hair.

"They have picked up speed," said Bergtora, impressed.

"I've talked to them. They are allowed to do Arnljot's hair three minutes every day. I don't want to scare him off."

"It must have been a shock to you when he suddenly decided to join Ravn."

"It was, but not anymore." Alma was already on her way down the stairs.

Bergtora was standing by the window, she wanted to look at everything that was going on from a bird's eye view. Alma and Arnljot disappeared around the corner of the house. Casper looked around to see if he could see her, he had no idea she was in the attic. At last, he went inside and Bergtora went downstairs to meet him.

"Do you have any regrets?" Casper asked when he saw her.

Bergtora stopped on the last step and held on to the railing with one hand.

Casper left her alone and went out into the garden again. That was all Bergtora needed. As long as Casper was willing to give her space, it would work.

"No," she said, when she came out into the garden.

"You needed time to figure it out," Casper said.

"All I needed was a few seconds. I'll never say anything fast, just because it's the right thing to do. If you ask me something, you will get an honest answer."

Sometimes too honest, Casper thought. "Maybe we should have some coffee in the garden?"

It was the safest question to ask Bergtora. They went into the kitchen together. Bergtora told him about the letter they had found.

"Can I see it?"

Bergtora gave him the letter.

Casper read it a few times. "How is it possible to hide love behind drunkenness?"

"Alma says the return address is located just behind the hill. Do you want to join us and investigate whether Fiona lives there with a broken heart?"

Casper was curious after reading the letter. What he found most fascinating, was the fact that the letter had most likely been mailed when Fiona was sober, why didn't she rewrite the letter before posting it?

Bergtora poured the coffee in a thermos and packed two cups in a small basket.

"What about the others, shouldn't they get any coffee?"

Bergtora just shook her head and smiled at him.

"From now on, this is a new tradition; you and me drink

coffee alone, at least once a day."

Casper looked at her for a long time, he needed time to realise that finally they were together.

Lagertha tried to swim in the burn.

"It doesn't take long to walk down to the beach in Bred-Vik," said Michael.

Fredleif stood on the ford, holding Michael's hand, he wanted to swim too, but not in the burn. Lagertha put on her blue dress and took Fredleif's other hand. They began to walk towards the beach. The weather was glorious.

Lagertha tied up her hair and stuck a stick through it to hold it in place when they reached the beach. Fredleif was already far out in the water, he appeared up and down in the water like a dolphin. The water was surprisingly hot.

"Have you seen any dolphins lately?" asked Lagertha of Michael.

"I saw a few the day you arrived."

"It's only a couple of weeks ago, but it feels like several years. I'm done being a shieldmaid, I'd rather just be here with you and Fredleif."

The blue sky merged with the water, it was only the structure that made it possible to see the difference between the two, the water sparkled while the sky was transparent. It was a beautiful day.

A life could change within a second, thought Michael. He didn't wake up alone anymore, there was a woman next to him, with long white hair. The hair was everywhere, Michael had even seen a spider use it in its web. It looked amazing, but it was the first time he had seen anything like it, the spiders never incorporated anything.

Michael swam towards Lagertha. They bathed for so long that the cold came creeping into their bodies, they had to get out of the water whether they wanted to or not.

"Tell me about what you are leaving behind."

"Imagine a river flowing quietly with sandbanks on both sides, with hundreds of ducks floating. They always lie and croak before they suddenly fly across the fjord. All of a sudden, they are back again, and the same thing repeats itself day in and day out."

"Are there any other birds?"

"There are crows, magpies and ravens." Lagertha could see that it caught Michael's interest.

"There's a place called Kongsviken, the bay of the kings, beyond there's a hill called Ravnåsen, meaning the Ravens Hill. They have settled at the king's favourite place to go ashore. The magpies have, according to the old people, lived in the same deciduous trees for generations, they are located between Kongsviken and Sjur's farm which lays down by the fjord. The crows live up in the hill, where Ravn comes from."

"Have you heard if Ravn has arrived on the island he was searching for?"

"Not yet, but it doesn't surprise me. There are only a few who travel where Ravn intended to go. If we're going to hear news about him, we need to go to the North. Isn't it time for some air under your wings?"

Michael envisioned a trip out on the open sea with giant waves, he didn't know if he was tough enough, but it was certainly not what he longed for.

"How about a trip around the island first?"

"I just have to gather the rowers first, it's not easy to sail around an island, it's easier to row."

Fortunately, there were twenty-two rowers who had been willing to settle on the island. They had been given land on Arran that the farmers didn't want, they said it was uncultivable. The first thing the rowers did, was to mix seaweed, straw and old horse manure into the soil. It was not possible to sow anything until the quality of the soil was good enough, it was going to take a year anyway. In the meantime, they had access to all the food on the island that didn't belong to anyone.

Only Lagertha was entitled to three farms, but she had left anyway. Most of the rowers had settled in Bred-Vik and Sand-Vik, but there were some in Lochranza, they were the ones looking after the ships. There had never been any doubt where the five ships were to lie, Lochranza was the only possible place, the crows would warn them if anything was going on.

22

They were finally ready to go on a trip to the other side of the hill. Fiona lived in a house nearby Blairmore burn in the village of Lamlash. There were small, white lime rendered houses with small gardens facing the fjord. Some of the gardens had tall palm trees.

Bergtora and Casper both thought it seemed completely out of place. They stopped in the street of the return address, and Bergtora, Alma and Fiona got out of the car, while Casper drove back to pick up the rest.

Fiona ran along the fence and stopped and talked to someone, they went to see who it was. Fiona stood and hung over the garden fence.

"What's your name?" she asked.

They heard a lady answering Fiona.

"That can't be right," said Fiona, "that's my name."

They heard the other Fiona say that she could come into the garden if she wanted to.

Bergtora and Alma were thrilled, it was the perfect invitation, they didn't know what they should have said anyway. Fiona went inside to get some ice cream; she came out again and gave Bergtora and Alma one as well. She said they could sit on the bench under the rose arch, the flowers were still in bud. Fiona licked happily on the ice lolly.

"What about you?" Alma asked. "Don't you want an ice cream?"

"I've lost my appetite lately since a good friend of mine died."

"That's why we are here," said Bergtora.

Fiona just looked at her incomprehensible.

Alma explained that they lived in the house of her deceased friend and told her about the letter they had found.

"Can I ask you a favour," Fiona asked cautiously. "Do you think it's possible for me to see where he lived?"

Alma and Bergtora thought it was a good idea They heard the unmistakable sound of an Aston Martin approaching.

"If you want to join, we will be picked up soon," said Alma.

Fiona went in to get her bag. When she came out again, she was wearing sunglasses from the '60s, and an orange scarf around her head. They went out on the street. Fiona was glued to the street when she saw it was Michael's car.

Casper opened the door and let out Holly and Emma. Bergtora opened the door on the other side, so Fiona could sit in front.

"Change of plans," said Alma. "We will drive Fiona back; she wants to see where Michael used to live."

"I'm driving," said Bergtora and took the key from Casper.

Fiona ran after Holly and Emma who were on their way to the beach. Casper and Arnljot ran after them. Bergtora started the car, and Fiona smiled broadly.

"Have you never been there?" asked Alma.

"Michael was married, and so was I. What happened between us happened a long time ago."

Fiona thought of all the years that had passed, and all she bitterly regretted.

"Didn't you tell Michael how you felt?" asked Alma.

"The letter you found was the closest I came. It was written after a night out in Brodick, but you have probably guessed that."

"Were you sober when you mailed it?"

"I was, I knew it was then or never."

Luckily, they arrived at the house and Fiona got something else to think about. Bergtora opened the door for her and Alma stood ready with the front door open.

"Welcome to Michael's house," she said.

"What about Michael's daughter?" asked Fiona. "Doesn't she come along sometimes?"

"That's one of the perks with the virus," said Alma. "It's easier to be left alone."

Fiona thought about how much she wanted someone to come and disturb her from time to time. She went into the house and Bergtora and Alma stayed in the garden.

"Come out when you are done," Alma said.

Fiona walked carefully around the house; she could still feel Michael's presence. A car stopped in the courtyard, Fiona went to the window to see who it was.

Typical, Fiona thought, *of course Margaret should show up right now*. She heard a tapping on the door. Bergtora and Alma heard nothing since they were in the garden. Fiona wondered if she should open the door or not, she had been looking forward to walking around the house alone.

The tapping stopped and Fiona could hear voices from the garden. She went to the window, hiding behind the curtain. It looked like Bergtora and Alma did their outermost to keep Margaret from the house, it seemed that they succeeded. Soon, Fiona could hear the car start and drive off.

She went into the kitchen and continued into the pantry. Fiona thought this was where his soul was. To get so much out of food as Michael had done, that was an art. They had only had one meal together. They had ordered fish, it was chalk-white with a white sauce and potatoes. Fiona had worn a tight black dress with a neck and long sleeves that ended at the knee. Michael had been impeccable in a white shirt and a black suit.

Fiona thought they had both been black and white that night. She with her light short hair and bright red lipstick, she even wore a long black coat, and he with his medium blond hair smoothly laid back, and a black jacket over his suit.

It had been a clear black sky when they ended the evening. The snow had laid a white blanket over the landscape. They had gone for a walk to the churchyard close by.

Fiona had a feeling that Michael had thought just as much of that night as she had. They had been young and naive, but the rest of their lives were marked by the few times they had been together. Now it was too late.

Fiona hadn't visited Michael's grave yet. She could ask if Bergtora and Alma wanted to drive her to the church in Kilmory. Fiona went out into the garden.

"Of course!" Alma answered as soon as Fiona asked. Bergtora started walking towards the car.

"Right now?" Fiona asked, confused.

"I have an ulterior motive," said Bergtora. "After we have been to Kilmory, we'll drive you home and pick up the rest."

"I can pick you up tomorrow so you can eat with us," said Alma. Fiona felt a happiness spread throughout her body. Alma and Bergtora didn't say what they said, just to have something to say, they meant every word.

Bergtora started the car and Fiona leaned back in her seat and enjoyed the sound of the engine. This time Bergtora had a hard time keeping to the speed limit, the car was made for speed but not the roads on Arran. A peacock or a sheep could suddenly cross the road. The landscape was unsurpassed with its slope hills and muted colours, Bergtora had to concentrate to keep her eyes on the road and not the scenery.

They approached Kilmory, but there were no signs of a church. Fiona said that a road would appear to the right soon. Kilmory church was the only church on Arran which wasn't close to the road. Bergtora found the way and soon the church appeared between rolling plains and fields, there was only one house nearby.

The church was built from a light local stone and had fine ornaments. Where the tower normally was, a bell hung in an opening made of stone.

Fiona got out of the car and went to Michael's tombstone. She had been to his funeral but had kept in the background. Fiona didn't think Margaret's mother McKenzie knew anything about her, but she didn't particularly want to meet her.

Bergtora and Alma kept an eye on Fiona from a distance. What they saw made them deeply moved, they could almost feel Fiona's grief.

"It's just like Arran has many time gaps," said Alma.

Bergtora agreed, there was something about all the places they visited, it was easy to see what had happened, it was still in the ground, and in the air somehow.

"It seems like the veil is extra thin on the island," said Alma. Bergtora thought it was a conversation they should have had with Ravn. Alma saw what Bergtora was thinking. She just squeezed her hand, there was nothing to say.

Fiona came walking towards them, she had nothing to say either. Bergtora's mobile rang, it was Casper who wondered if she was on her way. Bergtora told them to go up to Fiona's house again. She started the car and managed to arrive at Fiona's place at the exact same time as Casper, Arnljot and the bairns.

"Since you are here," said Fiona, "you are welcome to a meal in the garden. I have just baked a loaf of bread, and there are plenty of toppings."

Casper and Arnljot just smiled and nodded, they were starving. Alma followed Fiona into the kitchen to help her. She saw that Fiona took the teapot off the shelf and opened a box with loose tea leaves, she recognised the smell of ginger and lemongrass. Alma just smiled to herself. Standing in Fiona's kitchen smelling the same tea she had in Caithness, made everything fall into place. Arnljot came and asked if he could help with anything.

"You do not happen to have a handsome uncle who is available?" asked Fiona.

"I know a couple, we are not related, but I can vouch for them." Arnljot showed Fiona a picture of two men. "You could visit Orkdal when everything is back to normal."

Fiona just nodded, she felt strangely well with Arnljot and the rest of them. Arran was a beautiful island, but Fiona had never managed to find good friends here.

She could be honest now that Michael was dead, she had only stayed here for his sake.

23

Ailsa and Lundesol arrived at Lochranza in the evening. It was completely dark, the only thing they could see was the smoke from the chimney.

"When you get to my age," said Ailsa, "then you know that life has flattened out, there is nothing behind every turn anymore. It just goes on and on."

"I thought you were happy with your life."

"Age changes how you look at what is going to happen next. You are expectant in another way, more resigned perhaps."

They went in and sat down by the fire. Orm came and sat down between them.

"I met some people I think you know up in the mountains," he said.

"Who?" Ailsa asked.

"I don't know, they didn't say their names."

"Describe them."

"One had black hair to his shoulders, it was exceptionally nice, and smooth. He obviously liked my hair too, commenting on both the colour and the length. He himself had never been able to have such long hair. When I asked why, he said it would have been highly unsuitable."

Ailsa laughed; she knew who it was. "Tell me about the woman," she said.

Orm stroked his chin as he smiled a little. It was clear that he had a good memory of the woman.

"She was," Orm began, glancing at Lundesol.

"Can you get us some ale?" asked Ailsa of Lundesol.

Lundesol understood that Ailsa was trying to get her out of the way so Orm could describe the woman. She reluctantly went to get some ale, neither Orm nor Ailsa noticed that she had stopped to listen.

"The woman I met had slightly different colours than Lundesol. She had a darker colour on her hair, but it was just as long. The colour of her eyes was a little greyer than Lundesol's, which is more blue. If Lundesol is the sun, then that woman is the moon, if you know what I mean?"

Ailsa understood all too well what he meant.

"Who were they?" asked Orm excitedly.

Lundesol came back with the ale and the mood was broken. They drank in silence. Orm had a hard time not comparing Lundesol with the woman he had just met. They were similar and yet so different. Orm wondered if he would be with Lundesol if he could choose between them. The unknown woman won; she had a certainty about her that Lundesol didn't have. Orm said he needed to be alone for a while and went outside.

"Tell me about the so-called moon," said Lundesol to Ailsa. Ailsa knew she didn't have a choice. She topped Lundesol's horn and began to tell, "It's true what Orm said, you are the same, but different at the same time. You're probably excited about her name?"

Lundesol hated when she wasn't taken seriously, she looked angrily at Ailsa.

Maybe I'm wrong, Ailsa thought, *maybe the trip Lundesol took to Glen Rosa had changed something in her.*

"I can't tell you anymore," she said, "I have an urgent errand." She put on a cloak with a hood which hung by the door and went into the dark late evening.

This was entertaining, thought Lundesol. She put on the other cloak that hung by the door and snuck after Ailsa, she could hardly see her in the dark.

Ailsa went to the only house nearby; it was on the way down to the ships. It had some deciduous trees in front that hid the house completely from those who didn't know it was there. Ailsa went inside and Lundesol was left outside.

Ailsa told them about the change that had happened to Lundesol after she had been in Glen Rosa.

"Why has she changed," she asked.

"Lundesol got into an energy field that most people fail to be in, they move on. Lundesol stood there until she had all the pieces. Orm thinks that she is uncertain of herself, but everything fell into place when he told you about the woman he had met. Lundesol brought out a rage that ran like a plague in her body, it wasn't envy, it was an energy that came into her when she was in Glen Rosa. What Orm said activated the energy."

"How do you know all this?"

"I'm here because I know."

Somehow it made Ailsa understand exactly what he meant.

"Thank you for the help," she said and got up.

Ailsa didn't see Lundesol hiding behind one of the tree trunks. Lundesol waited until Ailsa had passed before she peeked at the man in the doorway. The light from the fire threw a tint over his face. Suddenly she understood how Orm felt, her heart was beating hard.

Lundesol did the same as Orm had done, she compared them. The unknown man won superiorly. Orm was too immature, she wanted a man who knew things.

She remained behind the tree long after the man had closed

the door. Orm had seen that Ailsa came out right after him. He had intended to follow her, but Lundesol got ahead of him. Orm had followed Lundesol instead. He went to Lundesol and said he knew how she felt.

"Should we go and knock on the door?" asked Lundesol.

Orm just laughed, he thought it was both unheard of and natural. The door opened at the same time, there was no one standing in the doorway, but the door was open.

Orm took a deep breath and began to walk towards the door. Inside was a large, long table with two benches on each side, the rest of the room lay in darkness. Orm recognised the woman and the man who sat at the table. Nobody said anything, they just looked at each other. Orm was the one who finally broke the silence.

"I'm Orm and this is my wife Lundesol."

The man and woman got up and came towards them. The man shook Lundesol's hand. Lundesol almost fainted, his energy was so strong, and his colours were completely beyond. She knew that black hair was a very common colour, the same as grey eyes, but on this man, there was nothing ordinary.

"Lundesol," she said.

"I know," he said and smiled.

Orm wondered if they would ever find out his name. The man stood for a long time with Lundesol's hand in his. "A name can't be that important," said Orm and turned on his heel and went straight back to Ailsa, Lundesol followed him. Orm wanted an answer, and he wanted it now. Ailsa could see how upset he was, she asked him to sit down. Orm sat down reluctantly, Lundesol did the same.

Ailsa began to tell them a story that went back to the time when mountains and lakes moved to create the lands that now existed.

The green stone in the mound where you are from, originally came from this place, it has to do with the incredible light you sometimes see across the fjord.

"How do you know all this?" asked Orm.

"It's in our genes, everything is stored in little boxes. It is only a matter of time before someone finds out that the particles in the air have a connection with the particles in the soil, including the stones. Some of the food we eat, can create new lines in the brain, and open up new channels. That's why I make ale with the white heather that gives hallucinations."

Orm waited anxiously for her to say the names of the two they had met.

"It doesn't matter what they are called," said Ailsa. "There's a reason why the house is so difficult to spot, they have gone into hiding."

"Is it necessary with all the secrecy?" asked Lundesol.

"We're going back," said Ailsa.

The door was still wide open. Ailsa went in first, Orm was not far behind, Lundesol stopped in the garden. She felt how open her senses had become since she had been in Glen Rosa. Lundesol became aware that the man in the house, was the man who had stood behind her in Glen Rosa, she recognised his energy.

Lundesol suddenly knew what he was called, she went inside.

"You are a crow," she said to him.

"That's my second name."

"You're the one who stood behind me in Glen Rosa."

"That's right. Come and sit, we can offer ale with a lot of white heather, I think we need it."

"I gave you a nickname, said Orm to the woman, it is Moon."

"It's nice, but my real name is Ravna."

"You have the connection to Lundesol anyway, Crow said to Ravna, "Orm was on to something when he called you Moon."

"I guess it's not your real name either," he said to Lundesol.

"No, she replied, it's Gudrun."

"It's not so bad to be named after God either, but I like Lundesol better, Gudrun is too hard."

"My name is Ravn Orm," said Orm.

"Wow! That is truly a strong name," said Ravna. "You are an animal that twists on land, and one that flies in the air, and they are both connected with a lot of strength and mystery."

"You have half the name," said Orm and laughed, "you only lack your second name, what is your second name?" he asked soon after.

"Rowan," she replied.

Rowan poured some more ale, he made sure they had enough to open up the special line in the brain. Lundesol wanted them to start telling what they had been waiting for, for so long.

"I was just waiting for the heather to start working," Rowan said, looking at her. "What we are doing now, is just the preparation for something that will happen in the year 1032. There is a connection in the Earth's crust from the time the volcanoes here sent off lava to your homestead. The green stone that's in the mound comes from here."

Rowan took a few sips and looked at Lundesol, she hoped he would stop, her heart was beating too hard.

Rowan continued, "What will happen in the year 1032 has to do with something that lies further ahead in time, but it doesn't concern you."

Rowan didn't know how to put it; he hoped the heather had

opened their brain enough, so they understood what he was talking about.

"Don't think about it, said Lundesol, just keep going." She had followed his thoughts all the way. Rowan had obviously not discovered that she could read his mind.

"It is the next generation it's going to happen to. Sølja and Sigurd are two of your descendants. They will be invaded by two druids, who will arrive at a place called Alvåsen."

Lundesol and Orm exchanged glances, they both knew where Alvåsen lay, it meant the Hill of the Elves.

"It doesn't concern us, but two of our descendants, so what are we doing here?" asked Lundesol.

Lundesol knew the answer as soon as she asked. What they had been told here tonight, would be stored in their genes, and sent off to Sølja and Sigurd, who needed to deal with the strange things that were going to happen to them.

Lundesol leaned her back against the wall. The evening had not turned out as she had thought it would, it had become much better. She was one of the pieces that mattered.

24

Casper went up to the attic, he wondered if there were more letters of any interest. He looked around and saw the two boxes Bergtora and Alma had looked in, they were pulled a little forward.

It was a brown slightly rusty coffee box that caught his eye. In the box there were small thin letters side by side, along the edge of the envelopes was slanted stripes in blue and red. Casper opened the first letter and read it, then he opened the next, soon he had read all of them. They were letters that had never been sent, they had no stamps on them. He sat down heavily on the floor with the wall as support. It was as if the letters were written to him. Casper looked at Fiona's address, she had been living in Cowgate, which lay in the Grassmarket in Edinburgh. He put the letters back in the coffee box and took them down to the kitchen.

Alma, Arnljot and Bergtora sat and drank coffee. Casper asked if they would like to hear what Michael wrote to Fiona, but never posted. They just nodded.

"Michael wrote that he regretted that he hadn't tried to stop Fiona when she moved to Edinburgh. He was so shocked that she left after they had decided to be together.

Here I think the crucial point lies, Michael writes about a night they had together. They laughed and danced and had the best time of their lives, that's when they promised each other to always be together. Both know that this is the one they have been looking for, but then something happens.

Fiona leaves the next morning without a word about what happened the night before. She only looks incomprehensibly at Michael when they say goodbye, he thinks she regrets everything, but I think there's something else going on. That's what I want to ask Fiona when she comes for dinner."

"Can we wait that long?" Bergtora asked.

"We'll have an early dinner," Alma said firmly. "Dinner at two o'clock, you can go and get her, but don't mention the letters. I want to be there when she tells us what happened that night."

"There's more," Casper said. "In the next letter, Michael writes that he is seeing another woman because Fiona isn't there, his pride stops him from visiting. In the next letter, Michael decides to visit Fiona in Edinburgh, but the woman he is with now and then, tells him that she is pregnant. Michael moves in with her."

"Is she Margaret's mother?" asked Arnljot.

"That's right, her name is Mackenzie. In the next letter, Fiona has obviously been home to visit. Michael doesn't know that she is coming so he is pleasantly surprised. Mackenzie is in hospital, it's nothing serious, but it allows Michael and Fiona to spend the night together. The next time Fiona comes to visit, Margaret is born, and Fiona keeps her distance."

"Why did he never post the letters?" Bergtora asked.

"I think the answer is that Fiona got too drunk," said Casper. "I don't think she remembered that they had decided to stay together. From her view, it was Mackenzie Michael chose to be with."

"If we hadn't rented this place, it's not certain that Margaret would have given her the letters," said Arnljot.

Casper looked at Bergtora; parts of the story were surprisingly similar, except he had swallowed his pride and showed up on Arran.

I have completely forgotten Sofie, Casper suddenly thought, everything had revolved around Ravn.

He called Sofie, she would probably use the suicide card again, but Casper didn't care anymore, not after reading the letters.

Fiona stood by the window and rubbed her hands hard together. She had hoped for so long that she and Michael would get a few years together, but now it was too late. Fiona regretted not telling him how she felt, her pride had stopped her. Michael had chosen Mackenzie, and that was something she would never understand.

Alma called and asked if it was okay that dinner was earlier, Fiona didn't mind. She had dressed nicely during all these years and been careful with hair and makeup.

To no avail, she thought. Fiona heard the car approaching, she put the orange scarf around her head and put on her sunglasses. Arnljot stood holding the door open for her, he smiled but said nothing, his long blond hair looked beautiful in the sunlight.

"It's likely that we will find a good man for you in Orkdal," he said.

"Do they have as fine hair as you?"

"Finer," replied Arnljot, "they have a silver wreath around the head like a crown."

They said no more the rest of the trip. When they arrived, Bergtora came out and showed her to a table that stood at the bottom of the garden. It was so mild that even the wind was warm. Alma brought a large serving dish with white fish and white potatoes.

"I hope you like it," she said.

Fiona nodded, smiled and supplied herself. Casper poured a rhubarb juice for her. The accessories were simple, it was flake salt from Orkney, dill and melted local butter. They tried not to stare at Fiona while she ate, but they were looking forward to the coffee, so they could ask Fiona what had really happened.

"You are not so good at dry talking," said Fiona. "What's going on in the big city you come from? Trondheim, isn't it?"

Casper looked at Bergtora, and Bergtora looked at Arnljot.

"I can begin," Arnljot said. "Trondheim has everything. It has been dragged screaming into the modern age we live in. It's a large university that provides influx and competence, and there's some high-level research going on.

"The hospital has been expanded with many separate houses. They are building tall houses by the fjord, it's possible they decide to keep a small stripe of the view of the mountain range on the other side of the fjord.

"Before you could see a line all the way from the great cathedral to the statue in the town's square and straight out to Munkholmen which is located in Trondheimsfjorden, but now you can see a huge grey bridge instead."

"What else? Any characteristics?"

"Low wooden houses with splendid colours," said Bergtora, "me and Ravn live…"

Bergtora stopped abruptly and got up and left. It was quiet for a long time. Casper went after Bergtora, Alma cleared the table, and Arnljot was left with Fiona.

"Then there were the two of us again. Is there anything else you are wondering?"

"Tell me about what happened between Bergtora and Ravn."

Arnljot told her what had happened the last few days.

"It's problematic sometimes," said Fiona.

Arnljot decided to let Fiona read the letters while they waited for the others to return. Fiona opened the box and took out the first letter. Arnljot brought her a glass of port and let her sit in peace and read the letters. He decided to go for a walk to the old trees standing in a row. He sat down at the root of a huge rowan, it wasn't in the middle of the old trees, but it was the tree Arnljot found most intriguing.

He closed his eyes hoping Frøya would contact him again. She didn't, but what he saw was just as intriguing. A woman called Flora planted the trees, and her husband Oak helped her. Arnljot could hear Flora tell Oak why.

"Dian will come back to this place on a day on a certain time, and she needs to find the trees exactly here. They will show her the line that goes through the landscape, and she will know what to do."

"Now I see," said Oak, "that's why we are planting a row instead of only the one rowan."

"It's a special rowan," said Flora.

Arnljot saw a different picture, Dian came to the rowan, Arnljot looked at her clothes, she looked like she belonged in his time. Dian didn't see him, he was in the future, he guessed she could only see the past.

She sat down beside him at the root of the rowan and looked at her watch, then she closed her eyes, and Arnljot could see the line of trees that continued up to Goat Fell. He must have held his breath, for at some point he started breathing again, and the image disappeared.

Arnljot went slowly back to the garden, he wondered if Fiona had read all the letters. Alma sat with her when he returned. He saw that Casper and Bergtora were on their way too.

Alma said Fiona would like to wait with the dessert. There

was beer and wine on the table.

"We have all read the letters," Casper said, "I hope you don't think it was rude of us."

"If it had been someone else, I would have, but not you."

"Do you think you can tell us about the pieces that are missing?" Alma asked. "We don't understand why you just left when you had agreed to spend your life together."

"That's what's so weird," said Fiona, taking a break. "I remember meeting Michael by chance at Ormidale, that was where all our friends and acquaintances were."

"Michael said he didn't know I was coming. After we went home to his place, and that's all I can remember. It was a huge amount of drinks that evening, and it didn't help that I started drinking whisky on the ferry."

"There was too much alcohol," Casper said. "You don't remember what you promised each other."

"Michael thought we were together, that's for sure. I must have missed something. I only remember a few seconds."

"It feels a bit strange drinking now," said Alma, "since that's what destroyed what the two of you could have had."

"No worries," said Fiona, "you have given me hope for the future."

25

Frøya felt she was happy to be with Heimdal, it was a mystery that she hadn't noticed him before. He had a charisma which made her in a good mood just by being near him. Frøya didn't have to fight anymore, the relationship with Odin had been an eternal struggle. Odin had chosen another, but Frøya had refused to accept it, now she felt it was all right.

"And here you are," said Heimdal. He had arrived without Frøya noticing.

"Here I am," said Frøya.

They sat on top of the mountain Creag Glas Laggar which was overlooking the beach. It was 444 metres high, and the perfect place to sit and watch what was going on in Lochranza.

"What really happened between you and Odin?" asked Heimdal.

"What happened between us is completely uninteresting. What's interesting is what makes you want to be with me."

"I have a rich inner life," said Heimdal and laughed. "I don't think too much, I live instead."

Frøya understood what he meant, every day with Heimdal was like meeting again for the first time.

"Looks like they're on their way to the ship," said Heimdal. Arnhild walked in front, with Olav, Orm and Lundesol behind, Ailsa was nowhere to be seen. The rowers were already seated in the ship.

"We have to find her," said Frøya.

They went to the house on the outskirts of the plain. Ailsa sat at the table with her head in her hands.

"Hold back the ship," said Frøya to Heimdal, and sat down carefully on the other side of the table from Ailsa. She looked up and met Frøya's green eyes.

"Do you have an errand?" asked Ailsa.

Frøya looked at the jug of ale that stood on the table. Ailsa poured ale in two horns that Orm had left behind. "I've always wanted to taste your ale," said Frøya.

Ailsa looked closely at Frøya, it was not just their age that was similar, it was also the eye colour and the long silver-grey hair. Ailsa asked if she needed a double.

Frøya just laughed, and asked Ailsa why she had chosen to stay.

Ailsa looked at Frøya shocked.

"I thought you understood who I was?" said Frøya. Ailsa just shook her head.

Orm came into the kitchen. "We have problems with the wind directions," he said. "First it blows in one direction and the second after it blows in another." Orm stopped suddenly, he had noticed Frøya.

"What are you doing here?" he asked.

"It's what hasn't happened I am here for," Frøya said.

"You want me to go with them to their homestead," said Ailsa and got up. That was what she was wondering if she should do when Frøya showed up.

26

It didn't help to sail around the island for Lagertha, she needed more wind in her hair, and the excitement of life or death during the crossing of the North Sea.

She didn't ask if Michael wanted to come, she understood that he was afraid of the sea. One ship was enough, there were not many of the rowers that had to have the sea underneath, they felt comfortable with soil under their feet.

Lagertha brought a sack of soil, in case the wind disappeared again and the fjord became beige.

"How long will you be gone?" asked Michael.

He had come to see her off.

"It depends on the weather, but before autumn comes, I'll be back."

The ship was moving fast, it looked like the wind was made for the journey home. Lagertha thought about how little Ragnar had occupied her mind lately, it seemed like she was finally free of him.

Michael noticed a figure standing next to him, she was not from this world.

"Frøya?" he asked.

"That's right," Frøya replied.

"Does Lagertha return?" Michael feared the answer, but he had to know.

"Lagertha comes back if she wants to."

"How long?"

Frøya could see how scared he was. "If you lose Lagertha this time, then you just have to wait for another 1200 years."

Michael didn't know if he should laugh or cry. "Are you serious?" he finally asked.

Frøya smiled at him now. "Not really," she replied. "Of course, Lagertha comes back, it's possible you have to wait until next fall, but no longer, I promise you."

Michael didn't know if it was possible to hug Frøya, but he took the chance. He lifted her high in the air, Frøya just laughed and said she had to go.

"Where are you going?" Michael asked curiously.

"You know," said Frøya and smiled at him.

She was gone in the blink of one eye, but Michael noticed that it was a cloud that landed on the deck of the ship, it sailed a little to one side and then the other, before setting a steady course towards the open sea.

27

Bergtora and Alma sat in the garden, departure was the next day. None of them could believe it was possible that the holiday had disappeared so fast.

"Are you satisfied?" Bergtora asked Alma.

Alma laughed a little before she asked, "What about you?"

"I thought of a riddle I used to play in my childhood. So much did I have, so much gave I away, and so much did I have left." Alma took a fist of sand in her hand and poured the sand into her other hand, she did so until there was not a single grain of sand left. They saw that Ravn and Arnljot came walking towards them.

"We never managed to get married," said Ravn to Bergtora.

"Is it too late?" asked Alma.

"Not really," said Ravn.

"You only have to apply if you want to get married between the stones at Machrie Moor, isn't it so?" asked Arnljot.

Ravn nodded affirmatively and tried to hide a smile; he knew what Arnljot was about to do. Alma had told them that Emil referred to her as his wife, but they were not married.

Ravn squeezed Bergtora's hand and looked excitedly at Arnljot. Arnljot went down on one knee and took Alma's hand in his. "I have never been bothered by jealousy, but when I saw you with Ardar my heart almost exploded. Fortunately, I'm used to hiding my feelings, otherwise no one knows how it would have ended. Love alone isn't enough; the right time must also be present. I hope you will marry me, Alma. I know for sure that there will never be anyone else."

Arnljot waited a while as he pondered what more to say. Ravn shaped I love you with his mouth.

Arnljot laughed and said, "I love you, Alma."

Alma gave him a kiss. Arnljot asked Ravn and Bergtora their thoughts about a double wedding. Both thought it was a great idea.

Bergtora called Angus Black, he was a Church of Scotland Minister. It was Fiona who had told her about him. He was born and brought up on Arran and he was one of the Arranach's. Angus replied immediately. Bergtora went straight to the point, and asked if he had anything special to do in the evening. He didn't. Bergtora's next question was whether he could marry two couples. Angus said yes immediately.

"Our wedding will be in the middle of the Standing Stones," said Bergtora and asked Angus to hold on. She asked Arnljot and Alma where they wanted to get married.

"Here," they both said at the same time.

"In the garden in Corriegills," said Bergtora.

Angus said it was a good plan, the only thing he wanted to know was where to go first.

"We take the garden first," said Bergtora.

Fiona had told her how well Angus looked in pink. Bergtora asked Angus if he happened to have a pink shirt. Angus just laughed; he took the hint.

"How many guests are we going to have?" asked Alma.

"One," said Arnljot and Ravn.

"What if you two pick up Fiona, I can take care of the food and Bergtora the clothes?"

Everyone agreed it was a good plan. There was no doubt

about who would fix their hair. Arnljot started the car, and Ravn got in. Arnljot turned into the road where Fiona lived, and stopped the car by the fence. Fiona was in the garden; she came over to them. She looked questioningly at Ravn, none of them had told her what had happened.

"How about a cup of coffee?" Arnljot said after they had greeted. "Ravn has a story he wants to tell you."

Fiona smiled and went into the kitchen to put on the coffee. Ravn wondered if it was possible to ask Fiona if they could make two bridal bouquets of the flowers that grew in her garden. He asked Arnljot first.

"You don't have to ask," said Arnljot. "As soon as we tell what we are going to do this afternoon, she will offer to make the bouquets herself."

Fiona came out with the coffee, and Arnljot invited her to two weddings.

Fiona laughed and said she thought it was great news. The next second, she asked who Ravn was to marry.

"This is where the story begins," said Ravn and took a sip of the hot coffee.

"Let's hear," Fiona said excitedly.

"I know Arnljot told you that Bergtora and I came here to get married, but then Casper appeared."

Fiona just nodded.

"I managed to open the front door to our house on Bakklandet when my mobile rang. It was Bergtora, she regretted that she had chosen Casper instead of me. Bergtora happened to hear a conversation between Casper and Sofie, who Casper lived with. The conversation had been so embarrassing that Bergtora didn't understand how Casper could talk at all with such a stupid woman. That's when she realised that Casper had chosen his life with Sofie after all; if she should continue to be with Casper, it would be only to rescue him."

"I don't quite understand," said Fiona. "I met Casper a couple of times, and it never occurred to me that he needed to be rescued."

"I've known him for many years," said Arnljot. "Casper is a completely different guy when he's with Sofie, it's hard to explain."

"I understand what you mean, I had the same feeling when it came to McKenzie. It wasn't because I was jealous, but Michael became another person when he was with her."

"Bergtora said the same," said Arnljot. "What was decisive was that she didn't want to save Casper, she wanted to be with a man who didn't need to be rescued."

"When did you come back?" Fiona asked and looked at Ravn.

"Like I said, I unlocked the front door when Bergtora rang. I put down my bag and sat down on the stairs to talk. When we hung up, I got up, took the bag and locked the front door."

"Then you ran down to Nyhavna," said Arnljot and laughed.

"That's exactly what I did," said Ravn. "The captain asked if it was okay if he wrote a book about us."

"Where's the captain now?" asked Fiona.

Ravn picked up his mobile and called him. The captain responded almost immediately.

"Homesick?" he asked.

Ravn just laughed. "Do you have any plans for tonight?" The captain replied that he hadn't.

"What about two weddings?"

"Let me guess, it's you and Bergtora, Alma and was it Ardar or Arnljot?"

"Arnljot. Are you coming?"

Fiona said that the captain could come and stay in the garden if he wanted, since it probably was complete chaos in Corriegills. Ravn said he would come and fetch the captain from the pier at once. Now it was the captain who was laughing.

"Then there were the two of us again," said Arnljot when Ravn left.

"Nobody stays behind if everybody leaves," said Fiona.

Arnljot sat back on the bench and put his legs on the chair Ravn had sat in. Fiona went inside and came out with two glasses and a bottle of port wine.

"It's not stupid for you to know the captain. You can visit us whenever you want."

"Do you think you will stay in Caithness or Trondheim?"

"It will be Caithness because of the bairns, but I want to celebrate Christmas Eve in Trondheim. I hope Bergtora and Ravn invite us every Christmas. You too," he added.

Fiona hoped the same.

"Let's celebrate Christmas together as often as possible," said Arnljot.

Fiona didn't know how much she had missed people who understood her, before she met all those who had rented Michael's house in Corriegills.

She heard the unmistakable sound of an Aston Martin that came driving down the hill and into her street. Fiona looked in the mirror in the hallway and put on some red lipstick before she went out to meet the captain.

He stood by the garden fence and rubbed eucalyptus leaves between his fingers before he smelled them. Fiona looked at him for a moment before she went out into the street.

The captain was a good looking man with a well-groomed

beard and short grey hair. Fiona saw he had green eyes when his met hers.

Arnljot and Ravn listened carefully, the captain had never told them his name.

"Fiona Black," said Fiona.

"Arthur Aurinko," said Arthur.

Arnljot and Ravn exchanged glances but said nothing. Fiona poured a glass of port wine for Arthur, Ravn got lemon juice.

"I've never been to a place where the tropical diversity has amazed me more than here," said Arthur.

"We only have four degrees below zero in the winter," said Fiona, "you can grow whatever you want."

"A kingdom of heaven," said Arthur.

"You are interested in plants," said Ravn.

"After the end of the Soviet Union, the living conditions in Cuba became deteriorated, so people started to grow vegetables on the roofs, in order to get enough to eat. I saw how much it meant for people to have access to their own clean and healthy food. That's when I realised how much joy you could have with plants. There's a greater diversity within plants than it is within us humans, just think about how small and how big a plant can be. Without them we wouldn't have existed."

"All the plants used to be purple once," said Fiona.

"That is strange," said Arthur. "What fascinates me the most, is the ferns that already existed in ancient times. You can see they are prehistoric before the leaves sprout."

Fiona got up and picked up a small stalk, at the end of the stem the fern leaf curled up like a snail. She fetched a glass of water and put the fern in.

"We have a question for you," said Ravn. "We need two bridal bouquets, do you think it would be possible—" He came no further.

"Of course," said Fiona, "pick what you want. You too, Arnljot. It's good to do it in advance, I will put them somewhere cold and dark, then they will keep."

"Hopefully in water," said Arthur and laughed.

He thought of the chain of events that had led him to sit here.

Fiona wondered if Arnljot had parents who were alive, since he had suggested that they should spend Christmas together.

"You're right, none of us have," said Ravn.

"Have what?" asked Arthur.

"Parents alive," replied Ravn.

"You have a standing invitation every Christmas," said Arnljot and looked at Fiona and Arthur.

"Bakklandet is lovely," said Ravn, "there is no nicer place."

"I can vouch for that," said Arthur. "I had an aunt who lived there, she was childless, so I was often there. I grew up in Strandveien, not so far from Nyhavna."

He suddenly smiled at Ravn and Arnljot. They didn't know how to respond; it was so unexpected. Fiona saved them, she raised her glass.

Bergtora had finished ironing all the clothes and tablecloths. Ravn had brought the wedding dress back again; he had never unpacked the bag. Bergtora looked at the fabric, colour and shape, she stood so long in her own thoughts that Alma shouted and asked what she was doing. Bergtora slipped into the wedding dress and went into the kitchen.

"Is this the first time you've seen the dress?" asked Alma.

Bergtora nodded and sat down on a chair. Alma poured her a cup of coffee. Bergtora looked at the dress once more. There were rowan berries and leaves all over the dress, the embroideries were in the same colour as the dress, it was made of silk in a beautiful beige colour, it was sophisticated in a relaxed way. "What are you going to wear?"

Alma looked at her in astonishment. "I don't know, do you think we will find a dress in the attic?"

Bergtora smiled and said they probably would. Alma suggested she took off her wedding dress first.

Alma went to the attic straight away; she was so excited that she couldn't wait for Bergtora. She had seen a rack of women's clothing in a corner, they had probably belonged to Michael's mother, they were mostly from the '20s. It was clearly not a poor home Michael was born into.

Alma saw a dress with some thin eggshell coloured lace hung on the outer layer, she had found the dress. Bergtora didn't manage to get up to the attic before Alma was on her way down.

"We don't have any shoes," said Bergtora, and went up to the attic.

Alma put the dress over a chair and followed. There were shoes and boots hidden under the dress rack. Bergtora pulled out a pair of thin light brown leather boots. She tried them on, she couldn't even feel them. Alma found a pair of shoes with a pointed toe and a pointed heel; they were surprisingly good to wear.

"What more do we need?" asked Bergtora.

"A suit and shoes for Arnljot."

Alma looked around; the men's clothes hung on the opposite wall. She took out a beige suit with brown thin stripes. A turquoise shirt and brown shoes. "Michael must have been a special man," she said.

"Hope it will not be too much for Fiona," said Bergtora.

Ravn called and said that they had invited the captain to the wedding as well, the only problem was that he had nothing to wear. Bergtora laughed and said it wasn't a problem.

"The captain is coming too," she said.

"And he has nothing to wear," Alma said and laughed. She took out a yellow suit with white stripes.

"That one is actually nice," said Bergtora. "Do you have a shirt too?"

Alma showed her a deep red shirt. She also found a pair of extra shoes in soft brown leather.

"Shall no one wear a tie?"

"No, there are no men who likes to wear a tie."

"That's it then," Bergtora said and helped Alma carry everything downstairs.

Arthur and Ravn sat in the kitchen when they came down. Bergtora put the suit and shirt in Arthur's lap and Alma gave him the shoes.

He got up and carried everything into the living room. It didn't take long before he was back again. Ravn had always had a suspicion that Arthur liked the clothes from Carnaby Street, now he had it confirmed, Arthur smiled from ear to ear.

"I saw what the clothes did for you. Now I understand what it feels like. I feel, to put it mildly; alive."

Bergtora gave him a cup of coffee. Arthur wanted to kiss her on the cheek, but he felt he didn't know her well enough.

"It's fine," said Bergtora.

"What's fine?" asked Arthur.

"If you want to kiss me on the cheek."

He leaned forward and kissed her on the cheek.

"Tell us about your upbringing in Strandveien," said Ravn. Arthur sat down and pulled his trouser legs up a little so he wouldn't strain the fabric on the knees. It was a gesture that was almost extinct, no one did it anymore. Ravn was moved, it was probably not an upbringing in abundance Arthur had behind him.

"There wasn't an upbringing in abundance," said Arthur, "there was often porridge for breakfast, dinner and evening, but occasionally we had fried herring with potatoes and dill. My mother grew vegetables in the small garden we had. There were dark blue cornflowers and red poppies between the vegetables. My mum always said that flowers lifted her spirit and made her feel less poor. She collected the poppyseeds and spread them further and further away from the house every year.

We appreciated that we had a bed to sleep in, as well as clothing and food. It was a hard upbringing, but we never lacked love, that's why I have a good life today."

Ravn jumped up. "I have completely forgotten Fiona and Arnljot, I said I would come back immediately."

"Let me," said Arthur and held out his hand so Ravn could give him the car keys.

Ravn gave him the car keys, and Arthur went carelessly over the courtyard. They hung in the kitchen window and saw him take a sit in the green Aston Martin. They saw a completely different man than the captain they had seen before. Arthur stepped on the accelerator pedal and span off.

28

Lagertha sailed into Korsfjorden, it was early in the morning, just before the sun rose. It was impossible to see the difference between the sky and the fjord. Lagertha looked carefully to see if she could see the beige colour, but it was absent. Orkdal lay on one side and Byneset further into the fjord, where the fjord was no longer called Korsfjorden, but Gulosen.

No gamboling of dappled fawns leaping this time, Lagertha thought and looked at Lunden on her left side.

Fredleif was glad to be home again, he ran into Sjur's arms, he was standing on the beach waiting for them. Fredleif had brought Sjur a gift. He put his closed hands in front of him and asked Sjur to choose. He chose the right hand and Fredleif opened his hand. It was a round white stone in the palm of his hand.

Sjur took the stone and put it in the middle of the palm of his hand, it felt good, almost like he and the stone had a secret together.

They went into the longhouse, the huge table in the middle of the room was covered with everything they could wish for. Sjur's men understood that something was going on. They glanced at Lagertha and Sjur. Finally, Sjur got up and told them what was happening.

"So, Lagertha and Fredleif are leaving, but you will remain?" asked one of his men.

Sjur nodded and said, "That's how it looks; one day, I hope

Fredleif will return. And we will make sure he has something to return to."

Everyone cheered and raised their horns to Fredleif.

Orm went ashore in Kongsviken. Lundesol got a feeling that everything wasn't as it should be. Ailsa and Arnhild followed Orm closely, while Lundesol and Olav went further back. Orm saw nothing suspicious until he came to the huge stone they used to sit on by the shore. Now there were three crows sitting on it, they sat completely still.

Orm made a sign that Ailsa and Arnhild were to hide with him behind a large beech tree, Olav and Lundesol did the same. Darkness came slowly creeping up around them. Orm still felt that it wasn't safe to go to the longhouse. There was smoke from the opening in the ceiling, but he saw no one.

"What are you feeling now?" asked Ailsa of Lundesol.

"It's too early," Lundesol said.

They sat down after a while. The evening came and went, and the night came and went. When dawn came, something finally happened. The door to the house opened and a man Orm recognised came towards them; it was a herse he hadn't seen in many years, Lundesol recognised him as well.

"What is he doing here?" Lundesol asked Orm. Orm hissed at her, hersen was close.

"I haven't taken your place, Orm," said hersen, "I have taken care of the place."

"Tell me what's going on," said Orm.

"I'm not your enemy, Orm. Håkon's men are. They say you killed both Håkon Jarl and the old gods during the same day."

"Sorry to disturb you," said Ailsa, "but I'm starving to death."

"Is it safe to show up?" asked Orm.

Hersen nodded. "I'm sorry I didn't tell you last night that it was safe. The truth is I wanted to be sure, I have had a feeling for a long time that someone was watching the place. I've never seen anyone, but there is something going on."

"Are you sure it's not the three crows over there?" said Ailsa and pointed at the stone.

Hersen looked at them carefully, then he walked towards them. They didn't lift from the stone, they just turned their heads and looked at him.

"Hi!" said hersen. "Is there something you want to tell me?"

"*Kra! Kra! Kra,*" said one of the crows.

Orm looked at hersen, but he just shrugged.

"Food," said Ailsa aloud.

"Food," said Orm.

They went inside the longhouse. There was a lot of food on the long table in the middle of the hall. Orm began to eat, the rest followed his example. Ailsa sat down next to Orm.

"The crow said there was danger ahead, not from without, but from within," she said quietly to him.

Orm looked at the people sitting around the table. He knew all of them, except for a woman who sat with a hood over her head. He got up and walked towards her.

"I don't think we have been presented," he said.

"I don't think so either," she said.

Orm couldn't remember seeing her before.

"What's your name?"

She looked at Orm for a long time before answering, "My name is Maria Lyrgja."

"Big sister?"

Maria nodded. "Then you probably understand why I'm

here."

"Inheritance," said Orm.

"Correct," said Maria harshly.

Orm sat down heavily on the bench and took a deep breath. He didn't know what to say.

"How do we know that you are his big sister?" asked Lundesol. Maria pulled up the arm on her dress and showed a tattoo of a worm and a raven.

"And what did you think I should be left with?" asked Orm.

"You get to keep Lundesol, and the ship you so conveniently docked with in Kongsviken. I suggest you leave right now; hospitality is over."

"Had it been possible to bring some clothes?"

Lundesol looked at Maria.

Maria looked closely at her. "I don't think so, I can have someone sew your clothes to fit me."

"They will never fit," said Ailsa, "you are too big and fat."

Maria stood up and howled, "Out!"

Lundesol got up. "With pleasure," she said.

Arnhild took Lundesol's hand, and they began to run back to Kongsviken. Orm got up slowly. His men looked down at the tabletop.

"Let's go," Ailsa said quietly to him. "Maria has a legitimate inheritance."

Orm looked at Olav, he had stiffened. Orm went over to him and pulled him to his feet. They walked slowly towards the door; they had just come outside when they heard Maria's laughter.

"Let her laugh," said Ailsa. "She's not the last to laugh."

"I don't want to drag you onboard the ship every time we are leaving," said Orm to Olav.

It looked like Olav suddenly woke up, he straightened up and started running.

"I think we should do the same," said Ailsa to Orm.

"Maria managed to chase me from my home, but that doesn't mean she's making me run."

"I know but it's quite cold. It's a good way to get the heat back in the blood."

Orm thought it was a good argument, it was actually quite cold. None of them had expected to spend the night behind a tree. There had been a fire in the hall, but it hadn't exactly been warm in the longhouse.

Ailsa breathed a sigh of relief as they reached the ship. She didn't tell Orm that she had seen some of the men exchange glances when they left. Ailsa had no doubt what they had been commissioned to do.

Lundesol had told the rowers to get in position, the sail was already hoisted. Orm and Ailsa barely managed to get on board before it sailed off.

Ailsa saw the men who were on their way to Kongsviken, Orm had not spotted them yet, but Ailsa could see that Lundesol knew what was going on. Orm looked like he needed time to recover from the shock, he just looked at his feet.

29

Bergtora sat in the kitchen, it was fairly early in the morning, a robin chirped outside in a holly. Arthur and Fiona slept over; it was late at night before they had caved in. They had played Michael's records in the living room, with the doors wide open to the garden, the lawn was the perfect dance floor.

The two weddings had been great fun and at the same time solemn. Everything had been successful. Casper was finally gone from her life and Ravn was back. Bergtora looked at the powdery pink colour of the kitchen walls, she wondered if it was Michael who had chosen the colour.

Alma came and asked Bergtora if she was okay.

"I have landed now," said Bergtora. "I have accepted that it is what it is."

"That's good. I have never experienced two who have been so equal."

"Neither have I," said Bergtora and laughed.

Alma fetched the port wine bottle and two glasses. She poured port into the two glasses and sat down. Suddenly, Fiona stood in the doorway, Alma got up and fetched another glass.

Alma had barely poured the glass before Fiona had drunk it all, Alma topped the glass once more, this time Fiona only took a sip.

"Here we are," she said. "In Michael's kitchen, with the pink walls he chose. I had a coat with that colour. I will never experience that kind of love again."

"How do you think Arthur feels when he learns that he's not the one?" asked Bergtora.

Fiona looked at her in astonishment.

"It's only a figure of speech that has become a habit. Michael never had the guts to leave Mackenzie, it's possible that I made him much better than he ever was."

She raised her glass and clinked it against Bergtora's and said: "Skål! Let those who want to be with us get a chance, and let's stop dreaming about what could have been."

"Hear! Hear!" Bergtora said.

Alma felt that it didn't concern her, she had been so lucky to be with her only choice, there was no one else behind the scenes. Ravn stood in the doorway with his hair to all sides. He walked over to Bergtora and pulled her up, then he sat down and dragged her down on his lap.

"Now we only need two more," said Alma.

Both she and Fiona looked excitedly at the door, but no one was standing there.

"Arnljot and Arthur!" howled Ravn.

They heard a commotion from the floor above. It sounded like they were both falling out of bed. At first, they heard intense swearing, then laughter. It didn't take long before they both stood in the doorway.

"Now I understand," said Arnljot. "It's a fairly early party."

Arthur just shook his head. "Are you sure you're going home tomorrow?"

"We have to," said Ravn. "I have to sell some cars in order to get some money."

"I have to go to Orkdal to pack," said Arnljot. "What about you, Arthur?"

Arthur was a little put out. He signalled to Fiona that he

wanted to talk to her alone.

"What do you think?" he asked when they stood in the living room.

"I hope you also go home and pack."

Arthur went into the kitchen and said, "Looks like I'm going home packing too."

All he heard was laughter and applause, Arthur had to sit down and wipe away a tear.

Arnljot began to summarise, "We're packing," he said and looked at Arthur. "Ravn and Bergtora are going back, but are not packing. That means," he said and looked at Arthur again. "We should arrange a time we can meet at Nyhavna after we have packed."

Arthur just nodded.

"Then we have clarified everything," said Alma.

"Except you," said Arnljot and looked at Alma. "You should go back to Caithness and pack as well, but first we should celebrate new beginnings."

30

Lagertha was ready to sail back to the Isle of Arran again. She had chosen to take her worm ship with her. Fredleif already hung around the neck of the worm.

Lagertha hoisted the sail with a black raven on a golden background. The raven flew to both sides, it depended on which side of the sail you looked. They were on their way out of Gulosen towards Korsfjorden. The sun was already high in the sky. Lagertha cast one last glance at Lunden and sent a kiss to Frøya.

"Don't be stupid."

Lagertha turned and saw that Frøya was standing behind her.

"I have been with you your whole life; I'm not going to leave you now."

"It's going to be a change of gods; do you still believe that?"

"It will happen, but not until a hundred years have passed. That time that grief, now we just have to enjoy ourselves, there are good things in front, and bad things behind."

"You sound just like Munin," Lagertha said and laughed.

"Oh my God, I do, I've been with him for too long. Fly back to Odin," she said to Hugin and Munin. "Greet him and say that I am happy with Heimdal. Hope Odin will be happy on my behalf," she mumbled to herself.

Hugin and Munin flew back to Høgsteinen where Odin stood tall.

31

"I'm wondering about one thing," Bergtora said to Ravn. "How happy do you think we will be without all those sitting around the table?"

Ravn looked at them, then he asked Alma and Arnljot if they could imagine living on Arran.

"If you and Bergtora live here too," said Arnljot. "What about you, Alma?"

"I feel the same."

"Then I ask you, Bergtora," said Ravn. "Can you imagine living on this magnificent island with me?"

Bergtora laughed and said, "It won't be only with you, but the answer is yes."

"Do you think we should start in the automotive industry?" asked Ravn of Arnljot.

Arnljot just smiled and nodded.

"What would you like to do?" asked Fiona of Arthur.

"It has always been a dream to work with plants, especially when I can cultivate all that my heart desires."

"Then there are only the two of us left," said Alma to Bergtora.

"That goes without saying," said Fiona and laughed. "You are working in a coffee shop," she said to Bergtora. "And you, Alma, you are a master chef at Michael's level."

Fiona felt to her satisfaction that she could talk about Michael without any hurt. A car stopped in the yard, Fiona looked out the window and saw to her astonishment that it was Mackenzie. There was a knock on the door and Fiona went to open it.

"What are you doing here?" asked Mackenzie.

"I've been to two weddings," replied Fiona. "The question is, rather, what are you doing here early in the morning?"

"Can I come in?"

Fiona opened the door wide open and let Mackenzie in.

Mackenzie went straight to the kitchen.

"I'm Michael's wife," she said and sat down at the table. Alma asked if she wanted a glass of port.

Mackenzie nodded and looked at Fiona.

"Congratulations," she said, looking at them in turn.

Ravn and Arnljot nodded to her, while Bergtora and Alma just looked at her. Mackenzie began to tell them how happy she and Michael had been together.

Bergtora got up and stretched, then she said, "I guess you stopped by because you saw the light in the windows, but we are going to leave tomorrow and would like to get ready."

Mackenzie got up and said harshly, "I have a lot to teach you when it comes to a happy marriage. No one was as happy as me and Michael."

Bergtora took her by the arm and opened the front door. As soon as Mackenzie was outside, she closed it and locked it, then she took a deep breath before she went into the kitchen. Mackenzie was like a bad version of Sofie. It was almost exactly what Sofie told everyone about her and Casper's relationship. Bergtora had to laugh, it was no wonder Casper had recognised himself in Michael.

Ravn looked at Bergtora. He saw how well she felt, Mackenzie was just as stupid as Sofie was. Bergtora also had

Fiona who understood exactly what she was going through.

Ravn hoped that he soon could say what he had gone through.

"You can say it now," Bergtora said and kissed him. She felt that it was the truth; Casper was in the past. Bergtora stood up and stretched her hands.

"Yes," she howled. "I'm free, there's only one Ravn in my life."

Fiona laughed, she felt exactly the same. Mackenzie had done her job; she had set them free.

Next day dawned with glorious sunshine. They made two trips down to the ferry berth. It was easy to leave Arran, they would soon be back again.

Fiona stood on the dock waving. Arthur stood for so long, waving back, that Ravn asked if the ship was off course. Arthur turned and saw that Ravn was right. He shook his head as he walked towards the bridge.

Fiona went for a walk along the fjord in Brodick Bay. She thought about how wasted everything had been. She still put on makeup every day and painted her nails regularly, but it was for a completely different reason than before.

Fiona walked past the hairdresser who was still closed, it didn't matter, maybe it would become fashionable soon, to not have perfect hair, she hoped so. Fiona had never seen so much messy hair as she had seen on the gang that was now her family, Bergtora was the one who beat them all, she really didn't care.

Fiona's steps were so light that she felt she could go for a long walk. She continued towards Rosaburn and the castle. Later on, the car needed to be returned, but for the time being it was safe at the ferry berth. The car had been Michael's dearest possession. Fiona picked up the phone from her bag and called Margaret. Fiona presented her request; she could hear Margaret laughing at the other end.

"I know someone who would be very happy if he knew what you were asking," she said.

"What do you mean?" asked Fiona.

"You're in his testament, the car is yours."

Fiona didn't know what to say, she just hung up. The car was in top condition and had hardly been anywhere, Fiona guessed it had been to the butcher in Blackwaterfoot and the distillery in Lochranza. It was the first car she had owned for years. Within a couple of weeks, she had a car, a boyfriend, not to forget a new family and friends.

Fiona sat down on a bench that stood by the old wooden arts and crafts house. The house was weather-beaten and naturally grey with an adventurous feel to it. She looked out over the fjord and tried to let it sink in that her life had completely changed. Fiona took a deep breath and thought it was so easy, why had her life been difficult for so many years?

Three crows came flying and sat down on the grass. Fiona followed them for a while, but they didn't do much. After a while the crows took off and flew towards Brodick. Fiona did the same, she got up and walked towards the fjord back to Brodick and the ferry berth.

Ravn stood and watched the three crows which came flying. He saw they were coming from Brodick. They sat on deck and didn't move. Arthur came and stood beside him. "I am half Kven," he said.

Ravn nodded and was excited to hear if Arthur would say anything else.

"The Kvens believe that birds are sent by the gods. I always feel safe every time crows or ravens follows me on the journey. It has never happened that I have been accompanied by magpies or eagles. The crows and the ravens have different tasks than magpies and eagles. Does it sound logical?"

"Logic may have the least to do with it," said Ravn and laughed.

"I think you are right," Arthur said seriously, "I've never met anyone who has the same faith as me."

"What faith is that?" asked Ravn curiously.

"It's the belief that the birds you see are not just here, there is something else behind."

"So true, so true," said Ravn. "We have a crow belief."

"That's exactly how it is," said Arthur and smiled broadly.

32

Lundesol was restless, something was clearly wrong, the colour of the fjord became more and more beige. Lundesol felt it was urgent. "Row all you can," she shouted to the rowers.

The rowers picked up the pace, and they rowed until the beige colour was behind them. Lundesol breathed a sigh of relief, she could see ten of Orm's ships approaching.

"What happened?" asked Ailsa.

"It seemed like the beige colour on the fjord swallowed the wind."

Ailsa looked at the ships behind them, they became smaller and smaller.

"How did you know that we had to get over the colour as soon as possible?"

"Just a feeling," said Lundesol.

"Sometimes that's all you need."

Orm's ships were completely gone. *They were no longer Orm's ships, they were Maria's now*, thought Lundesol.

"Do you think they intend to follow us to Arran?" Orm asked Lundesol.

"No, the beige colour saved us, why save us if it's of no use?"

"You're right," said Orm and sat down beside Ailsa.

"Never a dull moment," he said.

Ailsa said she didn't mind. "You know that boredom kills?"

"I have never heard that one before, tell me more."

"Nothing happens, you just eat and sleep, or you do things you don't want to do, or you talk to people you don't want to talk to."

"You're right, that sounds boring."

"This here, right now, that makes life worth living. Lundesol, who steers the ship towards your new home and my old home. It should have been the opposite, but that's what makes life so exciting."

"And far from boring," said Orm.

He understood what Ailsa meant. Some would say that he had lost everything, but for Orm it was easy. He had lost a lot, but he still had so much left.

All the sand had disappeared between his fingers, what he was left with was an empty hand that could be filled with things he wanted, and not what he had inherited. Orm felt completely free, for the first time in his life.

33

Michael stood on the beach in Lochranza waiting for Lagertha. He had dreamed of a flock of crows that had taken off to meet Lagertha halfway.

The flock of crows who always sat by the beach was gone. It was evening and still no sight of Lagertha. He decided to spend the night on the beach. Michael lay down on some sheepskins and looked at the stars. Orion had decided to stand straight across the place where Michael had first seen Lagertha's ship. It was not so long ago, it just felt that way.

He must have fallen asleep at some point, for it was morning when he awoke. He sat up and rubbed his eyes. The fjord was dark grey and completely shiny, everything was reflected, every little cloud. It was as beautiful as only a completely quiet and mirror-bright fjord could be. The flock of crows was back again, that usually meant that Lagertha would be back as well, but Michael didn't see her anywhere.

He took the sheepskins and the blanket and began to walk towards the house. The first thing he wanted to do was to smoke a pipe outside. He grew the tobacco plants he needed in front of the house. They looked great with their oval-shaped leaves, and clusters of white tubular flowers.

Lagertha had seen Michael on the beach. She wanted to surprise him, so she had told the rowers to go back a little. Lagertha managed to jump ashore without being seen.

Michael came out of the house with the pipe in his hand, he

went to the bench. Lagertha sat there already with two horns filled with ale.

"You have brought your son," said Michael.

Lagertha presented Fredleif, and Fredleif said hello before he started running, he had obviously intended to explore the island. Lagertha just laughed; it was just the way it should be. Fredleif would probably come back if he got hungry.

They drank the ale, and Michael smoked his pipe in silence. Lagertha wanted to go for a walk, Michael suggested they went up to Creag Gras Laggar. When they reached the top, they could see a small figure at the top of the highest mountain in Lochranza. Fredleif lay down on the side and began to roll down from the mountain.

Lagertha and Michael ran down from Creag Gras Laggar and along the meadow towards Fredleif. They expected to find him half-killed at the foot of the mountain, but what met them instead was a boy who shook his head and laughed.

"You're supposed to roll down a hill," said Lagertha, "not from the highest mountain you can find. You're only three years old, you have to be careful at least another year."

Fredleif nodded and looked at the ground. Lagertha took him by the hand and Michael took Fredleif's other hand, and together they ran back to the house. Lagertha sat down in the meadow with Fredleif and picked up a long grass and put it between her thumbs and blew on it. A loud sound came from the grass. Fredleif tried the same, and soon the howling sound sounded all over Lochranza.

Michael lay down in the meadow and watched the clouds rise across the sky. Maybe it was just now real life began, without all those he didn't want in his life. He thought of something he had heard not long ago: "If your relatives are not how you would like them to be, use then rather up your fortune, enjoy it yourself and let your friends enjoy it. Often one saves for the hated one what one has intended for the loved one."

Michael had fortunately had half of the people he wanted in his life, while the other half had only caused anger and frustration. For the first time he felt that he could free himself from them.

"What are you thinking about?" asked Lagertha.

"How do you think one should relate to people who want to take control over your life?"

"They will gather information about you to have something to say. If they don't know anything, then you are uninteresting to them."

"I think the best thing is to stay away from them."

"Or you can have so many nice people in your life, that there's no room for them."

"A herd of starlings came and flew over their heads, they flew in different formations, back and forth and around in the sky."

34

Ailsa thought about how ironic it was, that she only had one night in her new life. She took a deep breath and drew in the fresh sea breeze. The rowers sat with their faces towards her, they had been rowing for many hours already. Ailsa looked at each one of them for a long time. No one caught her interest until she looked at him who was closest.

"Did you find anyone interesting?" he asked.

Ailsa told him how fascinated she was by Olav and Orm's hair, she had hoped to find a man her own age with long blond hair.

"You're about forty-eight years old," he said.

"I'm fifty," said Ailsa.

"I'm fifty too, and I used to have long light hair, does that count?"

Ailsa looked at him carefully. She liked his shoulders which were just wide enough. He had a charming smile, and his teeth were white. The nose had a slight bend at the top, but it was long and beautiful. The mouth was attractive, as were the hands, thighs and legs. If she could have a serious conversation with him, in addition to having fun, then she would consider him.

"What is your verdict?" he asked.

Ailsa said she should think about it. She asked him for his name.

"Joen Pors."

"I'm Ailsa Craig. Both mean stone."

"Then it was a good thing you left, otherwise it would have

been Stone, Stone, Stone."

Ailsa asked what he was talking about.

"Have you never heard what the place Orm comes from is called?"

"*Stein* means stone?" Ailsa asked astonished.

Joen just nodded and looked out over the fjord as he rowed. Ailsa asked him how he imagined his future if he could choose. She noticed that the rowers around him were quiet, they were obviously listening.

"They are my brothers; they can hear what I have to say. I want a woman who lives on Arran, is fifty years old and wants a man like me, who is strong, willing to work, a good friend, has insanely good humour and knows a lot about hidden things that only a few know anything about."

Ailsa smiled happily and began telling him about her house, whether he thought he could thrive there or not.

"I'm thriving already," said Joen. "What's between us is going to work and we both know it. Since you know the area, are we close?"

Ailsa just shook her head. "You were not on the first trip, what made you decide to join this time?"

"You met Orm's big sister, didn't you?"

Ailsa smiled and nodded. "Do you snore?" she asked shortly afterwards. She heard a roar of laughter around her.

"This guy has kept an entire fleet awake," said one of the rowers.

Ailsa wasn't worried, she could give Joen some ale with white heather, it helped even the worst snorers.

"I can see you have a solution," said Joen.

"How would you like a horn of ale before going to bed?"

Joen just smiled.

35

Bergtora and Ravn had packed everything they wanted to take back to Arran, the rest they had given away or sold on. Arnljot was on his way, they were to meet Arthur within an hour.

"How is it to leave Nidarosdomen and the flock of crows that live there?" asked Ravn.

"Maybe there's a new flock waiting for us, I saw a flock in Lochranza. Do you think we can find a house there?"

"I was thinking we could look for a house in Blairmore," said Ravn. "Did you know that Lamlash used to be called Kirktoun of Kilbride in the old days."

"It doesn't surprise me; I have never seen so many churches in one place before."

"I haven't either. Now it's time to say goodbye to Trondheim, Nidelva and Domen."

Ravn had set the table by the river for the last time, there were three glasses standing on the green checkered cloth. Bergtora poured up sea buckthorn berry liqueur with a dash of vodka and gave Ravn a glass.

"Let's wait for Arnljot before we have a final toast," Ravn said, he sounded a little melancholy.

It may be sad, but Bergtora didn't feel that way. It was just something new, and something they wanted. Bergtora tried to think of a place she could imagine to live and work, Lochranza came popping up in her head.

A flock of crows had its habitat there and here. Lochranza

had everything she wanted. There was a small stone house at the end of the meadow, half the roof had caved in. It was possible to create a cafe there, and at the same time have a place to live on the first floor.

"Where are we going to live in the meantime?" asked Ravn.

"Maybe we can share the rent with Alma and Arnljot, they have decided to try and rent Michael's house."

"There's another house I think will be sold soon. I have a feeling the owners miss Edinburgh, they used to live there."

"Where is it?" Bergtora asked excitedly. She knew the moment she asked which house Ravn was talking about. "I sat on a rock with my feet in the stream, and you came even though I wanted to be alone."

Ravn just smiled.

"We get time enough to explore the island," said Bergtora, "now we have to get ready to leave."

"Cheers!" Ravn said, "we don't have to wait for Arnljot."

Ravn saw that Bergtora disappeared into her thoughts, she was still writing a book called The Bloodlines. Ravn didn't want to disturb her; he went into her mind instead. Bergtora was provoked by a lady, who believed the reason for cats being buried together with children during the Viking age was that they shouldn't be afraid of death. Bergtora suddenly looked straight at Ravn.

"You don't have to invade my thoughts, we can talk together like normal people."

Ravn laughed and clinked his glass against Bergtora's again.

"You have another theory," he said.

"We know that Frøya chose those who came to Folkvang, before Odin chose those who came to Valhall. I think the cats showed them the way to Folkvang."

Ravn nodded; it made sense. He came to think of all the ships that had dragon heads, some of them looked more like cat heads, they had ears and eyes like cats, even the long tongue.

"Do you think all the ships ended up in Folkvang?" asked Bergtora.

"As far as I know, there were not many ships in Valhall."

"What strikes me is that Valhall is known, but not Folkvang."

"Maybe Frøya wanted to keep it hidden."

"Perhaps, but it is still strange. It's said that her father had a shipyard, and her brother had the famous ship called Skibladner. Think about all the beautiful ships we had that are now gone, and all the stave churches that looked like the ships with their black tar. Its main use was to preserve wood against rot. That's why we have some left today."

"We once had more than two thousand stave churches, and nobody knows how many ships we had."

"And now we have one castle, and that's the only one. It's not like they have disappeared during the centuries."

"We had longships and longhouses; we were farmers and warriors."

"Have you forgotten all the kings and queens we have had?" Bergtora said and laughed.

"Why didn't they want to live in castles?"

"I think it's because of the old gods, they lived in great halls, even after they died. None of them wanted a castle."

"It's strange anyway," said Ravn. "France has more than forty thousand castles."

"They built the stave churches with a lot of the old gods hidden in the woodcarvings."

"Most of the time they didn't bother to hide them, they were in plain sight."

"When they started to build the churches in honour of the new gods, they were mostly white, they lime washed the stone churches to make them white as well."

"The old gods were worshiped with the use of black, and the new ones with white."

"Strange but true."

"I wonder why Frøya stood in the background?" said Ravn. "She taught Odin all the magic he knew, and she chose the dead first."

"The first one that ever lived who knew magic was Diana," said Bergtora. "Diana seduced Lusifer when she was in the form of a cat, they had a daughter together."

"That's interesting," said Ravn, "the moon god had a daughter with the sun god."

"Diana created the heavens, the stars and the rain, she also divided herself into darkness and light. The Queen of the Witches, she was called."

"What's interesting, is that when Lusifer fell to Earth, he lost a stone from his crown, it was an emerald. It's said that the holy grail was made from that particular stone."

"He was called the peacock angel," said Bergtora and laughed. "Lusifer was created from God's illumination, God told him to bow to no one. He also created six other angels, they were called the seven archangels, and Lusifer was their leader.

"God wanted them to bow to the first human he created out of dust, it was a test for Lusifer to see if he would do everything God asked him to do blindly. Lusifer passed the test, but the story later on became that he had disobeyed God, and therefore had to leave heaven. God and Lusifer were the first entities, and they made the balance with light and darkness just right."

"That balance is long gone," said Ravn. "The fight has never been about either light or darkness. Think of day and night, or the sun and the moon. Maybe God was darkness, and Lusifer was the light, and somehow Lusifer was connected to the bad darkness, but that wasn't the whole story."

"I don't think it's my story to tell," said Bergtora.

"I have a feeling that it's already told," said Ravn, "it's just waiting for the right time to approach."

36

Alma stood holding Emma's hand and looked at the almost black and white hollyhocks outside the stone fence which had sprung out. She had to tell Emil about her plans, she didn't know how he was going to react.

Emma began to pull at her hand, Alma couldn't postpone it any longer, she opened the gate and went into the garden. Emil sat and drank coffee and watched the ducks. Emma ran over to him and threw herself around his neck. Emil hugged her and smiled at Alma.

"How have you been?"

Emma began to play with everything she had obviously missed in the garden.

"I have made a decision," said Alma and looked at Emil.

"Go on," he said.

"I have decided to move to Arran."

Emil first looked at her in horror, but then he envisioned a different life. What he saw was not worse, it was just different. He would see the bairns on a different time schedule. It was going to be more intense, but at the same time, he was free when they were gone.

"It's going to be fine," he said, "we'll make it work. When are you leaving?"

"We have to sell the house," said Alma seriously.

"Or I can buy you out."

"Do you want to? Where did you get the money?"

"While you were away, my mother died. I didn't want to contact you, because I knew you never liked her. How are you and Ardar?"

Alma smiled and said she had replaced him with his friend named Arnljot. Emil got up and went into the house, he came out with two glasses and a bottle of port wine, he poured it into the glasses and gave Alma one. He lifted the glass.

"It goes fast now and then, but I have no doubt that it will be better than it was before."

"Hear! Hear!" Alma said.

"I have the money, you can go whenever you want."

"I'm only bringing clothes and a few cups; you can keep the furniture."

"I think you get space for what you intend to take with you on a trailer, and I happen to have a car with a tow ball. The bairns would probably want to bring some toys."

"We don't need a trailer," said Alma.

"You do," Emil said seriously. "I want you to take with you the furniture you inherited from your grandmother. Let's do it right the first time around, I'm happy to drive you. We can make a trip out of it, a last holiday together."

Alma put a hand on each of his cheeks and kissed him, Emil just laughed.

37

Arnljot stood looking out over the rolling fields from the family farm and into the fjord called Orkdalsfjorden which ran into Korsfjorden. Korsfjorden was called the Cross fjord, because four fjords met there. Trondheimsfjorden, Flakkfjorden, Orkdalsfjorden and Gaulosen, which the locals sometimes called Gulosen.

Arnljot wanted to take some heirloom furniture from the farm with him. It was a barrel that had contained grain, he could not determine the type of wood, but it was light. And two benches in rosewood that in some strange way had ended up on the farm. They had an edge on both sides and were brilliant for his collection of vinyl records.

It wasn't a farm with land that had to be maintained, the land had long since been sold to the neighbours. Only trønderlåna remained. His grandfather was still alive, but when the day came that he passed away, the long, white and wooden trønderlåne was Arnljot's.

His granddad came out into the yard and stood next to him.
"Ready?"
"I'm ready."
Ready could mean two things. Arnljot was not quite sure if his grandfather asked if he was ready to go, or if he was tired. It didn't matter, the answer was the same.
"I will miss you," said Arnljot.
"I'm coming to visit. You told me they have co-op there as

well; I miss it since it burned down here, I'm also excited to see how different the product range is."

"The biggest difference is that you can buy whisky. I was really amazed when I saw a whole shelf of different whiskies at the hardware store in Whiting Bay, which is by the way one of the seven villages on the island."

"Invite me to Christmas, and I'll come."

Arnljot didn't have the heart to tell him that he had plans to come home for Christmas, he could see how excited he was. Arnljot had to remember to take him to the hardware store in Brodick, you could go through the store and into the next street behind the store. A lovely street with old Scottish houses and gardens.

38

Arthur stood at the harbour and watched Dora which lay close by, Hitler had built Dora for his submarines. It was so massive with its three-metre concrete walls, that it was impossible to blast away without taking half the city with it, but people had become accustomed to it.

Arthur turned around and went back to his childhood home, departure was in two hours. Bergtora and Ravn had already been with a load, but Arnljot was nowhere to be seen. He had talked to Alma the night before, Emil was going to drive her to Arran, Arthur didn't have to make a stop in Caithness this time.

He remembered there was a Pictish tribe called the Cat people, they used to live in the middle of Caithness. The earliest recorded name for Shetland was Inse Catt, meaning: Islands of the Cat people. And Orkney was called Innse Ork, and ness was the Norwegian name for a headland. Catt wasn't so different from the Norwegian word katt either.

It took him an hour to finish packing. He put on his captain's coat and went down to the harbour. Arthur turned one last time and looked at his childhood home. The large green wooden house with two floors looked like it always had. It was a bit melancholic, but mostly it was a good feeling. He had decided to sell the house, the real estate agent would take care of everything and wire him the money.

The only thing he had brought with him, besides his clothes and toiletries, were two large woven rugs. His grandfather Ismo had taken them with him from Tornedalen, where his family came from, they were Kvens. Ismo had moved to Strandveien in the 1920s, because of a good friend he had in Fjæregata. It was called the Tide Street, and Strandveien was called the Beach Street. Trondheimsfjorden had reached both Strandveien and Fjæregata in the old days, that was before they dammed up the area and built a railway.

The railway opened officially on the 22nd of July in 1881. He remembered the date and year, because he saw the pattern and liked the numbers, some numbers were impossible to remember, they didn't look good together.

There had been a long beach with chalk-white sand where they decided to build the railway. It hadn't only been idyllic with the chalk-white beach. Once, one of the horses that lived in the area had died and was just left on the beach, the next day it smelled of horse meat all over Lamoen. People had been cutting meat from the horse that they either fried or cooked. It was not just animal carcasses that lay there, most of the foul-smelling waste from the city was buried on the beach. One doctor had persuaded the women on Lamoen to clean their houses to reduce mortality. His name was long gone from the stone which lay on the graveyard beside Nidarosdomen, the doctor had made a huge difference, he deserved to be remembered.

Arthur took out one of the rugs from the bag and looked at the symbols which were woven into the rug. They looked like stylised roses, and triangles which were symbolising spruce trees. Sometimes, when he had looked at the rugs, he disappeared to Kvenland which lay in Bottenviken.

He had never mentioned it to anyone, but he felt that Ravn might understand him. The Kvens symbols were unknown to the outside world, that was why they were so powerful, they hadn't been used for the wrong purpose, like Hitler had misused the most powerful symbol that had ever existed. The sun cross was originally the symbol of the sun. Arthur had seen it painted on top of the wooden panel at the back of the Greyfriars Kirk in Edinburgh. The sun cross as it was actually called was painted in gold on a blue background. It had also been on a woven rug that was found in the Oseberg ship. He heard someone shout, he turned and saw that Ravn waved at him.

Arthur looked at his childhood home once more. He had been completely put out when he saw the pink kitchen in Corriegills. Fiona told him that Michael had chosen the colour from a coat she had.

Arthur hadn't told Fiona that his grandfather had chosen to paint the kitchen in exactly the same pink colour, he thought it was so strange that he had to tell Ravn.

"It's the lines that runs through the landscape, they are called the bloodlines. They connect people who are not related but have a connection anyway."

Arthur understood what Ravn meant. For most, it was just a coincidence, but for him it was a piece of a pattern that fell into place, and the pieces did not fall into place by themselves, there were some who pulled the strings.

There were still no signs of Bergtora or Arnljot. Ravn walked around restlessly; he didn't quite know what to do. They went inside the ship and sat down in the cabin, the rain had suddenly arrived in torrents. Arthur found two whisky glasses. Ravn was curious about what kind of whisky he had. Ravn smiled when he saw the bottle. It was called The White Stag.

"Whisky from the island we are going to," said Arthur, "I thought it might fit."

"Would you like to show me the two rugs you have with

you?" Ravn asked.

He had seen them sticking out of one of Arthur's bags, one rug had slightly lighter colours than the other. Arthur took them up from the bag and hung them over a brass rod which went across the wall.

"Done this before?"

Arthur confirmed that he had. Sometimes he felt the need to see the rugs. He wondered if he should tell Ravn that the rugs took you back in time and to another place, but he didn't.

"You don't need to," said Ravn, "I already feel the rugs pulling me towards them."

He sat right in front of one of the rugs, and Arthur sat right in front of the other. Ravn looked at the stylised roses, there were eight petals on each of them. Arthur had already disappeared into another sphere. Ravn disappeared soon after.

Bergtora and Arnljot came into the cabin and looked at Ravn and Arthur who were sitting in front of two rugs. Bergtora looked carefully at the rugs, they were bright red and white with a slight difference in the colours, the one Ravn sat in front of had lighter colours.

After a while Arthur looked at them. "I'm back," he said, "we have to leave Ravn until he's ready to come back."

Arthur and Arnljot went to remove the ropes and prepare the ship for departure. Soon after they came back, and they were on their way.

"Don't you need to stand on the bridge?" Bergtora asked Arthur.

"No need, my heir is standing there, this is my last trip."

Ravn shook his head and came back to them.

"Then it's time to tell you what it's all about," Arthur said.

"It's about a balance that has been interrupted. The hidden

forces that have gone via the genes for centuries, started to go wrong five generations ago. People who used to be close to nature got a close relationship to power instead. How it happened, no one knows, but something developed in the wrong direction.

Now everything is starting to come to the surface, the layer that protected them before is gone, they are visible for all to see who they really are for the first time. No one likes to be exposed, so it is dangerous times we have in front of us.

You can recognise them by the milky coating they have on the iris in their eyes. They have the greatest knowledge and great powers but use it the wrong way." Arthur took a deep breath; he didn't know how to continue.

"What did you experience?" Arnljot asked Ravn.

"I ended up in Tornedalen. I followed the old Kven route up to the Lyngen Alps and back again." Ravn didn't know how he should continue either.

"We have to wait," said Arthur, "it's not the right timing." He looked at Arnljot. "Have you and Alma decided to buy Michael's house yet?"

"Margaret hasn't decided if she wants to sell, we can rent it until further notice."

"We will rent it with them," said Bergtora.

"That's a bad deal," said Arthur, "you should look for something else."

Ravn felt dizzy, he had to sit down, Bergtora felt the same. Arthur said the time had come to tell them what was so special about the rugs.

"One night I saw my grandfather Ismo sitting right in front of the rugs. He disappeared, but at the same time he was there, I remembered shuddering because I didn't understand what was happening. Ismo opened his eyes, but it took a while before he was himself again. He asked if I wanted to know a secret. I was ten years old at the time." Arthur took a short break, and Ravn poured him another whisky.

"Ismo wanted me to sit in front of the other carpet. We sat in the dark, and after a while I was in a different place. It was a large bay with spruce trees and heavy snow. Ismo wasn't there, but I wasn't afraid, it was just exciting. There was snow on the ground, with some hare tracks that went across, and an owl that perched in a tree. I remember it was cold, nothing happened but it wasn't boring. After what felt like years, a figure came walking from the forest.

He had almost no hair, only on the sides, the nose was slightly curved at the top but not short nor too long, his eyes were big and blue. The man had broad shoulders, but not too wide, he was wearing a dark blue raglan sweater and black trousers. He looked at me for a very long time, then he asked what I was doing there. I told how I had come there, and he finally told me who he was. Heimdal told me how time worked. It could move inside a spiral if there was anything that needed speed. Time has three stages; the spiral is the one with the most force. When time is elastic, it goes back and forth. The third way time moves, is in a circle."

Ravn asked if there were any special ethnic groups who knew that time moved inside a spiral.

"Kvens."

"And when the time moves in a circle?"

"Druids."

"And the last one, when time moves back and forth?"

"Vikings."

Ravn disappeared into his mind. What if one could find an

event that could unite the three ways time moved? Maybe there were a connection between the Kvens, the Druids and the Vikings. Maybe there was a bloodline between people who had known each other once, then the same people met generations later with the same genes that remembered the events, how would time then relate?

"Do you remember the stone you sat on?" said Ravn, elated to Bergtora.

"I sat on a rock close to Ormidale with my feet in the river when you suddenly appeared. I remember you saying that Lagertha and Lundesol most likely had been sitting on the same rock."

"Exactly," said Ravn, "they probably knew some druids, that means they have been sitting on the same rock as well. Then we only need you, Arthur."

Arthur understood what Ravn meant, he would unite the three ways time could move, through a common ground which was a rock and a river.

Arthur tried to imagine that time went in a spiral, and at the same time in a circle and back and forth. What he saw was a treble clef. Some people sang before they spoke, the music was as old as time itself. If time was united in the right way, then maybe the light tones could overcome the dark ones.

Arthur could not wait to sit on the rock, but he had to wait, they were in the middle of the North Sea.

"What happens when time moves back and forth?" asked Ravn.

"Time stops, it moves back to pick up what hasn't happened yet, and then it moves forward again," replied Arthur.

"What happens when time moves in a circle?" asked Bergtora.

"The same that happens when you get lost, you move in a circle until you find the right track, then you are back at the starting point again, and you can try and find the right way once more." Arthur came to think of something Heimdal had said to him. If you found the right stone, then time would stop where the three rivers met. Time went back and forth just where the water ran past the stone.

Arthur told them what Heimdal had said.

"I think we have the wrong stone," said Ravn. "You have all seen pictures of Glen Rosa where there is a square stone almost down in the river."

"Where the three rivers meet," said Arthur thoughtfully. "That must be the Paras River, Upper Finne River and Lower Finne River. It's where the culture of the Sami people meets the culture of the Kvens and the Norwegians. It is also where you have the border of Norway, Sweden and Russia. The Paras River runs into the Sigdals river which runs into Storfjord by the Lyngen Alps. We have a powerful spot there, but if we want to find the place where the Druids, Vikings and the Kvens met, it has to be the stone standing in Glen Rosa Water. Maybe the stone there will stop the time by the three rivers. What if time can travel to other places?"

"What about where the four fjords meet?" asked Arnljot.

Ravn laughed and said, "Arnljot, you bugger, you're talking about the places where we all come from."

"What are you talking about?" asked Bergtora.

"I come from Trondheimsfjorden," said Arthur, "Arnljot comes from Orkdalsfjorden, Ravn from Gulosen, and you?" Arthur looked at Bergtora.

"My family comes from By."

"That's excellent," said Arnljot, "the fourth fjord."

"It is," said Bergtora proudly, "I am from the fjord that connects us all."

"You see, that's where you are wrong," said Arnljot. "Rye is the place where Korsfjorden begins and Flakkfjorden ends."

"By is just before Rye," said Bergtora. She had to sit down; her head was spinning. She had always thought she came from Korsfjorden, that's what she had heard her whole life, but it was wrong, she came from Flakkfjorden. They all came from four different fjords, and they all connected in Korsfjorden, that's why it was called the Cross fjord.

39

Fiona had taken the trip to North Sannox. She followed a trail by the river up to the mountains. The weather was grey but not sad. It was sometimes lovely with a grey-weathered day; it cleared the mind. She wanted to take Arthur to all the places she used to go alone. The path leading to the place where the three rivers met, was the first place. Then she wanted to show him Sannox glen and the Devil's Punch Bowl, and of course the two distilleries. All the paths on Arran were beautiful, the same were the villages.

They could take the train to Edinburgh where they could enjoy an Aberdeen Angus steak at the Outsider restaurant with a castle view, then they could go to all the small and strange bookstores which lay in small dark alleys.

Fiona kept looking for Arthur's boat. It was expected any time now. She lay down on the grass and chewed on a straw. There was a gap between the clouds, she could see the sun behind a thin veil. Fiona decided to go to Lochranza. The village was reputed to have the least hours of sunshine, it was the most shaded village in the entire world.

Arthur would call her half an hour before they arrived, so she had plenty of time to drive back. Fiona hoped she got to see some dolphins by the castle, she had seen a pod there a few years ago. She stopped at the distillery and bought a cup of coffee before she drove down to the beach. Arthur called when she drank the last sip.

Fiona delivered the empty cup to the distillery and drove

back to Brodick. She arrived just as the ship docked, Arthur jumped overboard and put his arms around her.

Bergtora and Ravn came and greeted her. Arnljot didn't say anything, he just hugged her.

"Would you like some venison casserole?" asked Fiona. Ravn shouted yes, and the rest started to laugh.

"There will not be room for all the luggage," said Fiona, "we can eat first and pick it up later."

They all agreed, and not long after, they sat around the table in Fiona's kitchen and ate. None of them said anything, it looked like they were thinking hard about something. In the end Fiona asked if something had happened.

"You can tell her," said Arthur to Bergtora.

Bergtora told everything they had experienced to Fiona.

"I understand that the rugs can take you to another place and time," said Fiona. "You get information that is related to you and your life. What I don't understand is what is true about the things you are told, and what is complete bullshit. How do you know the difference?"

"You use your intuition," said Bergtora.

"That's simple enough," said Fiona, "but some people have a great gift, and they use it the wrong way. Why do they get information from the other side, shouldn't it be for people who know how to treat sensitive information?"

"The world isn't perfect," said Arnljot. "You are saying that only sensible people should get information, and not the dangerous ones who destroy lives, because they don't know what's real or not."

"Maybe they know what's real," said Ravn, "they just don't understand what they should keep quiet about."

"They have intentions that are not compatible with what they hear," Arnljot said.

"Explain," said Arthur.

"They want to use the information they receive to become famous and rich; they want people to look up to them, all they want is to be important."

"It's not the first time," said Fiona, "I think it's much more common than you think. There are very few who can handle sensitive information. It's easy to say that there are charlatans, but the question is, why do they get through to the other side at all?"

"I think it's because they should learn to distinguish between what is right and wrong," said Arthur.

"And that's not possible if you have nothing to choose from," said Fiona.

"Let's drink coffee in Glen Rosa," said Ravn. "I want to find the square stone as soon as possible."

"I know where it is," said Fiona.

She put on her orange scarf and white sunglasses.

"It's not a long trip," she said encouragingly.

Fiona could see how they struggled in the back seat and decided that Arnljot could drive. They changed places and soon they were on their way. The only things they saw and heard were some crows flying along the road. A blue sky started to show between the grey clouds, it looked like it was about to clear.

Arnljot parked the car close to the path that went yonder into Glen Rosa.

They continued alongside Glen Rosa Water to the Blue Pool where the stone lay close to a small waterfall. The stone was perfectly located on the left side of the river, it looked as if the stone itself dipped its feet in the water. Fiona and Arthur sat down on the stone first.

"Do you feel anything?" asked Arthur.

Fiona just shook her head. Arnljot gave them a cup of coffee so they could drink it on top of the stone. Arthur told Fiona about the four fjords, and the three rivers.

"We have the three rivers here as well," said Fiona. "It's located nearby."

"We have to leave," said Arthur, "Fiona knows where the three rivers are.

Soon after they could see the place where the three rivers met. It was a beautiful place, but the ambience wasn't. The landscape lacked its soul.

"This is the place," said Bergtora.

Ravn sat down on a small rock, and took off his shoes, he stuck his bare feet gently into the river. Bergtora sat down next to him and stuck her bare feet in the river as well. The water made a spiral around their legs.

"There you have the spiral," Bergtora said happily.

40

Joen went ashore, he followed Ailsa slowly. She had tied her grey hair in a knot in the middle of the head and put a stick through. They all had a fresh taint in their faces, the sun hadn't shone from a clear sky during the crossing, but it had been there. Joen gazed at Ailsa's body. The waist was there, not narrow, but it was there. Her shoulders were soft, the thighs tight, her buttocks were located in the right place. The bust was nice, a little old and worn, but still nice. The wrinkles had begun to come, but Joen liked the twinkle in her green eyes. He wasn't looking for a young body, he was looking for a home, and Ailsa was that home.

"Finished," asked Ailsa. "What's the verdict?"

"It will do," said Joen and started walking faster.

Ailsa followed him, she wanted to see if he found the house on his own. They passed the house of Ravna and Rowan. Joen shuddered when he suddenly turned his head and saw straight into Rowan's blue eyes, which were sometimes grey, but now they were bright blue.

"Hi! You old eagle," said Joen, "so this is where you live?"

"Welcome to the island of the many stags," said Rowan and went over to Joen and gave him a hug.

That was the last thing Ailsa had expected, it was impossible that the two of them knew each other from before.

"You don't know everything about me," said Rowan and smiled.

"Obviously not," mumbled Ailsa.

Ravna received them and hugged Joen hard. Ailsa just gazed at them, but she said nothing. Ravna had set the table with freshly baked bread, mushroom soup and of course ale with white heather, on the long wooden table. The three of them sat chatting at the table while Ailsa stood and listened.

"Don't you want to come and sit down?" asked Joen after a while.

The only thing Ailsa could think of was that Ravna and Rowan pulled the strings more than she had been aware. She sat down and began to eat, the crust on the bread was hard and golden, and the soup silky soft. The ale had a bitter taste, but together with the food it was perfect. Ailsa didn't think it was possible to feel as good as she did right now.

"You're right," said Rowan, "we are pulling some strings, that's how we know Joen. Mister Pors has also pulled the strings, but not on the level we operate."

Ravna and Rowan looked at Ailsa. She was changed, she looked much younger than before. Joen had always been very self-conscious. Ailsa had first started to care how she looked after she turned fifty, and that was only a few months ago.

Ravna had helped her rinse her hair with greater burdock, it helped to get the shine back, the rest Ailsa had done herself. Rowan had come over to her once she had obviously decided to get a more feminine gait. Her hips rocked so violently from side to side that she had almost lost her balance. Ailsa had mostly been with men; she had never thought that she was the opposite sex. Something had happened during the last couple of months. Rowan thought it was because Ailsa finally wanted to share her life with a man, and she had found him in the middle of the North Sea.

"Tell me everything," said Ailsa.

"We met Joen twenty years ago at Høgsteinen. He received us when we arrived on a wet October night. Joen thought Bergtor, Lundesol's father was the right man for us. At that time there were turbulent times in Norway, Joen knew that Håkon Jarl wouldn't welcome us."

"Joen is Orm's uncle and Bergtor is Lundesol's father, I understand what it's all about," said Ailsa. "You prepared the ground for Orm and Lundesol."

"That's right," said Rowan, "Joen understood what we were talking about, it was worse with Bergtor. He understood what the gods in Lunden were doing, but he couldn't understand why there was a line in the landscape which went through the stones of the landscape from ancient times.

"We understood that Bergtor would never understand what we were talking about, but it was enough that one in Orm's bloodline understood. After all it was his blood that was going in a straight line to Sølja. It's Ravn Orm who is the descendant of Lagertha and not Lundesol."

"Who is Sølja?" asked Ailsa.

"Two druids from Arran will take up residence in Sølja and her husband Sigurd for a little while in the year 1032," said Rowan. "There are hidden bloodlines and hidden visits we are talking about."

"You've never told me why it's so important," said Joen.

"I told you there were two druids, who knew most about numbers."

"I have always felt that there was more to the story, but if you don't want to tell me, that's fine."

"Do you want to sleep here tonight?" asked Ravna. "I reckon it's a little raw in your house, Ailsa."

"I think Arnhild and Olav would appreciate some privacy,"

replied Ailsa. "Orm and Lundesol will sleep there as well."

"It sounds like there could be a house shortage," said Rowan.

"If there are any trees you want to fell, then I'm happy to accept the timber in exchange for what you want," said Joen.

Rowan nodded towards Ravna.

"I'm the forest owner in this family. What I want in exchange for timber is a ship."

Joen nodded contentedly.

Neither Ailsa nor Joen managed to stay awake any longer. Luckily, the bed was already made so they could plunge into bed. Ailsa fell asleep as soon as she put her head on the pillow. Joen lay awake for a long time. Finally, he got up and went outside. He took the road past Ailsa's house. Joen wasn't surprised when he saw that Lundesol stood and looked at the moon, it was big and white.

"Can't sleep?" he asked.

"I can never sleep when it's as big as it is now."

"Do you want to go for a walk?"

Lundesol nodded and went inside to get her cloak. They started walking inland. Joen told Lundesol that Ravna had offered them timber in exchange for a ship.

"Are you building it, or shall Orm give her his ship?"

"I will build her a new one, Orm has lost enough."

"Or he has gained a lot, it deepens on how you look at it," said Lundesol. "Orm has been juxtaposed with the rest of the rowers, maybe that's not a bad thing."

They had reached Sand-Vik. Joen looked up at the mountains, there was a path yonder.

"Shall we go up through the mountains?"

Lundesol had already begun the ascent. They chose the path

that went to the right when they reached the peak, soon they were in a valley which had mountains on both sides, and a river in the middle.

They continued walking until they came to a square stone that stood by a small waterfall. The water was high, there must have been a lot of meltwater from the mountains earlier in the year. Lundesol took off her shoes and went into the river.

The wind stopped blowing and the river stopped flowing, it failed to decide which direction it should flow in. Lundesol and Joen stopped talking and held their breath. Joen went into the river too, he stood looking upwards, and Lundesol stood looking downwards.

Orion's belt stood on one side of the full moon while the Plough stood on the other. Lundesol noticed that the zodiac signs were in line with the moon with an exact equal distance.

Now it's happening, thought Lundesol, Joen thought the same. The river began to flow again, but it didn't flow in the same direction. From where Joen stood the river ran upwards, and from where Lundesol stood it ran downwards.

They stood for so long that their feet became icy cold. The wind returned and they decided to leave. Lundesol and Orm started walking towards Lochranza, it took the rest of the night. When they reached the second highest peak, they sat down, and looked at the rays of sun that hit the water and the meadow.

Rowan was up, he waved at them.

"If we are lucky, we get breakfast," said Joen, and got up. They began to walk down towards Rowan and Ravna's house.

"Do you have a feeling that we did something important last night?" asked Lundesol.

"Not so much, it was just strange."

Ravna had also risen but her eyes were still tired.

"Was it nice?" asked Rowan.

"Very nice," replied Lundesol, "it feels like the most important thing has already happened."

Rowan and Ravna exchanged glances. Both of them thought that Lundesol would have laughed if she knew what vanishingly small part, she and Joen had performed. It was an important part, but it had not been particularly complicated, they had just taken off their shoes and stood in the river for a little while.

Joen didn't feel he had accomplished anything; that's why the bloodline went through him via Lagertha and not through Lundesol. She easily lost her head, while Joen understood that what had happened, was only a grain of sand. The symbol of time was that you had sand in one hand and moved it over to the other, and so on until there was no more sand left, not even a grain of sand.

41

Michael stood stretching towards the sky.

"Have you stretched your shoulder?" asked Lagertha.

"I found that I get a good posture if I stretch every day."

"For how long?"

"Until I'm satisfied."

Lagertha just nodded; she didn't know what to say. She started to clear the table. Michael asked if she would go for a walk to Glen Rosa, there was a rock there he wanted to show her.

Lagertha was ready, the clearing could wait. They walked the path that went to Sand-Vik by the fjord and further along to Glen Rosa. It was a nice day with scattered white clouds. Lagertha did the same as Michael had done, she stretched. It was a strange feeling, it was as if the body was hung on a string.

"It's the same feeling you get when you pick apples," Michael said. "Did you know that the island is called the island of the apples?"

Lagertha shook her head. She had seen many apple trees on the island, it was reasonable to think that was why. Michael had a lot of apple trees in his garden.

"It's your garden as well," Michael said, "I saw you brought some seeds, what kind of plants will they be?"

"I brought only one kind. The farmers in and around Trøndelag have at least one specimen in their garden. You are considered to be a thief if you steal one plant."

"Maybe it can thrive together with black elder."

"It will be a good mix, since they have the same colours and shapes."

"Maybe we can plant them on each side of the trail down to the fjord, then we can plant black elders behind."

"Sounds like you want to plant a protective row up to the house, do we need to?"

"No one knows what comes next, the answer goes without saying."

Michael pointed at the stone in Glen Rosa, they had arrived. He saw two figures sitting by the river, Lagertha had seen them too. She waved to them, and they waved back.

"You found the way," Rowan said as they approached.

Michael nodded and sat down by the ford. Rowan and Ravna greeted Lagertha.

"Now time should go in a circle," said Rowan. "It shall not go into a spiral yet, it's important that it goes in a circle first. Stand on the ford on the side of the stone, and Ravna and I will stand on the other side of the river."

They did so, and soon after the water began to change direction. It ran from right to left down from the rock; upwards the water ran from left to right. It worked.

Rowan said it was important to make time go up and down from the rock at a given time that lay into the future. Ravna said that now everything was prepared for the future.

Lagertha asked what was prepared. As far as she had heard, there were two druids who should hide inside two Vikings a wee while for protection. She always had a feeling that there was more to the story, but no one would tell her what it was. Ravna stretched before she sat down on the large rock.

"I can tell you parts of what is going to happen," she said. "It's all about the Earth. It needs to change fast, if it doesn't, it will enter a downward spiral. The Earth must have enough power to go up, at the same time as it starts to go down, only that way the Earth can retain its balance."

"Time is running out in the sand," said Rowan, "to make time go back again from the sand then water is needed, think of it as high tide."

"We only help time to put everything in order," said Ravna.

42

Ravn wondered how Alma was doing, he called her and asked.

Alma replied at once.

"It's going very well, we decided to pass through Ullapool, it's a place I've always wanted to visit. We can go for a swim in beautiful turquoise water and eat the best fish and chips on the west coast."

"Ullapool is a very unusual name, isn't it? Do you know its origin?"

"It means the circle of devotion; it's known to be an old secret place. Ulla derives from the Gaelic word Alla, the Saxon wrote it Holy, from Haly and Hallow. The Egyptian Helopol was the city where creation itself was believed to have taken place."

"That's interesting," said Ravn, "I know the Greek called Helopol Heliopolis which means sun or city."

"Helopol and the Gaelic Ullapool are synonymous," said Alma.

"Heliopol is also called On, and Onn in Gaelic signifies a stone."

"The origin of the city was probably a stone set up in the honour of the Deity."

"All the ancient cities were circular, like Troy, Carthage, Acropolis, Rome and thousands of other cities."

"That's true, the origin of Rome is the Greek Romē, and not Romulus, it means to surround or encircle."

"Isle of Skye has the same problem," said Ravn, "the origin

of the word sometimes disappears."

"They all agree the name has a Norwegian origin, but I don't know how they connect that Skye means a wing with a Norwegian word. Do you?"

"No, but I think there's a simpler explanation. Sky means clouds in Norwegian, isn't that a more plausible explanation, that it was a clouded island, instead of a winged island?"

"How old is the word sky?"

"It is mentioned in the poetic Edda, or the old Edda. I have the book here," said Ravn. He started to read from the "Lay of Alvis":

"Tell me, Alvis!

How the clouds are called, which with showers are mingled in every world.

Alvis:

Sky they are called by men."

"And you can see in Norwegian that the translation is correct," said Alma.

"I can," said Ravn and laughed. "I will make a venison casserole till you arrive."

Alma just laughed, and Ravn hung up. He went to see if he could find the others.

Arnljot sat on the grass and looked out over the fjord. Bergtora came and sat down next to him.

"The meaning of life," said Arnljot, "is to find the one you want to be with."

"We are meant to be with someone, but it can be unbelievably tiring trying to find the one. If you have the same humour a lot is in place. You haven't got cold feet I hope?"

"Not at all. I'm just amazed that I really appreciated life before too, it was difficult at times, but that's part of life, isn't it?" Bergtora took a deep breath. What she wanted most was an ordinary day, but she didn't know if it would work. Life had a life on its own, all you could do was to hang on.

"What is it, Bergtora?" Arnljot asked worriedly.

"The fear that life can be too good, is it an irrational emotion?"

"Too good to be true didn't arise out of nothing, but one can hope it goes well."

"How many times can you fall before you can't get up again?"

"I haven't told you who I met on the ferry when Ravn and I left."

"Before you came back without leaving the ferry," Bergtora said and laughed, "I don't forget that so easily, who did you meet?"

"I met Frøya. She gave me some good advice how to comfort Ravn, who at that time was inconsolable. Her unknown story is that she stayed with Heimdal, she got tired of grieving."

"Did Heimdal become a replacement for Odin?"

"You know how it is when someone takes the spotlight, you don't see those behind."

"Heimdal has been in the shadow of Odin, the same way Frøya has been in Odin's shadow."

"Frøya said I had to be there for Ravn and go on a road trip. If you fall, then you and I will go on a car trip."

Bergtora took a deep breath again, but this time it was different, she felt safe. She squeezed Arnljot's arm and put her head on his shoulder.

Ravn came and sat down beside them. Bergtora turned to Ravn and put her head on his shoulder instead. The fjord was both gold and silver, the sky was white, grey and light blue.

"What do you say about going to Glasgow tomorrow?" Arnljot asked Ravn.

"You want a car?" asked Ravn.

"Don't you?"

"A turquoise old ford is what I want, what about you?"

"A yellow old ford."

"Thunderbird?"

"Nope! Mustang. You?"

"Thunderbird."

"I think it's best we go early; car auctions tend to start at eleven o'clock."

"Maybe we should buy electric cars instead," said Ravn.

"We should," said Arnljot, "but we can have a nostalgic look around for old times' sake. An era is definitely soon over."

Arthur stood suddenly behind them. Ravn told him about their plans.

"I can drive, I don't think Fiona will mind lending us the car. Is the house hunt starting now, or are you just going to rent?"

"It's just a base, Mackenzie has decided to keep the house, but we can stay here for a week," replied Arnljot.

"I have found the perfect house for me and Bergtora," said Ravn to Arnljot, "it is big enough for you, Alma and the bairns to stay there as well."

"Excellent," said Arnljot and smiled.

43

Joen had almost finished building Ravna's ship, it was light and subtle, yet elegant. She only needed eight rowers, but Joen thought that Ravna didn't need any, she would always have the perfect wind. She wanted a ship so elegant in shape that it needed no carvings. The sail would be completely white, in contrast to the tarred ship. Joen was happy, he hoped Ravna was too.

Rowan came and inspected the ship.

"Is it you or Ravna who wanted the exquisite shape of the ship?"

"Ravna, she has helped the rest of the rowers with the design of the houses they are building too. She wanted them tarred as well."

"I've seen them, they are exquisite. It was a good idea to put the forge in the middle for the heat, but I don't know if it was so wise when you think of the fire hazard."

"No worries," said Joen, "Ravna made a double stone wall around the smithy. What I like the most is that the houses lie in a horseshoe facing the fjord, with the mountain range behind."

"How do you intend to make a living?" asked Rowan.

"I can build a ship and trade it into what I need, what do you do? I have never met anyone I know so little about."

Rowan stroked his chin, he would rather not talk about himself, but he liked Joen.

"I know a lot and need little," he said in the end.

"That's good, then I know a lot more about you," Joen said

sarcastically.

"There's nobody I trust, except Ravna."

"You can trust me."

Rowan sat down on the beach and watched the flock of ravens. He took a deep breath, he knew Joen was right, maybe it was time to open up.

"I can move through time," he said at last, "and Ravna can do the same."

Joen sat down with him. He wanted Rowan to tell more, but he knew he couldn't be pressured. Only time could get Rowan to tell him more.

"Time is both my friend and enemy. It waits for me sometimes, but sometimes it goes ahead. The hardest part is letting things take the time they need."

Time was all you really had and needed, thought Joen.

"I don't think you completely understand what I am saying," said Rowan. "We don't choose if we have time, time has us."

Joen laughed out loud.

"Then there's absolutely no problem," he said.

Now Rowan laughed too. After they were done laughing, Joen felt angry, he didn't understand anything, and it made him feel restless and out of his comfort zone.

"What is the point of living every day, as if it was the last, when we most likely don't have a last day? If time has us and not the opposite, then there's absolutely nothing we can decide. It's no hope and no meaning. Why are we here if we have nothing to say after all, what's the point?"

Rowan didn't feel like responding to Joen's long tirade.

"Let's take a bath," he said instead.

He started to undress, so did Joen. They jumped into the water at the same time and howled and screamed, it was impossible not too because the water was so cold, the summer was almost over, and the water temperature was marked by it.

"Ice cold," Rowan said to himself, he was lying and floating on his back. Joen, who was accustomed to considerably colder water, took a long swim towards Catacol.

When they finally lay on the beach after getting dressed, Joen began to wonder if it was possible to get to know Rowan. He looked at his black hair that was glued to his skull, he looked like a drowned cat.

Rowan turned his head and looked at Joen. "If you want to know who I am, you have to answer the following question. Do you keep quiet with what you get to know, or do you have to share it with someone?"

"I keep quiet," Joen said without hesitation.

"I work in secret, but you probably understood that. It's not just a matter of preparing the ground for the future, there is more at stake. It's possible to control the Earth, but it requires that things are done in secret, and continue to be kept secret."

"Why?"

"There are enormous forces on both sides. God is not standing alone; he stands with the Devil by his side. They are the two, that holds their hands over the Earth. We talk about a war that can destroy the Earth. What can help Earth is numbers, everything in nature is made up of numbers, without them we don't exist."

"Explain."

"What the numbers can do is to make things happen or stop them. If a person in the right place at the right time say the right numbers, then anything can happen."

"Because the numbers are the building blocks, then they can be used to initiate a chain reaction," said Joen.

"That's just the way it is. The numbers will help people to travel to the moon."

Joen just gazed at him, but he didn't say anything.

"It becomes understandable to people how they can travel to the moon with the help of numbers, what they always will struggle to understand, is the numbers that seem random. You see a pattern of numbers in your daily life, but you don't understand how it's possible, there's no explanation.

"Lundesol thought she had done something big that changed everything, you understood that what you did was only a grain of sand in the big picture. It has to do with your genes, they are like a link that collects what is useful and pass it on to the next generation.

"You need to be completely open to the fact that you know something, but it's not because somebody has told you about it, or you have experienced it. It's from a source outside yourself, but at the same time it's inside of you."

"It's in your genes," Joen said thoughtful, "it's inherited."

"The numbers are also inherited, that's why it's so important that the two druids who know most about numbers, can hide inside two Vikings for a while. If the two druids die young, everything will be lost."

"And the two Vikings will accidentally get my genes," said Joen. Now they both laughed.

"It's actually only one who has the great knowledge, and that's the female druid called Dian. Her boyfriend called Purple is only there as support.

And the same goes without saying for your descendent Sølja. Her boyfriend Sigurd is only there for support, and he's from Lundesol's branch, so you see it adds up."

"Why can't the two druids bring the knowledge they have

via their genes to the next generation of druids?"

"You have understood more than I thought you would," Rowan said seriously. "In order to hide what will happen, it's not a druid that will execute what the numbers can do.

The druid who will inhabit Sølja, transfers the knowledge into her genes. It's too obvious that it's a druid who knows most about numbers, but it's not obvious that it is one from your bloodline." Joen lay down in the grass and thought about what Rowan had said.

"Tell me more," he said at last.

"One last thing," said Rowan. "I will tell you about the protection the numbers can give you."

Joen sat up and looked at Rowan excitedly.

"The one from your bloodline is called Dian Rowan, she is born as a druid, but she can travel through time. So, the next time, she will be born as your relative, and she is also your ancestor. At some point, Dian will live next to a mountain that is four hundred and fifty-eight metres high, the numbers will protect her."

"Not the numbers," said Joen dryly, "the mountain itself will protect her."

"That's right," said Rowan impressed.

"Go on," said Joen, "tell me more."

"There is a churchyard close by. The graveyard is closely packed with four hundred and fifty-eight monumental stones within the chapel ruins."

"The stones and mountains give the best protection," said Joen. Rowan suddenly understood why Joen knew so much. He and Ravna had always thought that they could control who the information went to. Obviously Joen's genes had picked up some of the information.

Joen took a deep breath and said, "You need a friend you can trust, who understands the strange and incomprehensible things you have to relate to on a daily basis."

"That's exactly what I need, I need a friend more than you can imagine. I'm really glad you decided to come here."

"And Orm's horrible big sister had nothing to do with it?" said Joen and laughed.

"I have absolutely no idea what you are talking about," said Rowan and laughed too.

Ravna looked at Rowan and Joen, she understood that Rowan told Joen their secret, she didn't mind, she trusted Joen. Rowan turned his head and smiled at her. Ravna wondered if he had told Joen that they were the two druids who could travel through time, she didn't think so. They still had to be careful who they told. A cold wind came and blew her hair in her eyes, she took hold of the long hair, and gathered it in a knot and put a stick through it to hold it in place.

Ravna looked at the sun behind the clouds, she had always been fascinated by the light. The Earth tilted 23.5 degrees, and created light and shadow when it orbited around the sun. Because of the north-facing glen and the rainfall, Lochranza was the place on Earth with most shade in the whole world.

Rowan came over to her and took some of her long sand-colour hair that had loosened from the knot, away from her face.

"What's on your mind?"

Ravna told him.

It dawned on Ravna and Rowan at the same time, it was in Lochranza the tilt would play a role, someday in the future.

Joen suddenly stood by Ravna's side and stared at her.

"What is it?" she asked.

"You look different."

"How different?"

"There's something about your hair."

"It's in a knot," said Rowan dryly.

"It's more than that, there's something about your energy."

"Can you feel a change?" asked Ravna of Rowan.

"Joen's right, you are changed, why, I can't answer."

Orm and Lundesol came and stood staring at Ravna as well.

"You are changed," Orm said, he had heard the last they said. "Your energy is different."

"That can't be right," said Ravna.

"It is," said Lundesol, "I can see it as well."

"You opened up your heart to me," said Joen to Rowan, "that's what changed between the two of you."

"What we had together was special because of what was secret to everybody else," said Rowan thoughtfully.

"I liked Joen's explanation," said Orm. "You tend to complicate things."

44

Bergtora sat and read Voluspå. Ravn sat by her side.

"Do you think Frøya and Heimdal are the most powerful gods?" Ravn looked at the book and read out loud:

"*Hearing I ask from the holy races,*

From Heimdal's sons both high and low; Thou wilt, Valfather, that well I relate Old tales I remember of men long ago."

"It looks like Heimdal is the ancestor, and it was Frøya who could choose from the warriors who fell in battle first, Odin could choose from the warriors Frøya didn't want."

"I saw some rock carvings in an old book," said Ravn. "If you look at the carvings which are three thousand years old, you see a lot of ships similar to the Viking ships that were built much later. Why do carvings of ships if they didn't exist?"

"You think they built ships that looked like the ones the Viking built three thousand years ago?"

"It makes sense. They also had two horns on their heads on some of the old carvings."

"The oldest symbol of life and fertility," said Bergtora, "some took the symbol from the stag."

"And the oldest female symbol is?"

"A circle, what else could it be, everything continues without a beginning or end."

"The Fimbul winter was 2556 years ago in the year of 536 AD. The Fenris Wolf ate the moon and one of its cubs attacked the sun. It was just before Ragnarock, and it was predicted in the younger Edda. The sun didn't shine for almost three years, it lasted longer in the North than it did in the South. A lot of gold was buried during that period, the craftsmen and blacksmiths were so good, but most of them died. People wanted to give their goods to the gods, in return for the sun."

"It's not true that it was a volcano that caused it," said Bergtora, "it was a cosmic event."

"I think you're right," said Ravn, "a volcanic eruption couldn't have made the sun disappear for so long."

"The sun shone differently, it wasn't gone all the time, that's why they thought one of the Fenris Wolf cubs had tried to eat it."

"How did they know in the early Edda that the Fimbul winter would arrive?"

"They had three years without a summer in between, and it was due to something that happened out in space," said Bergtora thoughtfully.

"When the glaciers are melting now, I guess a lot of the gold that was buried in 536 AD will emerge. The glaciers can dig under the sea level, rivers can't, that's why we have so many deep fjords."

Arnljot stuck his head into Ravn and Bergtora's bedroom. He sat down at the foot end of the bed.

"I am the stepdad of three girls, and I have absolutely no idea how to raise them?"

Bergtora went down to the kitchen to Alma.

"What's going on?" Bergtora asked Alma lightly.

"Nothing."

Alma looked at Bergtora for a long time. "Say something, she said in the end."

"How are things between you and Arnljot?"

"Good as far as I know, why?"

Bergtora didn't reply.

"Say something," Alma said again, hard this time.

"Arnljot doesn't know how to raise Emma, Holly and Fiona."

"And that's all?" Bergtora nodded.

"You can tell him what I told him, I will handle it." Alma sat down heavily on a chair.

"I want him around me all the time, and it scares me. Of course, I want him to give my daughters a sensible upbringing."

"Arnljot can handle anything if you are honest with him."

"Is it that simple?"

"With him it is that simple."

Arnljot stood in the doorway, and Bergtora went upstairs to the bedroom again. She lay down on Ravn's arm, she could see that he was in a long row of thoughts.

Ravn had big plans; he had talked to the two owners of the house he wanted to buy. He was right when he thought they wanted to live in Edinburgh again. They had given him a tour of the land and the house; it was one of the historic houses on the island that was listed, but it was possible to build a stair up to the first floor on the outside of the building.

Sound insulation was another thing Ravn had investigated. It was legal to lay an extra floor over the old one as long as it was preserved underneath. On top of the sound-insulating boards Ravn wanted white linoleum with a little grey marbling in the pattern. Linoleum came from the Latin name oleum lini. It contained linseed oil, resin, wood flour, limestone flour, colour pigments and jute. Ravn loved the white, soft floors that were so easy to keep clean. The only thing he had to keep in mind was not to clean them with green soap or ammonia, he had to use

Castile soap.

Ravn looked forward telling the big news to Bergtora, but she had fallen asleep. He got up and went down to Arnljot and Alma who were sitting in the kitchen. Ravn couldn't help himself; he told them about the house.

They heard Fiona's car park in the yard. Arthur was standing in the doorway soon after.

"Someone told me you needed a driver," he said.

Ravn just laughed. Alma went to tell her daughters that Emil would watch them for a couple of hours. They wanted to come too, and Emil offered to drive them in his car.

Arthur was standing by the car holding the door wide open. Alma hurried to give each of the daughters a pair of shoes before she ran after the others. Arthur pressed the accelerator pedal, and soon after they were in Brodick.

Alma asked Arthur to wait for Emil. He parked the car by the boardwalk. Soon they could see Emil, and Arthur stepped on the gas again. They passed the Ormidale hotel and continued on a bumpy road yonder. Soon they saw a large old square house with two floors that was firmly planted in the ground.

Arthur stopped the car, then he went straight to the burn. Ravn followed him while Alma and Arnljot stood and looked at the house.

"What do you think?" asked Arnljot of Alma.

"I think it's stunning."

A peacock walked past them and showed them its spectacular feathers. Emil had arrived at the house, the bairns calmly got out of the car.

"Shall we live here?" asked Holly.

"I hope so," replied Alma.

Two gentlemen came out of the house, they held the door

wide open.

"Welcome," said one of them, he presented himself as Percy.

"Scott," said the other one.

"Where is Ravn?" asked Percy. "I thought he was the one who was interested in buying the house."

"He is," said Arnljot, "he went to the burn, but he will be here shortly. I don't know if Ravn mentioned anything about buying the house with someone?"

Scott nodded and said, "He did, I presume that is you?"

"Except me," said Emil.

Scott showed them the ground floor, while Percy was ready to show them the first floor. The house was exactly what they had imagined it to be, dark wooden floors and wallpapered walls. It was impossible to imagine that they wouldn't live here.

Alma opened the window in the bedroom on the first floor, there was a large eucalyptus tree outside. She rubbed a leaf between her fingers before she smelled them. All the rooms were big and square, Alma had already moved in.

Ravn stood suddenly beside her. "What floor would you like?" he asked.

"First," said Alma without hesitation, the eucalyptus tree had made all the difference.

They went to find Arnljot, he was sitting on a wrought iron bench in the garden. A yellow clematis with small simple flowers climbed around the bench, and further up into a magnolia tree that had lost its flowers and only had green leaves left.

Ravn asked Arnljot the same question.

Arnljot thought it would be rude to say. Ravn smiled at him, and Arnljot took a chance and said, "First."

Alma and Ravn started to laugh.

"It looks like me and Bergtora ends up on the ground floor," said Ravn lightly.

"Don't you think you should ask her?" said Arnljot.

"I will call her right now."

Bergtora sounded tired, but she had answered straight away. Ravn had the mobile on speaker so Alma and Arnljot could hear what she said.

"I love living on the ground floor so I can go straight into the garden. Do you think you can come and pick me up?"

"I will come and get you," said Arnljot. He went to fetch Arthur, he was talking to Scott, he wanted to hear if Arthur could move their furniture by sea to Edinburgh. Arthur rejected it, as he didn't have a ship anymore.

Arnljot asked if they should go and fetch Fiona as well as Bergtora. Arthur agreed, and they walked towards the car, the peacock saw them and hurried to spread its plumage.

"We're in Scotland," said Arthur, "but there's something weird going on. They have peacocks and palm trees and shrubs that are almost 6.5 feet. There's something strange about the whole island, if you ask me."

Arnljot agreed, it was a mysterious island.

Arthur didn't call Fiona, he wanted to surprise her. He parked the car by the fence and Arnljot rang the bell on the door.

Fiona opened at once, she had heard the car. Arnljot told her that they had found a house they wanted to buy with Ravn and Bergtora. He knew it wasn't necessary to ask Fiona if she wanted to come. Fiona sat in the back, and they went to fetch Bergtora. She had walked down to the road that went on towards Brodick. Arnljot stopped and Bergtora sat down next to Fiona.

"What floor did Ravn choose?" asked Bergtora.

"I don't know," said Arnljot.

"I know," said Arthur. "He told me by the burn."

"Which floor did he choose?" asked Bergtora again.

She knew the answer in the same moment as she asked. Ravn hadn't chosen, it was enough for him to be with the people he most wanted to be with.

Ravn was so excited to show Bergtora the house, that he walked down the road until he came to Brodick, there he stood by the side of the road waiting for them to pass. Arthur stopped the car, and Ravn crawled in and sat down next to Bergtora.

Arthur was excited whether the peacock would welcome them again. It didn't stand in the courtyard this time; it waited till they had almost reached the front door before it came running and frightened them.

"They are nice birds," said Fiona, "but they don't like squirrels."

"Squirrels," said Bergtora surprised, "why not?"

"Look," said Fiona quietly, she pointed at a squirrel in an oak tree by the entrance.

The squirrel looked at the peacock, then suddenly without any warning, it jumped down right in front of it. The peacock jumped straight up and ran away.

Arthur lay on the ground and bounced while he laughed and held his hands on his stomach. Scott and Percy came running to see what was going on. Fiona knew them from before, she explained that Arthur had never seen a squirrel game before.

"Then we have clarified that," said Scott. "Would you like some refreshments in the garden?"

"Good idea," said Ravn, but he followed Bergtora instead, she was headed towards the first floor. She went inside the bedroom and took her hand out of the window and touched a leaf on the eucalyptus tree, just like Alma had done.

"Do you have regrets?" asked Ravn.

Bergtora shook her head. "I have always thrived best with soil underfoot. When will the house be ours?"

"We just have to discuss the transfer with the Bank of Scotland, I guess it will take a couple of days."

"You know I've always missed a good friend?"

Ravn nodded. He looked inquisitively at Bergtora, he suspected that she was afraid that life would be too good.

Bergtora smiled and said, "I don't want to waste any more time being afraid, I want to enjoy being with Alma."

They went outside to the garden. Arthur asked Bergtora if there was something he could contribute to the cafe they were to open.

"We have to ask Alma," said Bergtora, "she's the chef."

They found her sitting at the foot of a tree by the burn. Bergtora didn't want to disturb her, but Arthur had already asked her. Alma got up, and they sat around one of the wrought iron tables that stood in the garden.

"It's perfect," said Alma. "I can write down a menu, and we can see what we need. Do you know if Fiona has a recipe for a good cake?"

"I know an exquisite cake. The filling is a mixture of cream, butter, flour, milk, eggs and vanilla, with a few drops of lemon, and of course dark chocolate pieces, I prefer the Queen's Chocolate from Freia. The recipe ended up in Fjæregata at one point, and found its way to Strandveien, my mother used to bake it."

"What was her name?" asked Alma.

"Åshild."

"We can call it the Hill cake, since Ås means hill," said Bergtora.

"I guess you want me to bake it?" asked Arthur.

"Only if you want to," replied Alma.

"It would be my pleasure, but I don't want to get paid."

"You and Fiona can come and eat for free whenever you want to," said Alma.

Percy came and asked them if they were hungry, he had brought sandwiches with turkey, pickled red onions and lettuce leaves. He had also brought apple juice in large bottles.

Fiona, Emma and Holly came running and took a sandwich each.

Alma took a deep breath and looked at Bergtora. She recognised Bergtora's fear, they were both afraid it wouldn't last. Bergtora took two sandwiches with her and went to find Ravn. She found him down by the burn.

"You got scared when you saw the forces that were hiding in the rugs," said Ravn. "Those forces are not only there, they are everywhere, also here."

"Anything in particular you're thinking about?" asked Bergtora.

"Maybe what one fears will happen, but never does. I'm worried too, but I have decided not to nourish it."

Bergtora took off her shoes and went into the burn, the water was freezing, but it felt good. Ravn did the same, he needed the cold blood to the brain, it was refreshing.

45

Lagertha was on her way home to Lochranza from Glen Rosa. She needed time to think about what had happened, it was weird and natural at the same time.

Her blood that went through her body, should help one person in the future that wasn't even born yet, to carry out something that was almost impossible.

There was a lot she needed to understand on a basic level. It was unnatural for some and natural for others, it depended on who you were talking to. One thing was for sure, the gods were going into hiding, until the Earth had gotten up to the level it needed to be, in order to survive.

It was no stranger than that, thought Lagertha and laughed to herself.

The path along the fjord from Sand-Vik, wasn't the shortest path, but Lagertha needed time to finish her thoughts. She passed the mountain Creag Ghlas Laggan and wasn't surprised to see Frøya there.

"Be greeted, great shieldmaiden," said Frøya and laughed when Lagertha approached.

Lagertha sunk down beside her; the sun was about to do the same. Frøya stood up and stretched. Lagertha thought it was more than strange that everyone she met that day stretched.

"Why do you stretch?" she asked.

"It's a pattern. It starts with small things, like everyone you meet, is stretching."

Lagertha's thoughts came back at full speed, she decided to take a bath. She got up and walked quickly down to the beach. The crows lifted and started to fly in a ring above her head. Lagertha didn't notice how cold the water was. It was just a relief to get all her thoughts washed off.

Frøya watched Lagertha who swam further and further away from the beach. She swam fast with her face into the water and her arms in an arc in front of her, before they broke the water surface in an arc again. Her feet went up and down faster and faster.

There was a pod of dolphins on their way towards her, but Lagertha didn't see them, she had her head underwater.

46

Ravn had just read Voluspå. The fifth stanza fascinated him. Both the moon and the sun made high tide, but it was the moon who took all the credit. The sun had half the power compared to the moon when it came to making tides. The moon made sure that the Earth didn't spin so much that it affected the climate, it stabilised the Earth. Ravn was sick of his thoughts; he didn't know where they were headed.

Come, Bergtora, and bring coffee, he thought. He knew Bergtora could read his mind.

Bergtora did, it took five minutes, just as long as it took to make two cups of coffee and get to the burn.

"What's going on?" she asked.

Ravn told her how sick he was of his thoughts; he gave her the book and showed her the fifth stanza.

"Do you think it's strange that the sun and the moon are siblings?" Bergtora asked after reading the stanza.

"I don't know anything anymore. I don't give a damn if the Earth and the moon have a core that contains iron, and the sun only makes half as much of the high tide as the moon, I'm just so sick and tired of my thoughts."

"Iron doesn't react with cold or hot water, but with steam, and it's in group 8, and the atomic number is 26."

"Which is 8," said Ravn and looked at her in astonishment. He needed another cup of coffee. Bergtora got up and took the empty cup from his hand. Ravn only used a small part of his brain at the moment, but Bergtora had no doubt that another cup would get Ravn's brain back to full capacity. Ravn was still in deep thought when she returned.

"I think I've solved it," he said. "It's about speed, the moon never shows the dark side because of the speed it goes around its own axis. The Earth and the sun show all their sides, the dark side is only special for the moon. We have three elements, if we call the sun, the moon and the stars an element, the Earth is the fourth. The sun is the fire, the moon the water, the stars the air, and Earth is the earth."

"The sun contains iron as well, but it's only 0.2 per cent and it's not in the core."

"In a supernova the iron gets to the finale, it's the heaviest element because it's an energy-intensive process and not an energising process."

"When a supernova explodes, heavier elements are formed which don't exist on Earth, and when iron is formed the star loses its hydrostatic equilibrium," said Bergtora.

"What is hydrostatic equilibrium again?" asked Ravn.

"Hydrostatic equilibrium is the reason the stars don't collapse or explode. The forces that work upwards are equal to the forces that work downwards. Hydrostatic is the name of the balance."

"The stars lose their balance when iron is made, and iron is in the core of the moon and the Earth but not the sun."

"Sometimes it is difficult to remember who goes around who," said Bergtora. "Recently I've been thinking about the Earth as a pig that's being roasted on a fire."

"That's clever," said Ravn, "it turns around to be roasted equally on each side. The sun shines on the Earth that spins around its own axis."

"The moon is the Earth's moon, so it goes around the Earth, but it uses 29.5 days and nights, for every ecliptic round it makes."

"And the Earth uses one year around the sun, that's why we have the seasons."

"Do you remember the time and the shapes?" asked Bergtora. Ravn nodded, but he wasn't shore what Bergtora meant.

"Time moves in a circle, up and down and in a spiral. A hydrostatic equilibrium has movements similar to time that moves up and down, and it's connected to the stars and to air, the third element. Water as the second element, is widely distributed across the lunar surface and has the spiral form in its fluids." Bergtora poured some milk in the coffee, and they both looked at the spiral. "It needs oxygen to make a spiral, that's why you never see a spiral in old coffee."

"The circle is time moving like the sun and fire," said Ravn. "And the last is where time can be presented with all three of its forms on Earth, which is in this case is the fourth element," said Bergtora.

"When time moves up and down, then balance occurs.

That's why the stone in the Blue Pool in Glen Rosa is so important, it makes time move up and down the river."

"The most compact shape in existence is a sphere, and it occurs when the isotropic gravitational field pushes the star together. It means equal characteristics in all directions."

"The tide's energy is one of the common denominators when we talk about the moon, the sun, the Earth and the stars," said Ravn. "The stars are affected by the tide's energy if there are large planets nearby."

"Or the sun, which is a great star, like Venus. Luckily the sun hasn't enough mass to explode. A car showed up the other day with an interesting number plate."

"Which number?" Ravn asked.

"444," Bergtora replied. "Isn't that the same number as the height of the mountain Creag Ghlas Laggan?"

Ravn nodded.

Bergtora still didn't think the number made any sense, maybe a pattern would emerge later on. Ravn got up and gave her his hand.

"Would you like to go for a swim in Lochranza?"

"Maybe we are like the other building blocks in the Universe," said Bergtora, "we seek to fill up what we lack."

"Iron is a lucky substance, it reaches an end, an explosion, then something new is created."

Bergtora thought of the hydrostatic equilibrium. The forces acted both upwards and downwards. It was something she couldn't get hold of.

"We all strive for balance and equilibrium," Ravn said. "Life goes up and down."

They were able to borrow Emil's car, he and his daughters had planned a trip to the beach in Brodick, it was within walking distance of the house they had bought. Ravn didn't know why they had to go to Lochranza instead of just walking down to the beach in Brodick.

They drove via Corrie and Sannox, Ravn loved the narrow streets in Corrie with the old stone houses by the road. It must be so difficult to drive a bus there, he admired the bus drivers' skills. Sannox had one hotel, some seals and a beach. Further up the path to the mountains, lay the Devil's Punch Bowl.

They arrived in Lochranza. Ravn took off his clothes and went for a swim, Bergtora did the same. She crawled until she reached Ravn. He disappeared for a long time under water, when he reappeared, he had returned to the beach. Bergtora continued to swim yonder, soon she got company.

Ravn regretted that he had swum back again. It was a pod of dolphins that joined Bergtora, there were seven dolphins in the pod.

Lundesol went for a swim, she wanted some time alone, none of her thoughts made any sense. Lundesol saw that Rowan sat on the beach, she didn't have time to talk to him, the water was too tempting. She took off her clothes and ran into the fjord, Lundesol swam with her hands like paddles in front, and her face in the water. Her feet hit the water hard and fast up and down. She swam for a long time, Rowan was impressed, he had felt how cold the water was, it was enough with a short swim for his part.

Ravna came and sat down next to him. There was something wrong with the picture of Lundesol who swam, but neither Ravna nor Rowan understood what it was.

Frøya stood on Creag Ghlas Laggan together with Heimdal. Time had brought together the three different times. Lundesol swam in the same direction as Bergtora and Lagertha. Two of them swam together with dolphins, Lundesol didn't.

"It is Ravn Orm who is the lineage from Lagertha to Bergtora, not Lundesol," Frøya said suddenly. "If Orm had gone for a swim, the dolphins would have arrived."

"Is it too late?" asked Heimdal.

"We can turn back time," said Frøya.

Heimdal nodded, he wanted to see what would have happened if it was Ravn Orm who swam and not Lundesol. Ravn Orm joined Ravna and Rowan on the beach.

"Do you want to go for a swim?" he asked. Ravna and

Rowan shook their heads.

Ravn Orm began to undress and walked calmly into the water and continued to walk until the water reached his waist. His long light hair reached the water. Ravn Orm swam outwards, it didn't look like he realised how cold the water was.

A pod of dolphins joined him. Ravn Orm didn't see them before one of them jumped over him, then he lay on his back and laughed.

His laughter resounded all over Lochranza, it was a happy laugh. It wasn't a long time Ravn Orm had left on earth, but Ravna was quite sure it was this moment he would remember when he died. She didn't think sadly of what was going to happen, Ravn Orm was not gone for good, he was to return to the island.

"Now it's in place," said Frøya satisfied to Heimdal.

They saw that the three times adapted to each other. Ravn Orm, Lagertha and Bergtora swam in a straight line across the fjord. Lagertha was the undisputed winner, she swam twice as fast as Ravn Orm, Bergtora lay far behind.

The dolphins appeared at the same time. The only thing that separated what happened next, was that one of the dolphins jumped over Ravn Orm.

"What is the purpose of letting three people do the same thing at three different times?"

"It's simple," said Frøya. "It's an enormous force that is created when the same thing happens several times. In this case, it's the numbers that decides. It's the number four three times which is equivalent to three people. So difficult and so easy, if one discovers the physical laws that apply.

The numbers came to Casper, Alma and Bergtora on three different number plates. It hasn't happened to just anyone, they have a short way in to us, they can easily pass through the veil which connects our world with theirs. Ravn Orm and Bergtora are two pillars which support Lagertha, she's the fastest swimmer and has the most guts."

"You're right," said Heimdal, "she has nothing that stops her."

"She has just as much that stops her as everyone else. The difference is that she doesn't allow herself to be stopped."

Heimdal didn't fully understand the importance of someone speeding up time and stabilising it, but it was clear that this was what Lagertha was doing.

"Imagine a supernova," said Frøya. "It's in perfect balance just before it explodes. Lagertha is in perfect balance when she swims."

"Explain!" said Heimdal, "he didn't understand what Frøya meant."

"It has happened before, it's not the first time someone creates balance, and thereby creates something new."

"So, the balance creates something new, and the explosions don't create something new?"

"Wrong, they both do. Once you get the balance, you can change the world."

Finally, Heimdal understood what Frøya was talking about, it was so simple. It was not about equal characteristics in different directions, it was about different characteristics in the same direction. "What's with the numbers?" he asked.

"We are sitting on this mountain which is 444 metres high. Bergtora saw a car license plate with the same number. They shan't be added with other numbers, they must stand alone."

"Why?"

"It's in context with what will happen next for Lagertha and

Ravn Orm, for Bergtora it has already happened."

Heimdal nodded, he understood what had already happened. It had been the wrong year the Maya Indians had been given. The year when everything was supposed to happen, wasn't 2012, it was 2015.

"Lagertha and Ravn Orm laid the groundwork for what was to happen in 2015," Heimdal said thoughtfully.

"Not only them, there were thousands of others too, it was a chain reaction. You've obviously been too busy to notice what's been going on."

Heimdal just laughed. He lay back in the grass, chewing on a straw, he would tell Frøya later that he was the only one of the old gods, that had been present when the events in 2015 had taken place.

Frøya came to think of one thing. What if the three of them swam at the exact same speed, what would happen then. A new sphere might emerge if the isotropy was in place. Now the direction was the same, but the characteristics were different, regardless of direction, or were they?

The three of them shared the same DNA. Frøya couldn't help herself, she let Lagertha slow down and Bergtora gain more momentum. The only one who swam at his own pace, was Ravn Orm.

Heimdal wondered what Frøya was up to.

"Watch!" said Frøya.

She stacked the three times and the three events on top of each other, they both held their breath while they watched Bergtora, Lagertha and Ravn Orm swim.

"You want to create a new sphere," said Heimdal. "Isotropy implies equal properties regardless of direction, but here they swim in the same direction. You will most likely get a new dimension."

"What about some divine intervention. What if we swim as well?"

"How fast do you want me to swim?"

"As fast as you can, maybe you can blast the boundaries of iron."

"You mean I'll be the star and lose my balance? Or do you mean I will demand energy to merge or split?"

"I think of iron as something that is subjected to other laws than all the other chemical substances, I wonder whether you will create balance or destroy it."

They undressed on the beach and went swimming. Frøya kept up with Heimdal for a while, but he won superiorly. They got dressed again and walked up to Creag Ghlas Laggan.

"Go and swim one more time," said Heimdal.

He was so determined, that Frøya did what he said. She had almost reached where the others turned, when a pod of dolphins appeared. Heimdal created a huge rainbow above Frøya and the dolphins. The colours from the rainbow were reflected in the mirror-bright fjord. Some of the dolphins jumped over the lower part of the rainbow. Frøya came shortly afterwards and sat down next to him.

"We have the number four three times," she said.

Heimdal nodded and said, "Bergtora saw a number plate, which had the same number, as the height of the mountain we are sitting on."

"444 is the height of the mountain," Frøya said, "and that fits, what doesn't is that Bergtora, Ravn Orm and Lagertha represents number four, and I don't. The fourth four doesn't exist."

"The number plate that showed up before, had four sevens,"

Heimdal said thoughtfully.

"The dolphins," said Frøya excited. "I cut myself out of the occasion but keep the dolphins, then it will be seven dolphins four times, which is the same as the number plate Alma saw." Frøya put the times on top of each other so they could see what happened.

They heard a rumble from the depths of the fjord, the sky darkened, and the fjord turned black. It became a violent spiral which went round as a maelstrom. The dolphins, Bergtora, Ravn Orm and Lagertha disappeared into the maelstrom.

The most difficult time to create had appeared. It lay there until the time came to bring it up again, but that time lay far, far ahead, into the future.

"What about the number plate Casper saw?" asked Heimdal.

"22356," said Frøya. "Two and six are the number first and last, and it makes eight which is eternity. 235 is the tilting of the Earth as it orbits. 23.5 to be exact, so you see you have balance. 23.5 is 5.5 on both sides, and that is the balance between light and shadow.

The Earth, the sun and the moon are the three deities. During the full moon or new moon, when the sun, Earth and moon are aligned, we have spring tide which is the largest difference between high and low tide possible. The Earth also has the four seasons, that relate to the moon."

"The four three times," said Heimdal and laughed.

"You're absolutely right," said Frøya. "The three deities, the moon, the sun and the Earth are related to the seasons, without them we would live in complete darkness."

"You said the moon was related to the seasons?"

"The moon pulls the Earth towards it, and makes it tilt 23.5 degrees, the tilt creates seasons. If the moon wasn't there the tides would fall, nights would be darker, and the seasons would disappear."

"The sun is four hundred times wider than the moon, but it's four hundred times further away," said Heimdal.

"By 2015, the annual global CO_2 levels will exceed 400 ppm, and there you have the four the third time, and that can end the world. Four times three is twelve, which is three, which stands for the three deities, the sun, the moon and the Earth."

"Now I understand," said Heimdal suddenly. "The moon helps the Earth with the tilt, and it creates the seasons, and the sun helps things to grow to keep the Earth inhabitable. The Earth, which is the daughter of Night, gave birth to the siblings the moon and the sun, it makes sense."

"One can't exist without the other two, it's as simple as that. Therefore, we need the spiral to be in balance, it needs to go downwards into the dark, in order to help the light spiral upwards on the 14th of Mars in 2015. And here you have the same as with the tilt, you get five if you add the first two numbers, and the number five stands at the end."

"And in the middle, you have three two one, which is the numbers for a countdown," said Heimdal and laughed out loud.

"The energy is strong here in Lochranza where it's more shadow than anywhere else in the world, that's why the spiral was so strong, dark and wild."

"You are still talking about the tilt," said Heimdal, and laughed again.

"It's all about the tilt," said Frøya and smiled.